"A tightly constructed, well-written, and suspenseful whodunit. Raines, a relentless but all-too-human hero, is an intriguing character who can withstand the scrutiny of subsequent episodes in what promises to be a fine series of novels."

—Booklist

MURDER AT MANASSAS

"[Killian] captures the chaos, confusion and horror of war, and he effectively handles the irony of a quest for justice in the midst of mass killing . . . Engrossing."   *—Booklist*

"Harry is an engaging character. He and his freed slave Caesar Augustus are an amusing pair as they try mightily to disguise their underlying ideals and bravery with a cloak of cowardice and greed."   *—The Denver Post*

"Michael Kilian has triumphantly opened his Civil War mystery series. The story line reflects strong research that includes trivia that adds period depth to the plot. The flawed and guilt-ridden Harry is a wonderful hero. The author's Herculean task to write a series of mysteries that chronologically follow the war to its conclusion gives this series a fascinating twist."   *—Midwest Book Review*

"A believable context . . . an absorbing period piece."
—San Antonio Express-News

MORE MYSTERIES FROM THE
BERKLEY PUBLISHING GROUP . . .

THE HERON CARVIC MISS SEETON MYSTERIES: Retired art teacher Miss Seeton steps in where Scotland Yard stumbles. "A most beguiling protagonist!"
—*The New York Times*

by Heron Carvic
MISS SEETON SINGS
MISS SEETON DRAWS THE LINE
WITCH MISS SEETON
PICTURE MISS SEETON
ODDS ON MISS SEETON

by Hampton Charles
ADVANTAGE MISS SEETON
MISS SEETON AT THE HELM
MISS SEETON, BY APPOINTMENT

by Hamilton Crane
HANDS UP, MISS SEETON
MISS SEETON CRACKS THE CASE
MISS SEETON PAINTS THE TOWN
MISS SEETON BY MOONLIGHT
MISS SEETON ROCKS THE CRADLE
MISS SEETON GOES TO BAT
MISS SEETON PLANTS SUSPICION
STARRING MISS SEETON
MISS SEETON UNDERCOVER
MISS SEETON RULES
SOLD TO MISS SEETON
SWEET MISS SEETON
BONJOUR, MISS SEETON
MISS SEETON'S FINEST HOUR

KATE SHUGAK MYSTERIES: A former D.A. solves crimes in the far Alaska north . . .

by Dana Stabenow
A COLD DAY FOR MURDER
DEAD IN THE WATER
A FATAL THAW
BREAKUP

A COLD-BLOODED BUSINESS
PLAY WITH FIRE
BLOOD WILL TELL
KILLING GROUNDS
HUNTER'S MOON

INSPECTOR BANKS MYSTERIES: Award-winning British detective fiction at its finest . . . "Robinson's novels are habit-forming!" —*West Coast Review of Books*

by Peter Robinson
THE HANGING VALLEY
WEDNESDAY'S CHILD
INNOCENT GRAVES

PAST REASON HATED
FINAL ACCOUNT
GALLOWS VIEW

CASS JAMESON MYSTERIES: Lawyer Cass Jameson seeks justice in the criminal courts of New York City in this highly acclaimed series . . . "A witty, gritty heroine." —*New York Post*

by Carolyn Wheat
FRESH KILLS
MEAN STREAK
TROUBLED WATERS

DEAD MAN'S THOUGHTS
WHERE NOBODY DIES
SWORN TO DEFEND

JACK McMORROW MYSTERIES: The highly acclaimed series set in a Maine mill town and starring a newspaperman with a knack for crime solving . . . "Gerry Boyle is the genuine article." —*Robert B. Parker*

by Gerry Boyle
DEADLINE
LIFELINE
BORDERLINE

BLOODLINE
POTSHOT
COVER STORY

THE
WEEPING
WOMAN

MICHAEL KILIAN

BERKLEY PRIME CRIME, NEW YORK

THE WEEPING WOMAN

A Berkley Prime Crime Book / published by arrangement with the author

PRINTING HISTORY
Berkley Prime Crime edition / June 2001

All rights reserved.
Copyright © 2001 by Michael Kilian

This book, or parts thereof, may not be reproduced in any form without permission.
For information address: The Berkley Publishing Group,
a division of Penguin Putnam Inc.,
375 Hudson Street, New York, New York 10014.

The Penguin Putnam Inc. World Wide Web site address is
www.penguinputnam.com

ISBN: 0-425-18001-8

Berkley Prime Crime Books are published
by The Berkley Publishing Group,
a division of Penguin Putnam Inc.,
375 Hudson Street, New York, New York 10014.
The name BERKLEY PRIME CRIME and the BERKLEY PRIME CRIME design
are trademarks belonging to Penguin Putnam Inc.

PRINTED IN THE UNITED STATES OF AMERICA

10 9 8 7 6 5 4 3 2 1

For John de Groot,
the old master,

and for Paige Price,
who keeps on dancing.

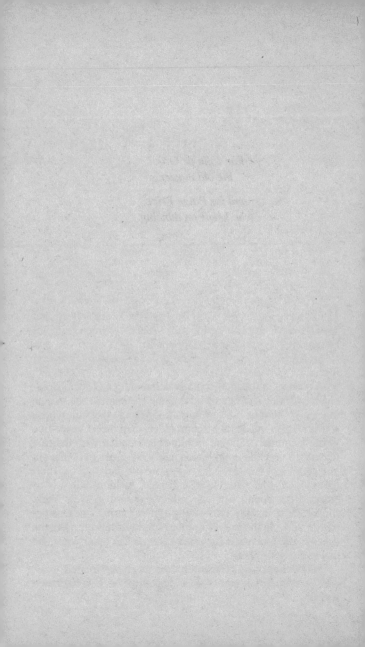

CHAPTER 1

U PON arriving at his West Eighth Street art gallery that warm spring morning in 1925, Bedford Green immediately noticed something terribly amiss:

Sloane Smith, his very beautiful young assistant, was crying.

A product of the intellectually demanding and socially exclusive women's college whose name she shared, she was an unusually serious and thoughtful young woman whose somber mien made her seem older than her twenty-five years. Extremely tall and fashionably slender, with delicate features, a very fair complexion, and gray-green eyes that put one in mind of northern seas, she wore her dark hair cut short and sleek in the latest Louise Brooks fashion and was as "modern" a young lady as could be found in New York. Sloane could display a disarming and endearing smile on occasion, making those eyes seem to sparkle. But rare were the times in the four years they had known each other when she had actually laughed.

Yet neither could he recall a time when she'd cried.

The sound of it now was as unsettling as if it had been screams.

Since leaving his job as celebrity columnist for the ratty tabloid *New York Day* and opening this little art gallery just off Washington Square, Bedford had been an exceedingly happy man. Having this remarkable young woman in his life was a big part of that. Her unexplained sorrow now caused him pain.

Certainly Sloane was no stranger to sadness. An insistently modern woman, she threw herself into amours, political causes, and radical cultural movements with much abandon, seldom with happy result. She seemed to choose her friends for their melancholy—or penchant for trouble—including, Bedford supposed, himself. She had difficult relations with her parents, who disapproved of her chosen lifestyle. But whatever she suffered, she usually bore it silently and privately. She prided herself greatly in being "a strong woman." She was from the Midwest—Chicago and Lake Forest.

The sound of her weeping was coming from the alcove in the back of the gallery that served as their workroom.

He hesitated, not sure how offering her comfort would be received. Setting his straw boater on the desk by the door, he flicked a speck of New York City coal dust from his otherwise immaculate white trousers. He wore both white flannels and white bucks with his blue blazer, though it was shy of Memorial Day and the prescribed official opening of the warm weather, white shoe season. Bedford was a man who dressed well, but always to suit himself. Never convention.

Stepping into the alcove, he found Sloane still oblivious to his arrival. Bedford wondered if her tristesse was over some new beau who was worse than usual—or perhaps a past one who'd given her sad memories.Her last young man, a verse libre poet with poor health habits, had died of influenza a few weeks before.

Bedford considered whether it might be a painting that had caused her distress. He'd just acquired a work he knew she would find disturbing. It was an oil by a young Austrian named Egon Schiele, unfortunately also deceased. If brilliantly rendered, the picture was pretty rough stuff—a study of a ravished, naked, wanton young woman seated sprawled in an almost obscene pose, her eyes reflecting every horror of life, her haunting face emptied of emotion, looking all but dead. The canvas had just arrived from Germany the day before.

Sloane had apparently had a look at the thing before he'd come in. The work now stood turned against the wall.

Steeling himself, he entered the alcove. She was seated at the work table, the morning mail before her, gazing forlornly at an odd, photographic postal card she held tenderly in her long-fingered hand.

"Sloane?"

Her hand dropped and she looked up. It worried him that she had not noticed him until then. Sloane had many feline qualities, and cat-like awareness of her surroundings was among them. The source of her sadness must be distracting indeed.

"I'm sorry," she said. She sought a handkerchief.

He gave her his neatly pressed one, then set his hand gently on her shoulder. "Is there anything I can do?"

She shook her head, wiping her eyes. He felt as though he had stumbled upon a very intimate, private moment, which was of course precisely what he had done.

Without another word, he squeezed her shoulder and returned to the front of the gallery, seating himself at the desk that was Sloane's usual station and turning his attention to the morning newspaper lying atop it—the very one for which he used to write his silly but popular columns until fired by the newspaper's owner—Margaret O'Neal—a formidable lady who had then been his fiancée.

The most prominent story that morning related the arrest of a Tennessee school teacher named John Scopes on the ridiculous charge of teaching evolution. According to the article, the state intended to try the man as an example to others so blasphemously and liberally inclined.

Like Sloane, Bedford lived in Greenwich Village. The speakeasies he favored there wouldn't lack for talk that night.

He read through the story—and another in similar vein. The Florida state legislature had passed a bill requiring daily reading of the Bible in public schools. Sin was being routed everywhere.

Not in New York, however. His Honor Jimmy Walker, a politician sometimes referred to as "the night mayor" of New York for his boulevardier ways, saw to that.

Hastening on, Bedford turned to the sports pages. The lovely Helen Wills, on whom he had a crush, had won a tennis championship in Newport. Less happily, a horse named Coventry, on whom Bedford had not wagered, had won the Preakness down in Baltimore, at odds of 22 to 1. The horse on whom he had rashly lavished his money had finished seventh. Coventry was expected at the forthcoming Belmont Stakes, but Bedford had his eye on another entry in that race, American Flag.

As he knew would happen, Sloane was standing before him, still holding her postal card. Her eyes were now dry, but her lovely face very drawn, and frighteningly pale.

"I want to go to Paris with you," she said.

Bedford sighed. "We've been through that, Sloane. I really need you here. Desperately."

"You could close down for a little while."

"A trip to Paris isn't a little while." He brushed a tear from her cheek with the back of his hand. "I haven't paid last month's rent. If we don't swing some decent sales pretty soon, I may have to close down for good."

"I don't think you're all that interested in running an art gallery, Bedford. I think you enjoy chumming around with your old newspaper pals a lot more than you do trading in art—not to speak of chumming around with showgirls."

"Claire Pell is not a showgirl. She's an actress. And a star."

"She is not an art collector."

Her expression gentled.

"I'd pay my own way," she said. "Both our ways. Anyway, Bedford. I've offered to help with the rent."

She spoke the words softly. It was a contentious matter with them. Sloane's family had enough money to buy a hundred galleries like his, but he had made it a point of honor never to touch a penny of hers. New York loan sharks had been another matter.

"Sloane . . ." He shook his head wearily, then took her hand. "Why don't you just tell me what's wrong. What's all this about?"

She set the postal card on the desk in front of him. On its front was a photograph of a very blond young woman almost electric in her despair. Her light-colored but darkly lined eyes were widened wildly. Her small mouth was slightly opened, the bones of her cheeks and brow casting hard shadows over her flesh. And the image was just a little out of focus, accentuating the suggestion of madness.

Something odd had been added to this bizarre likeness— small, sparkling tears below and beside the eyes. But they weren't really tears. On closer inspection, they appeared to be clear glass beads. The picture was a trick. But her crazed appearance seemed utterly genuine.

Bedford gazed upon the bizarre image for a long moment, until the poor woman's mad expression began to make him uneasy. He turned over the card. It was postmarked Paris, and addressed to Sloane at the gallery.

The card bore only one message, "*Douleur. Le dernier cri.*" It was signed simply, "*Fou.*"

"'Pain,'" said Bedford, translating. "'The latest cry.'"

"No," said Sloane, somberly. "She's not talking about fashion. She means, 'the final cry,' as in crying out. I fear she may be in some terrible trouble."

"Because of this picture?"

"I know her. Better than you know me."

Bedford let that pass.

"And 'Fou'?"

"'Fou,' meaning 'crazy.' That was our name for her in college. At Smith. She was a free spirit, don't you know. Dancing nude on the lawn in the moonlight sometimes, very late at night. Things like that."

"What's her real name? Isadora Duncan?"

"Polly. Polly Swanscott. She's a good friend. She stayed with me here for a time, before she got her own place."

Bedford looked at the postmark. "Her own place in Paris?"

"Her own place in the Village. Over on Bleecker. In Paris, I think she hasn't an address. I think she's been living with a man."

As Sloane well knew, he was sailing for France within the week, to search out paintings for clients and a possible chance for the one big sale that would put his gallery on its feet. As he thought upon it, there'd be some tempting benefits to bringing Sloane with him. With her help and expert eye, he might make some real finds. But the only find she had in mind was this madwoman.

"I don't understand any of this," he said.

She went to the end of the desk and sat down, gracefully crossing her legs. Women's hemlines had risen shockingly high that spring—to midcalf and a bit higher. Sloane's skirt barely reached the top of her knees when she was standing. Now the hem lay upon her thighs.

"I need your help, Bedford. Simple as that. I want to find Polly—if it's not too late."

"But what is it you think might have happened to her?"

"That's what I want to find out."

"You were crying, Sloane. You never cry."

The look she flashed him was a warning.

"Help, Bedford. Not prying questions."

"Are you being cross with me?"

"Yes I am."

"You know I'd like to help, but . . ."

"You know people, Bedford. You know everyone. You've been a newspaperman. You know police detectives, and gangsters. You know people in Paris—that Negro aviator you flew with in the war who runs a café now."

"Sloane, I'm going to Paris to buy art. On business. My time over there's limited. So are my resources."

She dabbed at her eyes. He couldn't tell if these were fresh tears.

"Won't you at least tell me why you think she's met misfortune?" he asked.

"No. I made a promise." She shook her head sadly, then

got to her feet. He feared for a moment that she was going to take her purse and walk straight out, never to return. Instead, she went to the canvasses stacked against the wall, turning the Schiele out toward the room. "We shall never get away with hanging this up," she said.

Bedford studied it. "Does that painting bother you?"

"Yes."

"Why?"

"This girl reminds me of Polly."

CHAPTER 2

THEY didn't speak of Polly Swanscott—or much else—the rest of the morning, though no clients or customers entered and there was little to interfere with conversation. At noon, Bedford suggested they close the gallery and take lunch together. Sloane demurred at first, then accepted, though without great enthusiasm.

She remained reticent as they walked along Washington Square and on down MacDougal to Minetta Lane and a restaurant they both favored. As regulars, they were given a table near the front. Sloane studied the menu at great length, though she should have known it by heart.

"I haven't had this scintillating a conversation since I last sat down with Calvin Coolidge," he said.

Sloane's eyes remained on the menu. "You've never even met Calvin Coolidge," she said.

"Are you sure? With him, it would be hard to tell."

He saw the quiver of an incipient smile on her lips, but it vanished.

"You said your friend Polly lived here in the Village," he continued.

She persisted with her contemplation of the luncheon entrees. "Yes. For a time. Too brief a time." Closing the menu at last, she turned to study one of the posters on the wall, a torn and dusty sheet advertising a masked ball in the Village that had been held the preceding October. Bedford tried to draw some hint of her thoughts from her eyes, but they were shaded by her cloche hat.

"Where?" he said.

"I told you. On Bleecker Street. East of here. On the edge of Little Italy."

"Why there?"

"It was safe."

"Safe? With all those gangster families in residence?"

She shook her head. "Safe because no one would look for her there."

"No one meaning . . . ?"

"Her family."

"And who are they?"

"I don't know much about them, except that they're very rich, and think the world of her. I think to a fault."

"But not enough to let her live *la vie bohème* in the Village."

"They had other plans, as mine did for me. They were planning a big wedding for her, but something went amiss."

"I daresay, if she's gone off to Paris. Or is the prime catch the man she's living with?"

Sloane was little amused. "Hardly. He's some nice boy she dated a little in college. His name's Nick Pease. Rather nice. And nice-looking. Went to Harvard."

"Perhaps she just didn't want to be Polly Pease."

He smiled. Finally, gingerly, she did the same, but then said, "This is serious, Bedford. Very serious. I mean to find out what's happened to her."

"I know. I'd just wanted to see you smile."

"She could be dead."

"Aren't you being a little overwrought?"

"No, I'm not. I know Polly. She's . . . I want to find her before anything happens. If it hasn't already."

"But you haven't told me why you think something would happen."

"I just know her. That's all."

The waiter came. Sloane ordered a salad. Bedford chose a small pasta dish. He also asked for grape juice for them both. They'd be served wine—in teacups. It would be a house red, perhaps of dubious origins, but they'd be glad for it.

Six years of Prohibition were proving a real nuisance. The Volstead Act had been lobbied through Congress by a Methodist clergyman from Virginia. Bedford resented this meddling by a church in matters of state. His own relations were Presbyterian, but there were certainly no temperance zealots among them. His Aunt Geneva in Albany was still known for her toots.

"I've heard of some Swampscotts in Boston," he said. "Any connection?"

"These are *Swanscotts*, and they're from the Midwest, like me."

"Farm implements?"

Sloane shrugged. "I don't think so. Dry goods. Drugstores. Something like that. Not codfish, like your East Coast 'old' money. Anyway, it doesn't matter. Our friendship didn't have anything to do with that."

Sloane's father was managing partner of a very large law firm in Chicago, one specializing in bonds.

"What brought them East?"

She shrugged. "I suppose they find it elevating."

"Elevating?"

"People here look down on the Midwest."

"Not the people here." Bedford made a circular gesture with his hand, indicating not only the crowded little restaurant but the street and neighborhood outside.

Sloane wrinkled her nose. "Before Polly moved to Bleecker Street, I'm not sure the Swanscotts even knew Greenwich Village existed."

"And now?"

"I suppose they wish it didn't."

Their food, accompanied by "grape juice," came very quickly. It was one of the reasons they were fond of the place.

SHE took his arm as they neared Little Italy. As she seldom did this, even when in a good mood, he looked at her curiously.

"Gangsters make me nervous," she said.

"As you observed earlier, you are describing some of my associates."

"That makes me nervous, too."

It was a bit disconcerting walking with Sloane. In her stockings, she equaled his six feet of height. Wearing her high-heeled pumps, she was several inches taller, and she had a very erect carriage. He was used to towering over most women. Sloane made him feel oddly small. And it had to do with more than height.

A block later, they reached their destination. Polly Swanscott's former residence was a particularly shabby tenement—a noisy, crowded, narrow structure, five stories high and full of children and cooking smells. They stood for a moment on the sidewalk outside the entrance, looking up. Bedford tilted back his straw boater.

"She lived on the top floor," said Sloane.

"That's sure elevating."

"She preferred it."

"To get away from the din of Italian street festivals?"

"For the light. I told you she was a painter. At least, she was trying to be one. She worked hard at it, but not everyone thought she had a lot of talent. You, too."

"I don't remember any paintings by a Polly Swanscott."

She shook her head. "I didn't tell you her name, but I showed you two of her canvasses and asked what you thought of them."

"What did I say?"

"I think the words were 'amateur' and 'melodramatic.' You may have included 'meretricious.'"

"Then I'm sorry. What did you think of her paintings?"

"I thought she tried really hard."

"But why would a woman bent on becoming a Greenwich Village 'artist' waste her time going to Smith College for four years?"

"Her parents' idea, I've no doubt. Her father gave the college a very generous gift. It helped get her in—along with the fact she was extremely intelligent and had straight A's."

He tilted his head back still further, studying the roof line. "Speaking of elevating, I don't suppose there's an elevator."

"I don't suppose you've ever lived in a tenement, Bedford."

He had, in fact, lived in worse than that. During the war. As a police reporter, he'd climbed the stairs of many a tenement—often with the most squalid carnage his reward. But he let her remark pass.

"Where do they dwell now?" he asked. "These Swanscotts from the Midwest?"

"Up in Westchester. Scarsdale."

"Scarsdale." He considered the name—and what it represented. "And Polly didn't like it there?"

"She liked it here. Her parents thought she was living at the Barbizon. When they found out the truth, they were very upset. They'd always hoped she'd marry well. Polly is very pretty. You can't tell it from that postcard, but she is."

"Did she have any boyfriends down here? Boys who didn't go to Harvard?"

"Yes. One. I don't know much about him. A Village guy."

"I'm a 'Village guy.'"

"Not like you."

She turned to go, but Bedford didn't budge. Looking again to the top story of the building, he noted a corner of the one of the window panes was broken. All the windows were grimy, two or three almost opaque.

"Is anyone living up there now?"

"I don't know. Just before she went to France, someone broke in and tore up the place. Wrecked everything. They didn't take much. There wasn't much to take, I suppose. Fortunately, she wasn't there at the time, but it frightened her."

"I daresay. Is that why she left? Because she was afraid?"

"Let's not talk about it anymore."

"But you want to find her . . ."

"Please!"

PASSING through Washington Square on their return, Bedford paused by the chess players congregated at the park's southwest corner, wishing he could forget the gallery and spend the rest of the afternoon lolling in the sunshine. He would have been happy just sitting on a bench, immersing himself in the spring day. Perhaps there was a reason for his lack of business success.

"Polly said some letters were taken," Sloane said.

"Love letters? Billets doux?"

She nodded.

"Did she tell you who they were from?"

She shook her head.

"Did she call in the police?"

Sloane brushed some hair from her eyes. "Yes, but they weren't much help."

They stopped at the Washington Square Arch, looking up Fifth Avenue toward the skyscrapers to the north, the Flatiron Building at Twenty-Third Street looming largest of all. Bedford's favorite painting in all the world was of that area up around Madison Square—George Bellows's *New York, 1911*—a great, vibrant, bustling canvas, full of smoke and steam and energy. He wondered who owned it now—not that he could afford to buy it.

"May I borrow that postal card for a bit?" he asked. "I'd like to show it to someone."

"I want it back." She reached into her purse.

"Of course."

"Are you going to help me, Bedford?"

He carefully placed the card in the breast pocket of his blazer, then took her gently by the shoulders. "Of course. I'll do whatever I can. Talk to some people. See what I can learn. But I'll need you to take over the gallery for the rest of the day." She often left in midafternoon.

"Yes. All right." She touched her face, as though something had just occurred to her. If so, she didn't explain.

"Thank you."

"I can't promise anything," Bedford said.

"And when you're in Europe?"

"Let me find out what I can here first. Maybe I can satisfy your curiosity about all this before I leave."

They started across the street. She took his arm once again. He hoped for a cheerier expression, but saw that the sadness had settled in once more.

CHAPTER 3

BEDFORD had small confidence that he could learn enough about Polly Swanscott to alleviate Sloane's distress in the short time left before he sailed for Europe, but he'd try. If nothing else, he knew where to start.

One of his favorite haunts in Midtown was the very avant garde and influential art gallery operated by the arts impresario and photographer Alfred Stieglitz. Bedford's little Eighth Street shop was such a small concern, but the two of them were in no way competitors. Stieglitz was more Bedford's friend and mentor, to the point of sending prospective customers Bedford's way when they showed insufficient interest in the "modern" works that were Stieglitz's forte and wanted something more traditional.

An older, spirited fellow, notable for an impish charm and inexhaustible enthusiasm, which sometimes took the form of Germanic bombast, Stieglitz was also something of a hustler, with a keen sense of main chance. Bedford still had friends in the newspaper business, and Stieglitz was well aware of the role that publicity and celebrity played in the formation of artistic genius.

The old man was most enthusiastic just then about the

work of a woman artist from Wisconsin and Virginia. He had married her the year before and her name was Georgia O'Keeffe.

Bedford found them now at work—both in the back, looking through several of Georgia's more recent paintings. Among them were two of New York skyscrapers Bedford had not seen before. Unusual, the canvases were rendered simply, the towering buildings painted sheer, without windows. But they gave the impression of soaring height and immensity—the awesome density of the city, its connection to the night heavens above and limitless universe beyond. The work was as powerful as the images were sublimely and immaculately beautiful. Bedford found himself staring at them transfixed.

"Magnificent, Georgia," he said.

O'Keeffe gave him a small grin, taking the measure of his sincerity, and then shyly looked away, apparently satisfied. The smile made her seem girlish. More commonly, there was a severity to her countenance that put Bedford in mind of a Pawnee scout examining a wilderness track or smudge of smoke on the horizon. She was one of the smartest women he knew in New York, yet very open, direct, and genuine, with little of the New Yorker's veneer of slick sophistication. Bedford liked her enormously.

Stieglitz stepped forward, eyes electric, slapping Bedford on the back.

"So then, Green, do you come to buy? Or are you hawking wares you can't unload elsewhere?"

"Neither," said Bedford. "I'm wondering if you might ever have heard of a young woman artist in the Village named Polly Swanscott."

"Name like that, sounds like somebody you'd represent for sure, Bedford," said O'Keeffe.

"I don't," Bedford said. "Not a very good artist, I'm told. Just a beginner. Used to live on Bleecker—near Mott."

He took out the Paris postal card.

"This is her. It's a very odd and distinctive sort of photograph. Would you have any idea at all as to who might have taken it?"

Stieglitz held the picture to the light, his enormously bushy eyebrows rising.

"Hmmm," he said, then turned the card over. "Paris."

"Mailed from there, anyway."

"A trick photograph," Stieglitz said. "But possibly the work of a master trickster. And a gifted artist." He turned to his wife, showing her the image. "It's Man Ray, wouldn't you say? Could be no one else."

O'Keeffe studied the photo even more carefully than her husband, then handed the card back to Bedford. "I've seen a Man Ray picture very much like that, but it was of a model he likes—someone called Kiki—Kiki de Montparnasse. This could be a Man Ray photo, too. But I don't think picture postal cards are his line."

"You can make a postal card of anything," Stieglitz said. "Note the French and their erotica."

"This is not erotica," O'Keeffe said. She went to a shelf and returned with a bottle of sherry and three glasses. "The picture Man Ray made of Kiki with bead tears is serene. Full of grace. This blond woman, she's frantic, fretful."

"Possibly he was yelling at her," Stieglitz said. "He's a small man, but he can be frightening sometimes when he loses his temper."

"He doesn't do that when he's working," O'Keeffe said. She pronounced that assertion as firmly as though it were courtroom testimony.

"Ray is still in Paris?" Bedford asked.

"Happily in Paris. Permanently in Paris. I wonder if he'll ever move back to New York." Stieglitz went to a drawer, and commenced a rummage. "Manny's from Brooklyn."

"Maybe he wants to forget that," said O'Keeffe, pouring Bedford a glass of the sherry.

"Do you think he might have an interest in society girls?" Bedford asked.

"Manny has a sizable interest in girls," said O'Keeffe. "Obsessive, you might say. And he's very ambitious, but not about social status." She pronounced the term as though it were an affliction. "He's making good money on his own."

"He has pictures in this month's *Vanity Fair*," Stieglitz said. "Crowninshield loves his work."

Bedford sipped, calculating how much of Ray's bad temper it might have required to have produced Polly's tormented expression. He studied O'Keeffe's, worried by what he saw.

"What's wrong?" Bedford asked.

She sighed. Georgia did not like to speak ill of her friends. "Manny can be possessive sometimes . . ."

"If you want to contact him," Stieglitz said, "here's his address. In the Rue Campagne Première. It's in Montparnasse—near the cemetery."

"Thanks a lot. You're aces with me, you two."

"Do you want to tell us what this is all about?"

"Wish I knew. I truly do."

◆

AS he'd quickly come to discover, Bedford's newspaper-owning fiancée had attached herself to him in considerable part because his mother came from an upstate "old money" family with cachet in all the right stuffy places, including the Social Register. But the family was so old they hadn't had any money for decades. Bedford had studied briefly at Hamilton College but had never finished, and his parents had died leaving him only two things of value: a rambling old farmhouse in Cross River up in Westchester County some fifty miles north of the city—and the family lawyer, Dayton Crosby, who now served as something of a stand-in father for Bedford.

An unkempt, resolutely eccentric curmudgeon in his early seventies, Crosby had once been a senior partner in one of the city's oldest, most prestigious, and insufferably establishmentarian law firms. But he cared little for that, and had gone into semiretirement at an early age to pursue more interesting interests, which included an animal welfare charity he had founded and books he wrote about celebrated New Yorkers. His knowledge of Eastern society and its tribes was without peer. Bedford had often called upon him as a resource for his newspaper column.

Crosby lived in an old brownstone house facing Gramercy Park, a few blocks east of the Flatiron Building. Ringing the bell several times, Bedford feared he'd have to go searching for the man at one of his clubs. He belonged to so many that it might be a chore lasting days.

Happily, Crosby's craggy old face at last appeared in a window beside the doorway, peering out suspiciously, as though Bedford might be a magazine salesman, or worse, someone from his law firm come to bother him about business.

"Bedford Green," he harrumphed, disapprovingly, after opening the door. "I thought you'd sailed for France."

"Next week."

"Then why aren't you hard at work in your gallery? As the President says, 'The business of America is business.' Or are you styling yourself a member of the leisure class these days?"

"Too much leisure at my gallery these days, Dayton. And probably not enough class."

Satisfied with Bedford's self-deprecation, which he held as a mark of a true gentleman, Crosby admitted him.

"Come in, come in, come in. Are you by any chance here for a game of chess?" Crosby was one of the city's best players, as Bedford lamentably was not.

"I'm in need of your help, Dayton."

The old man scowled, a predictable response.

"It's for Sloane," Bedford added.

Her name transformed the man's dour expression into an unreservedly boyish grin.

It had been said of Crosby that he always looked as though he had just taken a shower—with his clothes on. He was one of the most thoroughly rumpled individuals with whom Bedford had ever been acquaintanced. His hair was constantly in disarray, and he dressed with far more of an eye toward comfort than elegance, wearing an old pair of slippers when in his house and often out on the street. Yet, for all that, he had a naturally genteel manner and ease with people—

especially ladies. Despite his age, he enjoyed flirting with young women, and with Sloane Smith he was utterly smitten.

"And how is that lovely lady?" he asked, padding down the house's main hall and bidding Bedford to follow.

"Still very lovely, but not very happy."

Finding no other convenient place, Bedford set his straw boater on a stack of books on Crosby's hall table, then followed along. There were such stacks everywhere. The man could have done without furniture.

Crosby led Bedford into his study, brushing dust off one old velvet-covered chair and removing two sleeping cats from another. A sheepdog was stretched out on the hearth, though in the springtime there was no fire.

"Why not happy? And how can I help you—and Miss Smith?" Crosby asked, when both were seated.

"What can you tell me about a family called Swanscott?"

"Swampscott. Yes. I know them. They're quite decent people. Been in Beverly, Massachusetts, almost since the Mayflower. Have they somehow made Sloane unhappy?"

"Not Swampscott, Crosby. Swanscott. A family from the Midwest. Now living in Scarsdale. Lots of money."

"That's all?"

"All that Sloane can recollect, and she's a friend of the daughter."

The older man shook his head. "I've never heard of any Scarsdale Swanscotts. But then, I've never heard of anyone from Scarsdale. Lots of money, you say."

"They have a daughter named Polly. Went to Smith College—with Sloane."

Crosby shook his head once more. "Sorry."

"How about Nick Pease?"

"I knew a Nick Pease at Harvard. Very grand fellow."

"This would be his son." He hesitated. "Or perhaps his grandson."

A cat jumped on Crosby's lap.

"I'll make some inquiries. You know my niece, Jill? She knows everyone in Westchester. Certainly knows some disreputable things about you. I talk to her every day. Perhaps

I'll have something for you tonight." Crosby scratched the animal's ears. "A quick game of chess?"

Bedford rose. "Thanks, but a quick game would be one I'd surely lose."

❖

If no longer a welcome visitor at the midtown office of the *New York Day*, Bedford had remained a regular, if discreet one. Its resources, particularly its clipping morgue, had proved very useful to him—in the art business, and in other business. The fate of Polly Swanscott was not the only troubling matter friends had brought to him.

Slipping into the building from the loading docks, he passed through the bustling din of the press room and ascended to the equally chaotic but more decorous editorial offices above, taking care to avoid the precincts favored by the higher-ups, including especially Margaret O'Neal.

The erstwhile colleagues who noticed him gave him the benefit of a wink, a few of them were even happy to provide him with a glad hand and good word, if not the offer of a nip from a desk drawer flask of top quality hootch—as long as neither Margaret or her brother Patrick—the *Day*'s publisher—was near.

Nodding and smiling politely, but declining refreshment, Bedford made his way to the back of the newsroom and the paper's morgue. Behind the counter was the gruff old woman who ran the place. A large, bespectacled, gray-haired grandmother named Ruby, she kept a cigarette in the corner of her mouth, its aroma mingling with the faint scent of bourbon that was a constant part of the ambience. In addition to serving as mistress of the many rows of file cabinets, repositories of clippings dating back to the paper's nineteenth-century origins, Ruby ran a bookie operation out of there and had enough bottles of liquor stashed in it to supply a speakeasy for a week.

All this was gladly tolerated by everyone up to and including the managing editor. Ruby's knowledge of the contents of those archives was encyclopedic. It would have been idiocy to replace her—not that the O'Neal family wasn't capable of that.

"Hiya, Bedford. Want a drink?"

He tipped his boater. "No thanks, Ruby. Just a quick look-up. Scarsdale family named Swanscott. Daughter named Polly. Anything you've got."

"Society news?"

"Anything."

"How far back?"

He shrugged. "A few years."

She rummaged in the files only a few minutes.

"Slim pickings," she said.

All she laid before him was a single, brief clip—a routine story filed by one of the paper's cop house reporters. He read it through quickly.

"This is all?"

"Yup. Not what you were looking for?"

He studied the clip a moment.

"Actually, I think it is." He smiled. "Thank you very much."

"You got a horse in the Belmont?" she asked, as he turned to go.

Bedford hesitated. "American Flag."

"You don't like Coventry?"

He put a five-dollar bill on the counter. "A fiver on the Flag—to win."

Shaking her head, she took up the money.

"Liked your column better when you wrote it," she said, as he went to the door.

BEDFORD headed across town to the carnival tumult that was Times Square. Plowing along the crowded sidewalk, he at last reached his favorite theater district haunt, Lindy's, where he abruptly found himself on the brink of an encounter with a man he most definitely had not come to see—the gambler Arnold Rothstein, who was seated at a table in the back.

Bedford owed him a not inconsiderable amount of money.

A dapper gent with a flamboyant style, but a hard case criminal nonetheless, famed for fixing the 1919 World Series, Rothstein was cavalier about his own debts, but a bit strict as concerned his debtors.

Engaged in conversation with a couple of newspaper reporters and a homicidal bootlegger of Bedford's acquaintance, the gambler hadn't noticed him. Bedford halted at the cashier's counter, quickly turning his back.

"I'm looking for Joey D.," he said to the large woman at the cash register.

"Not here, Mr. Green."

"He usually is, this time of day."

"Well, he was here, but he got called back to the precinct. Something about an old case of his."

"Okey doke. Much obliged."

Keeping his back to Rothstein's table, Bedford went to the pay telephone near the men's room, calling up the precinct house's number and asking for the detective section. Joey D'Alessandro answered the phone himself.

"It's Green," said Bedford, quickly. "I'm at Lindy's and I need a favor."

"Do yourself a favor and get out of Lindy's. Rothstein is looking for you."

"He only has to look about fifty feet, but he hasn't seen me yet. I'd appreciate it if you could check something out for me, Joe."

"It's kinda busy here, Bedford. Otherwise, I'd be over there with you."

"Just take a sec'." He read D'Alessandro the short newspaper clip. "I need to know what this is all about. Stuff they wouldn't have put on the sheet."

D'Alessandro hesitated. "You think there's some funny business here?"

"I'm sure the New York police department did its usual first-class job. But there's always more than meets the eye—especially with official case reports."

As a reporter, his first story had been about a woman shot twice through the chest whose passing the police had listed as a suicide.

"Hmmm," said the detective.

"My thought exactly."

The detective said something no newspaper would have printed, made a vague promise, and hung up. As Bedford did the same, he felt a hand on his shoulder. A glance at the pinkie ring told him all he needed to know.

Rothstein smiled, a cat with its paw on a mouse.

"You'll get your money," Bedford said. "I promise—if I have to cross the deepest sea to find it."

The gambler's smile got broader—and more menacing.

"I've let you string me along, Green, because you used to do me favors when you had that newspaper column. But that's beginning to seem like a real long time ago."

"You'll get your money, Mr. Rothstein. You needn't worry."

The gambler stepped a little closer. "That's right. I don't have to worry. I don't because I can always sell your markers to one of my friends. Now, I know it'd be really stupid for someone as well known as me to cause harm to someone so close to the publisher of the *New York Day*. But some of my friends, they are that stupid." He looked over his shoulder, something Bedford thought the man ought to do more often. "I've been informed that you've made travel plans, Green, and that you're sailing for France real soon." He leaned very close. "Just don't come back without my money."

He stepped back, brushing off the shoulder of his expensive suit, as though his contact with Bedford had made it dusty.

"Don't worry," Bedford said again, adding, "By the by, I'd go with American Flag in the Derby."

"You're telling Arnold Rothstein where to play his bets? You?"

"Just a hunch."

Rothstein shook his head in amazement and walked away.

T HERE were times when Bedford felt he was still in love with Margaret O'Neal, who was bright, witty, and—when

not obsessed with the society pages—a lot of fun. There were
times when he found himself as bewitched by Sloane Smith
as Dayton Crosby was. Like all the men in New York bohemia capable of such a thing, he also had a mad passion for
"the Golden Girl of Greenwich Village," Edna St. Vincent
Millay.

But the women who loomed largest in his life were two
Broadway actresses, equal in his affections, but as different
as Piper Heidsieck and a fine Chianti.

Tatiana Chase was the offspring of an American financier
and a Russian ballerina whose czarist family had had the
foresight to get out of Russia long before the revolution. A
blue-eyed blond with somewhat Slavic features, she was a
daffy, fun-loving, very grand and highly cultured ingenue
close to Bedford's thirty years. She had been a "Debutante of
the Year" and a big name on the New York social scene until
boredom had set in and she had turned to the stage. She much
preferred the company of theater folk to anyone whose name
might appear in the Blue Book's listings, a publication she
dismissed as shabby, pompous, and common.

A clumsy but determined horsewoman, sailor, tennis
player, and golfer, Tatty Chase was a creature of boundless
enthusiasm. This, plus a marvelous sense of humor, served
her career in lieu of acting talent. She was well suited to light
comedy, especially the witty, class-conscious works coming
over from London by the likes of Noel Coward. But her two
attempts at serious drama had drawn the biggest laughs of
her career, and come close to ending it.

Her biggest parts now seemed to be in plays she personally and generously invested in. Tatty had made a few valiant
tries at the moving picture business now thriving across the
river in Astoria, but with small success. The only film parts
offered her were in slapstick comedies, which she feared
might be viewed as demeaning, though Bedford thought she
might have been brilliant in them. Directors had not been
pleased by her stubborn insistence on wearing her long pearl
necklace—which she claimed her mother had been given by
the Czarina Alexandra—no matter what the costume or occasion. Tatty wore her pearls even in the bath.

Claire Pell was in far greater demand on the New York stage—especially for musicals. She had a throaty, alluring singing voice, with an above average range, and her dancing ability was equal to the dazzling good looks of her legs. She, too, yearned to do serious dramatic works, but producers insisted on thinking of her only in terms of musical comedy. She couldn't object, for they had made her a star.

She had large, soft brown eyes to go with her dark blond hair, and played ingenue parts with ease, though she was as old as Tatty Chase. Her parentage was a mixture of Hungarian and Italian. Close-up, her face had something of an exotic cast to it. Bedford thought she might do well in motion pictures, and encouraged her in that direction. But Claire thought they offered little future—at least for her.

"I sing," she said. "They're silent."

It was a few minutes after five, a time that would find her in her dressing room. She had the starring role in a ghastly romp of a musical called *Belles Abroad*. She played a Southern vamp, a part she managed well, though she'd grown up in a working-class Long Island suburb, and had numerous relatives among the Italian immigrants living in lower Manhattan.

The critics had been unkind to her show, but the songs were pleasant, the girls showed plenty of leg, and the seats stayed full. As Claire observed, it paid the rent.

"Hello sport," she said, without looking up from her dressing table mirror, as he entered after a polite knock. "I'd give you a kiss, but I just finished my makeup."

She pondered her reflection a moment, then rose and turned to him.

"Hell with it," she said, moving close. "I've got more makeup."

It was a very warm kiss. They hadn't been together for a while.

She stepped back. "You look really swell."

"You always say that," said Bedford.

"Yeah, but sometimes I lie. Not today." She returned to her chair and set about making a few small repairs to her face, none of which seemed at all necessary. "Did you come by to invite me to dinner after the show?"

He paused. It was a delightful idea, or would have been. "That would be wonderful, but . . ."

"Gee, Bedford, you make a girl feel so wanted."

"I'm occupied tonight—trying to help a friend."

"Is the friend you're helping by any chance named Tatty Chaste?"

The mispronunciation was deliberate.

"It's Sloane. Someone she knows seems to be in trouble, and she's asked me to help her find out what it is."

"She doesn't know?"

"Apparently not."

He handed her the newspaper clip. She read it quickly, frowning, then returned it.

"I don't understand."

"The girl whose apartment was broken into—she's the one in trouble."

"How is it I'm supposed to help you?"

"This happened in Little Italy."

"A lot happens there. You think I know people who do things like that?"

"No, Claire, but I wondered if you might have friends or acquaintances who know people who do. You've told me how people of that interesting sort are always after you to arrange theater tickets for them."

"If I got them tickets to this bow-wow of a show, they'd be after me, period."

"Sloane's really upset over this. The girl is a friend of hers."

"And you're sticking your oar in? I thought you were off to Paris?"

She stepped behind a dressing screen, changing from dressing gown to costume.

"I am. End of the week. As it turns out, this girl's living in Paris now. Before I go looking for her—if I do—I want to be well informed."

"Let me put you wise to something, Bedford," she said. "I don't like asking those people in Little Italy for favors."

He'd gone to a wedding with Claire once, and remembered well some of the more interesting gentlemen guests.

"Sorry, I really shouldn't be asking this of you."

"If I help you, you're going to owe me."

"Anything."

"Careful. I may take you up on that."

◆◆

THE evening proved as pleasant as the day, so Bedford walked home from the theater district, stopping at Luchow's on Fourteenth Street for dinner and then proceeding down to Sheridan Square and his apartment on Barrow Street. He bathed, changed into a fresh pair of white flannels and a white tennis sweater, made himself a gin and Italian, and then sat sipping it and listening to jazz recordings as he leafed through his art magazines and waited for his telephone to ring.

In the end, only Joey D. and Dayton Crosby called. The detective had found a police report pertinent to Polly Swanscott's Little Italy burglary. He read it to Bedford in its lengthy entirety—the length owing to a subsequent and related crime of far more seriousness. Crosby said his niece Jill had heard the Swanscotts were from Michigan and owned a chain of drugstores in the Midwest, but little else was known about them.

Still, Sloane would realize he had not been idle. He rang her apartment, baffled by the lack of response.

She lived only two blocks away on Grove Street. Walking over, he rang her bell three times. Stepping back into the street when there was no answer, he looked up to the third floor and the windows of her flat, finding them bright with lamplight.

There was certainly another place to look—their favorite Village hangout—Lee Chumley's speakeasy just around the corner.

The stout, wooden front door to the establishment bore only the street number "86," and might have served as access to some castle keep. Its one small window was barred and revealed nothing of the interior except a sort of vestibule.

Like most of the speaks in the Village, Chumley's had little to fear from enforcers of the Volstead Act. Mayor Walker, tolerant and indulgent to a fault, saw to that. The principal fear was the occasional raid by the Bomb and Alien Squad looking for "Reds." Leland Stanford Chumley, the proprietor, was a local organizer of the International Workers of the World. He and his fellow Wobblies would hold meetings upstairs and afterwards repair to his saloon below. John Reed was long gone from the Village and now buried by the Kremlin wall in Moscow, but the neighborhood was full of leftist writers just as subversive in the establishment view, and they were often to be found in Chumley's.

But the last Red Scare had quieted down, and life in bohemia had returned to normal. There were no wary eyes peering from the barred window. Chumley's door was unmanned and unlocked.

Bedford clicked it open, stepped into its little vestibule, turned left up a short flight of stairs, crossed a landing, passed through a velvet purple curtain, and descended into the yellow glow of the noisy, smoky, softly lit interior, which resembled an old English public house from the previous century. The floor and tables were of a wood so ancient it might have been laid by the original Dutch settlers. The walls were decorated with a continuous row of the covers of patrons' books. Cats were disporting themselves variously about the crowded main room and a fire was going in the corner hearth despite the spring warmth. An argument was enlivening a conversation among a large group gathered around the bar to the rear.

Bedford searched for familiar faces through the heavy cigarette smoke, recognizing Theodore Dreiser sitting with friends at a table to the side. His heart quickened to see Village golden girl Edna Millay holding forth at another table just beyond, her strawberry blond hair falling over her eyes as she read from a sheet of paper. She was with three men, one of them the literary critic Edmund Wilson.

Bedford looked further, spotting Sloane finally at a table

by the hearth, sitting all alone. She could have served as a study for two paintings Bedford admired—one, of a woman absinthe drinker, by Henri de Toulouse-Lautrec, the other, a sadder, lonelier work by Edward Hopper, the young protégé of Bedford's Eighth Street neighbor, Gertrude Vanderbilt Whitney. Called *Chop Suey*, it was of a sad young woman in a cloche hat in just such a New York setting, seated in just the same pose.

"I tried to reach you by telephone," Bedford said, standing before her.

Sloane looked up, warily, as though he were an intruder, but said nothing.

He seated himself. "I've put together a few pieces of the puzzle. Your friend Polly had good reason to be afraid after the burglary. It turns out there's a murder mixed up in this. But it may well turn out to be a good thing—except, of course, for the poor devil who got killed. He was the burglar who broke into her apartment."

Sloane simply stared, puzzled. The flickering light from the fire illuminated her gray-green eyes enough to reveal confusion and a melancholy more profound even than that he had observed that morning.

He paused to order a whiskey from a passing waiter.

"The Swanscotts own drugstores, by the way," he said.

"What did you say?" She spoke quietly, and a little vaguely, as though only slightly distracted from her thoughts by his presence. Her eyes were fixed on something not in that room.

"The Swanscotts are from Michigan," he said. "They own drugstores."

Sloane took a nervous sip of her drink, spilling some. "Yes, I know."

"They sent her to Smith to meet rich boys from Harvard."

There was laughter behind him—coming from Edna Millay's table. Sloane seemed utterly oblivious to it.

"I don't believe she went to Europe to get away from her parents," Bedford continued. "I don't think they're quits. When her apartment was broken into, the police made a list of what was taken. There were some letters and a piece of jewelry or two, but also a bank draft from her parents, made out to her. The parents are continuing to provide her with money. They may have disapproved of her life here, but they were supporting it and they're doing it now. I think she ran away to get away from New York. The burglary must have scared her plenty—especially with that burglar then turning up dead in New Jersey."

He glanced down at the table top. As with all the others, there were names and initials carved all over it.

"Sloane?"

Her eyes were now staring straight at him. "You said, 'dead,'" she said.

He leaned back. "Yes. The police found the burglar who broke into her flat in a dump in Jersey City. He'd had his throat cut. He's no threat to her anymore. Not to anyone."

"How do they know he was the one?"

"That bank draft from her parents. He was carrying it. The police say he was a common street criminal, but her parents told them they thought he must be one of her Village boyfriends."

"Boyfriends?"

"According to the police, the dead man's name was Henry Schultz. Did Polly ever talk about such a man?"

"She had only one boyfriend when she was here in the Village," she said, slowly, "his name is Norman Oritzky. I never met him, but I think he lived over on East Third Street."

"Not a nice neighborhood."

"No. But she may be in a worse one now."

She reached into her purse and set a postal card on the table, similar in size to the one Bedford was still carrying. He recognized the art on the front, a Bonnard portrait of a woman floating in a bathtub, her eyes vacant and staring. He turned the card over. It was addressed to Sloane at her Grove Street apartment, and bore only one word.

"'*Mourir*,'" he read.

"'To die,'" said Sloane.

Moving with sudden and unnerving swiftness, she rose from her chair and hurried from the room, pushing between the crowded tables. Bedford started to rise to go after her, but thought better of it, knowing his company would not be welcome.

The waiter brought his whiskey. He was a long time looking at it, and then a short time drinking it.

He passed by Sloane's Grove Street flat again after leaving Chumley's, but didn't ring. There was no light on in any of her windows.

Following Barrow Street to Seventh Avenue, he continued east.

❖❖❖

THE tennis whites he was wearing were not very suitable clothes for a burglary, but even in Little Italy the streets were largely deserted at that hour and Bedford's approach to Polly Swanscott's former residence was little noticed—or so he hoped. He loitered against the wall of the building as two autos passed by, but neither driver paid him much attention.

Finally, he stepped up to the door, which, as he hoped, was unlocked. A pungent variety of stale cooking smells assaulted him as he stepped inside. Creeping up the wooden stairs, he flinched at the creaking noise he made, and halted on the first landing—ready to make a hasty retreat at the first bark of dog or human cry.

But there was neither. He found that keeping to the side of the stairs eliminated most of the sounds. By the time he reached the fifth floor, his own breathing was the loudest thing to be heard.

With no light on in the hallway, he had to strike a match. It was obvious which of the three doors was Polly's. One of its panels had been knocked out. Reaching through the opening, he turned the knob.

From his earlier examination from the street, he had guessed the apartment was still unoccupied, and so it proved, though someone had made a half-hearted effort to clean it up. There were no dishes in the sink. The cupboards were largely bare. Most of the furniture had been removed.

But, lighting more matches, he found odds and ends lying

about—a chair missing two of its legs. A book of poetry with a stained cover and some torn pages. A broken wineglass lying on its side in a corner.

In a closet in the lone bedroom, he made a more interesting discovery: the remnant of a torn painting, still attached to its smashed frame. Perhaps a third of it was missing, but the center and upper portions were intact.

He struck one more match, leaning close, startled by what he saw.

A woman's face, with sad, haunted eyes. Oddly, it reminded him much of a Joseph Stella painting he'd seen at Stieglitz's gallery. But that work was sensual, an exotic, pleasurable fantasy.

This was a frightening work, more so than the postal card image in his pocket. Her skin in this was a mass of ugly red splotches.

Bedford pulled the remnant of the canvas free of its frame, folding it carefully.

He was running low on matches, but struck one more and held it high to give a look to the closet shelf. Something else had been left. A bottle of liquor. Pulling out the top, he smelled what he took to be a very good scotch. What burglar would leave that behind?

A dog finally did stir itself to a bark as he made his hurried descent of the stairs, but Bedford was out the front door before anyone could interfere with him.

CHAPTER 4

TATTY Chase owned a large yellow Packard touring car that she drove very fast and very badly. She was stage performer enough to make herself heard over the rush of wind, though Bedford had to lean close to catch everything. The proximity of her perfume and her beauty was intoxicating. As they careened around one corner, he gave her a quick and friendly kiss just below her ear—an intimacy she completed ignored. Tatty was annoyed, apparently by the very idea of the Swanscotts.

"Drugstores? People who trade in snake oil medicine and toilet tissue?" she said. "And you say they have social ambitions? What is wrong with Americans? This is a country founded on egalitarianism, *n'est ce pas*? The Constitution forbids patents of nobility! There are not supposed to be social classes here. But these people—this commercial riff raff—they make money in toilets, or meat packing, or breakfast cereal, and demand to be treated as aristocrats, as though they're better than the rest. *Mon Dieu!* Don't they know aristocrats are *born*, not *made*? Amazing. Utterly amazing!"

Bedford had the previous December been Tatty's guest at the Russian Nobility Ball at the Waldorf Astoria. He'd had a marvelous, vodka-enhanced time—involving, at one point in the evening, gavottes—but knee-deep in princes and countesses, he'd found himself the only commoner there. It was a suitably humbling experience.

"I'd appreciate it if you'd be nice to them," Bedford said. "I need for them to tell me some things."

"Of course, darling, of course. I'll help you anyway I can. Even that."

She patted his hand, allowing the car to swerve suddenly to the right. Correcting, she shifted down with a rasping movement of the gears and then accelerated around a chuffing Model A Ford. As she returned to her lane, the right wheels caught on the shoulder of the road and she swerved once more. When Bedford opened his eyes again she was grinning broadly, enjoying herself immensely.

◆

THE Swanscotts' house was huge, made all the more ostentatious by being set on a much too small plot of ground for its hulking size. There were large, pretentious gates at either end of the short circular drive that would have far better suited the sprawling country estates of Tatty's aristocratic forebears. To cap the vulgarity, a conspicuous wrought-iron sign bearing the Swanscott name was positioned at the nearer entrance.

"Are they a *hotel*?" said Tatty, wheeling the big Packard through the open gates.

The driveway was wide, but she still managed to bump over a curb and set one of the car's wheels on the lawn when she parked.

Bedford supposed the Swanscotts wouldn't mind. He'd brought Tatty along for the sole purpose of dazzling and disarming Polly's parents sufficiently for him to elicit some useful information from them. However modest her talent and infrequent her starring roles, Tatty was a certifiable celebrity with enormous social cachet.

Mrs. Swanscott proved to be a large, overdressed, pleasant-faced woman with graying blond hair who might better have resembled her pretty daughter twenty years and fifty pounds before. She was wearing far too much jewelry for early afternoon—in marked contrast to Tatty, who as always wore only her pearls.

"Mr. Green! Come in, come in!" Mrs. Swanscott trilled. "Please. Please."

"This is my friend, Tatiana Chase," said Bedford. "She was kind enough to drive me here from the city."

"Are you *the* Tatiana Chase?" asked Mrs. Swanscott, as though stunned to be in such proximity to a great personage.

"Dee-lighted," said Tatty, vigorously sticking out her hand in the manner of the late President Theodore Roosevelt, whom she had much admired for his vigor, straight talk, and lack of pomposity.

"There was an article about you in *Town & Country.*"

"Yes, I'm afraid there was."

With a nervous titter, Mrs. Swanscott led them down the cavernous entrance hall to an elaborate sitting room, which boasted three couches and a small divan, among lesser pieces. There was a larger-than-life portrait of Mrs. Swanscott above the fireplace mantle and, near it, a slightly smaller one of a pinched-faced, unhappy man Bedford took to be her husband. Bedford glanced about but found no painting of Polly, though a silver-framed photograph on the piano appeared to be of her.

Tatty was surveying the room as well. He presumed she was going to behave herself, but there was an impishness lurking behind her friendly expression.

The maid, who had vanished after taking Bedford's straw hat, reappeared immediately after they had all seated themselves, pushing in an enormous, rattling tea cart, laden with a tea service and a dozen different kinds of pastries.

"Refreshment?" Mrs. Swanscott asked, leaning so far forward in reaching for the teapot Bedford feared she was going to slide from her perch on her couch onto the floor.

Bedford contented himself with some tea. Tatty's choice was a too large piece of chocolate cake, from which she took only one small bite.

"Well," said Mrs. Swanscott. "What would you like to know?"

"Your daughter, Polly . . ."

"Polly is in Europe. The 'grand tour,' don't you know.

Starting in Paris. But what would you like to know about Haskell and me?"

Bedford gave her a blank look.

"Aren't you here for an interview?" she asked. "For your column? Aren't you doing a piece about us?" She looked through the doorway, as though he'd left someone behind. "Where is your photographer? Isn't this for the rotogravure section of your newspaper?"

He'd not made his purpose very clear—deliberately.

"I no longer write that column," he said, carefully. "I'm afraid I've severed my connection with the *New York Day*."

Mrs. Swanscott seemed nonplussed. Then at once her expression lightened. "Then you're representing a different newspaper? The *New York Times*?"

"I'm afraid not. I'm here about your daughter," Bedford said. "I'm here on behalf of a friend of hers—an associate of mine who was at Smith College with her."

The woman appeared stricken. "You mean you're not here to write a newspaper article about us? About our donation?"

"Donation?"

"To the Horticulture Society."

"Fifty thousand goddamn dollars!"

The voice came from the hall. An instant later, Mr. Swanscott entered—a short, stout, square-jawed man considerably less distinguished than the image in the oil portrait. He went to the side of his wife's chair.

Bedford smiled, as agreeably as he could manage, as Mrs. Swanscott hesitantly introduced the two of them to her husband. Bedford rose to shake Mr. Swanscott's hand, but the fellow didn't budge in his direction.

"Fifty thousand is a generous sum," said Bedford, finally. "And I'm sure it's quite newsworthy. But as I say, I'm no longer with the *New York Day*. I run an art gallery now."

"Art," said Mr. Swanscott. "You make money with that?"

"It's a marvelous little gallery," said Tatty, glancing about the room. "All the best people go there. You ought to visit it. I'm sure Mr. Green could assist you, uh, in completing your decor."

Mrs. Swanscott appeared flustered. Her husband's face deepened in color.

"Are you trying to sell us something?" he asked.

Bedford took out the postal card, presenting it carefully to the mother.

"Polly sent this to my associate—Miss Sloane Smith— who finds it worrisome. She thinks your daughter may be in some kind of trouble, and has asked me to help. Have you heard from her since she went to Europe?"

"What does this mean?" said Mrs. Swanscott, turning over the card and reading the message. " '*Doleur*'?"

She pronounced the word "dollar."

"It means 'pain,'" Tatty said.

Mrs. Swanscott blanched. "Oh dear."

"We hear from Polly regularly," her husband said. "She's taking a trip through Europe."

"She was enjoying it very much," said his wife. "She's said nothing about anything painful. Maybe this is a little joke."

"When was the last time she wrote?"

"Oh dear. I can't remember. But she's doing fine. We send her money, every month, and we know she's receiving it."

The husband snatched away the card, looking at it contemptuously for a few seconds, then thrusting it back at Bedford.

"This is not my daughter," he said. "My daughter looks nothing like this. She looks like that!"

He pointed to the framed photograph on the piano. Bedford went to it, noting a much younger and more contented Polly, wearing a white shirtwaist and straw hat and posed on a lawn before what looked to be a large summer cottage.

"Oh dear," said Tatty. "I'm afraid she's a bit behind the fashions in Paris."

The father scowled. Mrs. Swanscott looked extremely uneasy.

"It occurred to me she might have left the country because she was afraid—because of the burglary of her apartment," said Bedford. "But the police found the man who did it. A criminal type named Schultz. He was murdered. In New Jersey. Polly has nothing to fear anymore. You should make that clear to her."

"Oh, we shall," said the mother. "We shall."

The father was looking at Bedford hard.

"I think you'd better leave now," said Mr. Swanscott. "You came here under false pretenses. You told my wife it was an interview."

"Not exactly," Bedford said. "I told her I had a few questions. But I'm curious. You told police this man Schultz was a boyfriend. Is that possible?"

"I didn't say anything about a Schultz. I don't know any Schultz. I said there was a boyfriend. A Jew. Was Schultz a Jew?"

"Sir?" said Bedford.

"The dead guy. He was a Jew?"

"I don't know," said Bedford. "What matter . . ."

"She had some Jewish guy in New York . . ."

"Polly is engaged to Nicholas Pease, a nice young man from Connecticut," Mrs. Swanscott interrupted. "Their marriage was postponed, until she returns from Europe, but they are still betrothed. There is no other boyfriend."

Tatty was on her feet. "Oh, dear. I really must run."

"I'm sailing for France next week," Bedford said, making one last cast into these waters. "I'd be happy to look up your daughter for you. Make sure she's all right."

"She's fine," said the father. "Stay away from her. Now, if you don't mind . . ."

Bedford bowed, toward Mrs. Swanscott. "Thank you for your time, and the splendid refreshment."

"Dee-licious," proclaimed Tatty, pulling Bedford along toward the hall.

"Are you in a play, Miss Chase?" asked the mother.

"Yes, but I'm afraid I haven't any free tickets to give you."

TATTY gunned the engine and accelerated so rapidly that a tire dug a trench across the lawn and one of the flower beds.

"Pity we can't choose our parents," she said, as they were roaring along the street. "Those people are impossible."

Bedford gripped the chromium handle on the dashboard placed there for that purpose.

"I don't think Mrs. Swanscott is as impossible as she seems."

"Why's that?"

He raised his voice to overcome the engine noise as Tatty accelerated. "I'm not sure. But I think she's more worried about her daughter than they're letting on."

"All mothers love their daughters. My mother loved me. I think."

❖

BACK in the city, Tatty dropped him at Eighth Street and Sixth Avenue in the Village, then turned back uptown after extracting the promise to bring her back "something marvelous" from Europe. He hoped she would settle for a piece of artwork from one of the unknown painters he was going to browse among. He couldn't afford much else Tatty considered marvelous.

He walked the half block to his gallery thinking upon the Swanscotts. For a daft moment, he tried to imagine Mrs. Swanscott dancing in the nude in the moonlight at Smith College. The notion somehow cheered him.

❖

HIS good mood did not last long. Sloane was not at the gallery. He thought at first she might have left early but, unlocking the door and stepping inside, he found that the establishment had not yet been opened for business for the day. There was mail on the floor, though nothing from Sloane explaining her absence. Bedford stood considering this for a long, uncomfortable moment, then went to the phone.

After seven rings, he hung up. He remained in the gallery for another hour or so, but neither Sloane nor any sort of customer crossed the threshold. Exasperated, he locked up the gallery and went to Grove Street and Sloane's building. There was no response to his ringing of her bell, but after loitering awhile he encountered a neighbor.

"Miss Smith?" said the woman. "She's on a trip, I think. Saw her out the window this morning, getting into a taxi."

"Why do you think she's on a trip?"

"She had two suitcases."

Bedford thanked her, then went around the corner to his own apartment.

There was a note under his door. It bore only one word: "*Adieu.*"

THE Café Très Vite was a bistro just off Broadway that Bedford and Claire Pell patronized frequently. The dining room was large, dominated by faux marble Romanesque columns, yet cheery and warm—the walls painted a soft orange, the furnishings Art Deco, the pictures modern—after a fashion. Two of them had come from Bedford's gallery.

They had declined their usual table by the window and taken one in the rear instead. Claire was tired and not up to dealing with late night autograph seekers, and Bedford was in no mood for another encounter with Mr. Rothstein, and especially not his friends.

"You didn't call," he said.

"What are you talking about?" Claire asked.

"Last night. About the burglary in Little Italy. The body in New Jersey. What some people might have to say about it."

She leaned back. A chill came into her voice.

"I forgot all about that. Sorry."

She grimaced.

"Is something wrong?" he asked.

"I hurt. You try earning your living doing high kicks and buck and wings for two hours ten times a week. You'll soon want to switch to coal mining."

Neither spoke for a long moment.

"Sloane Smith has left me high and dry."

"Poor you. Did she run off with someone?"

"I mean she's left the gallery. And New York. I don't know where she's gone, or for how long."

"I'm sorry you're so unhappy, Bedford, but you have to admit she's a very strange girl."

"I find myself worrying about her the way she was about her friend Polly."

"There's nothing you can do about it. Anyway, cheer up. You're going to Paris."

She touched his hand. He took hers in his.

"You're absolutely positive your family friends had nothing to say about the late Mr. Schultz?" he said.

"I just told you. I completely forgot about that. And let's leave it that way, okay?"

He patted her hand. "Sorry. I'm being inexcusably persistent. This is beginning to preoccupy me."

"You know your problem, Bedford?"

"I could recite a couple dozen of them."

"Well, your big one is that you're in the wrong line of work. You shouldn't be running a store."

"Gallery," he corrected.

"You should go back to the newspaper business."

"No thanks."

The Très Vite had a small jazz band of three. Their last set had long concluded, but one of the musicians, a guitarist, returned and began playing. Claire's hand was still in Bedford's.

"When he finishes this song, let's go," she said.

"Don't you want to dance?"

She smiled, "No."

❖

V**ERY** late that night, but shortly after he returned home, Bedford's telephone rang. He'd mixed himself a nightcap and had fallen asleep in a chair. The insistent sound confused him at first, but his grogginess gave way to the realization that it might be Sloane phoning to explain herself.

Stumbling, he went to it, holding the mouthpiece close. "Sloane?"

There was a pause. For a moment, he feared she was having second thoughts and was going to hang up. Then he heard a woman's voice—soft and nervous and seemingly far away—and not Sloane's.

"This is Mrs. Swanscott," she said.

"Mrs. Swanscott?" Bedford blinked.

"I must speak quickly, Mr. Green."

"Yes, very well." He lowered the phone as he dealt with a yawn.

"I'm very concerned about Polly. If you're still going to Paris, I'd like you to try to find her for me—to make certain she's all right."

"But I thought you said you were in regular contact with her."

"We send her checks—to the American Express. They're received and cashed. But we don't hear from her. I'm worried now. Very worried. Our daughter isn't like this."

"I see."

"I realize this might inconvenience you—that you have more important business over there."

"Mrs. Swanscott . . ."

"I mean to compensate you for that inconvenience—and appropriate expenses. Would five hundred dollars be enough?"

"Mrs. Swanscott, I can't . . ."

"Six hundred then. I'll have a check to you tomorrow."

"But . . ."

"Please don't call me—not till you get back. If and when you find her, cable me. That's all I ask. I want to know she's all right."

"Very well, Mrs. Swanscott, but . . ."

"If you can make her come back with you—I'd like you to do that. I'll pay you a thousand dollars if you can do that. I'm more than worried. I'm frightened. She's mixed up with such strange people."

"They're just artists."

"I'm counting on you, Mr. Green."

"But Mrs. Swanscott . . ."

She had hung up.

❖

SLOANE was absent from the gallery again the next morning. He felt foolish for having thought she might turn up. He had to resign himself to closing the place down for the duration of his European travels.

There was work to do. He took off his blazer, rolled up his sleeves, and began removing his more valuable paintings to the storeroom in back, which had a stout oaken door and two very good locks. He'd leave a few cheaper pieces and prints hanging near the front window. For a moment, he considered putting the Schiele there as well, but even in Greenwich Village such a provocation might invite the police.

He was just finishing his task when he heard the bell above the door ring. Two days without a customer and now one just as he was about to leave.

A young man stood by the front desk, a highly presentable and pleasant-looking fellow, with dark hair parted in the middle and slicked back neatly. His clothing was a virtual duplication of Bedford's, though he wore gray flannels and black shoes with his blazer and striped tie. He held his straw hat in his left hand, declining to set it down without invitation.

"Mr. Green?"

"Yes?"

The young man took a step forward and extended his hand. "Nicholas Pease. I am friend of . . ."

"A friend of Polly Swanscott's."

Bedford shook the man's hand, embarrassed that he'd not had a chance to wash off the dust. The visitor appeared not to notice. He was, at least, very well-bred.

"More than a friend, sir."

Bedford hastily rolled down his sleeves and fastened the cuff buttons, reaching for his coat. He felt uncomfortable without it.

"So I'm given to understand. What can I do for you, Mr. Pease? I presume you're not here for a painting."

Pease glanced at a framed print on the wall. It was a rather macabre French theatrical poster. He turned quickly back.

"I'm afraid not." He paused, then looked Bedford quite

directly in the eye, as though he were about to confess something. "I'm in regular contact with Mrs. Swanscott. She tells me that you've received a letter from Polly."

Bedford decided to keep the postal card in his pocket. "It was a postal card, and it was sent to my assistant, Sloane Smith, with whom I believe you are acquainted. Unfortunately, she's not here. In fact, I've no idea where she is—nor when she's coming back."

Pease seemed puzzled by that, but continued.

"Mrs. Swanscott said it was from Paris, and that Polly's likely there."

"She was until recently, at all events."

"You're going to look for her?"

"Sloane asked me to—as did Mrs. Swanscott." Bedford was too embarrassed to mention the fact that he was being paid, and hoped Polly's mother hadn't. "I'll do what I can."

"I'd like to ask you a favor."

Bedford simply waited, trying to look agreeable—without agreeing to anything.

Pease took an envelope from his coat pocket. "If you find her—would you give her this."

Bedford took the letter. It bore only the name "Polly."

"Why not send it to her care of American Express in Paris? I gather she still goes there to pick up the money her parents send her."

"I'm not sure it would get to her."

He quite possibly meant he was afraid she wouldn't accept it.

"Very well," Bedford said, pocketing the envelope. "Though I certainly can't make any promises."

"I understand, but, if you do find her—no matter what— I'd appreciate knowing where she is. And how she is."

"That much I can do. And I'll certainly express your concern."

"My letter will do that."

The young man took a slight step backward, but moved no further.

"You know of our engagement, Mr. Green?"

"I do."

"Well, it wasn't my idea to break it off."

"Nor Mrs. Swanscott's."

"No."

"Are you saying it was Polly's?"

Pease appeared flustered. "Mr. Green, if you can—if you find her—there's something else I'd like to know. Need to know."

Again, Bedford waited.

"I need to know whether my mother had anything to do with breaking our engagement."

"She disapproved of the betrothal?"

"I'm not sure. I just want to know whether this is mother's doing—or if it's what Polly really wants."

Her running off to Europe should have been a pretty clear message, Bedford thought, but said only, "Once again, I'll try."

"I'll compensate you for your trouble."

Now Bedford was really embarrassed. "That will not be necessary."

Pease moved now toward the door, a little clumsily, his poise diminished. "Well, then. Thank you, Mr. Green."

"Mr. Pease, why not simply go look for her in Paris yourself?"

The young man looked sheepish indeed, now.

"I work for my father, in his firm, Mr. Green. If I were to run off like that—well, it would only make matters worse. A lot worse."

With that, he gave a quick bow of the head, then turned and hastened out the door, heading east toward Fifth Avenue, as if reluctant to linger in Greenwich Village any longer.

CHAPTER 5

BEDFORD'S ship, the *Aquitania*, was British and very fast, but two days out of New York the vessel piled into a nasty storm that slowed its progress and confined most of the passengers to their cabins. Traveling in Second Class in a cabin that lacked a window, Bedford preferred to be out in fresh air no matter how severe the ship's pitch and roll.

The gale, in fact, was enticing. His service in the war had been as an aviator, not a ship's officer, but he'd spent enough time at sea to know that the best cure for seasickness was to fill one's stomach full of bread and potatoes, on which he loaded up at breakfast.

Borrowing a foul weather jacket, he went out on the main deck and found himself the only passenger there, despite a thrilling vista of gray-green moving mountains marching along beneath a ragged sky of torn and racing clouds. Lunging to the rail, then struggling along it forward to the bow, he hooked his arm around a stanchion to keep his place in the strong, stinging wind, fixating on the roiling sea as it fell away and then returned in a great sloshing and thrashing rush that seemed to lick up to the very boards at his feet.

Heavy weather was what he liked most about going to

sea. He thought it the grandest imaginable recreation. Of all his friends, the only one who shared this odd enthusiasm was Claire, whom he'd once again left behind.

A young woman, bundled into an oilskin jacket much too large for her, of a sudden came sliding and tumbling to his side, her purchase so precarious he had to reach out to steady her.

She grabbed hold of the rail, then turned to look at him, her flushed and shining face very close. There was a wild look to her eyes he attributed to the excitement of the storm. He recognized her, but could not recall why. He was certain he'd never met her. Perhaps a newspaper photograph.

"Fun!" she said.

"Yes it is."

"Love fun!"

"Yes."

She leaned even closer, looking up at him.

"Do I know you?" she asked. "There is something very familiar about you. Are you at all famous?"

"Not at all. But I was thinking the same of you."

"Shouldn't. Not famous yet. But I mean to be. I'm studying the ballet."

She seemed well into her twenties; hardly an age to commence training for the dance.

"I paint and write, too," she said. "I'm very talented."

She was oddly featured—large hooded eyes, tiny nose, strong jaw, her face a little too square—but very pretty. The weird gleam in her look somehow added to her attractiveness.

Hunching over the rail, she bravely looked straight down into the sea.

"They talk of God on high!" she said. "What about down there? That's Godlike wrath and fury."

Her accent was decidedly southern, but she spoke more rapidly than was the custom in that region—almost as fast as a New Yorker.

A great wave came curving and whooshing along the side of the ship, its froth catching both of them in the face and running cold water down their necks. He shivered.

"You shouldn't have invoked the deity," he said.

She giggled, as might a child.

"I'm Zelda," she said.

"Bedford Green."

She looked at him curiously. "Did I meet you on the Bedford green? Are you from Bedford Village? We used to go to Bedford, when we lived in Westport."

"My name is Bedford Green."

"That is a very strange name. My husband's name is not at all strange. It's Francis. Francis Scott."

Of course.

"But he is sometimes strange," she said.

"You are Zelda Fitzgerald."

"That's right! How clever of you. Are you a detective?"

He shook his head, a little sadly. "I wish I was. Where is Mr. Fitzgerald?"

"In our stateroom, dead to the world. I don't call him Mr. Fitzgerald. Sometimes I call him Goofo. He's hungover. Again. He says he's seasick but we were awfully blotto last night and that's what it's from. He had whiskey for breakfast but it didn't help—and anyway it was at five a.m. I'm often ill but not today." She took a deep breath of the brisk, cold air.

"You will be if you don't get inside," he said. "That wave gave you a dousing."

"Will you come with me?"

How could he not? He nodded.

"Come have a drink with me. In the saloon. We'll survive the storm together. And talk about God."

❖

SHE led him up to the First Class section from which she had come but from which he was ostensibly barred as a denizen of mere Second Class.

"I saw you down there on the deck from my cabin window," she said, as they entered the First Class lounge and headed for a table in the center of the mostly empty room. "I wanted to be there with you. Out there with the sea. You seemed so thrilled with it all. I wanted to be thrilled, too."

"Glad you did," he said, pulling out a chair for her. "But better now to be warm and dry."

"Warm and dry and tight. We need gin."

Zelda seated herself. She was even prettier out of her oil-skin. She wore a wool skirt and tweed jacket, with a long collegiate scarf. Her hair was a dark gold in color, cut short to reveal the full length of her long neck, but very full and curly. She kept her eyes on him. God was no longer on her mind.

"My husband's famous," she said. "I'm going to be. I'm writing a book. It's about me. And him. You can be in it, too. Are you at all interesting? Are you famous?"

He knew all about the Fitzgeralds—from the few years when they had lived in New York. Though they'd been a highly public couple—riding on the rooftops of taxicabs and dancing in the Plaza Hotel fountain—he'd never encountered either of them. He wasn't certain whether that was good or ill fortune.

"Not at all. I'm an art dealer. A highly unsuccessful art dealer."

"Are you going to France to buy art? We know artists. Armies of them. They don't all like Goofo, but I like them. Some of them."

"That's my ostensible reason." He hesitated. If he were a detective—a good detective like his friend Joey D.—he'd remind himself that discoveries are made by turning every stone. "But I have another."

He showed Zelda the postal card of Polly, and told the tale again.

She gripped the card with both hands, as though she was afraid it was going to jump away from her. For a long time, she stared at the girl's image, hard. Then she turned the card over and pushed it away, looking horror-stricken.

"God," she said.

"Sorry?"

"She looks like God." Zelda shuddered.

"I don't suppose you and your husband ever ran into the girl?"

"No. No, I'd remember. Face like that." She lighted a cigarette, shuddering one more time. She exhaled. "I think I want to meet her. No, I don't want to meet her. But I must."

A sleepy waiter, who seemed amazed to find them there, was approaching.

"Gin fizz," Zelda said to him. "Gin fizz. Two gin fizzes." She turned to Bedford. "What would you like?"

"A gin fizz would be swell."

"Three gin fizzes," she said.

Bedford put the postal card in his pocket. He feared it was getting worn.

"You have a daughter," he said. "Little Scotty."

"Yes. My dear little darling. She's in Paris, with her nanny. We were in Rome, but we didn't like it there. We've moved back to Paris, but Goofo had to go back to New York about his new book. Now we're going back to Paris. But then we may go somewhere else."

"Your husband is a splendid writer," he said, recalling that he had read two of the man's books. *This Side of Paradise* was magnificently written, but youthfully pretentious and self-indulgent. *The Beautiful and the Damned* was also well crafted, but the overall cynical and self-pitying tone of the novel had bothered and depressed him. Fitzgerald's characters reminded him of too many friends and relatives—and perhaps a little of himself.

There was supposed to be tea dancing, every afternoon in the First Class lounge. Noting the lack of dancers and music, Zelda complained about the latter to the waiter when he brought their drinks. When he protested that pitching decks from the storm made that sort of entertainment impossible, she threatened to go to the captain, whom she insisted had become a close friend.

Shaking his head, the waiter disappeared. In a surprisingly short time, three musicians came forth, grousing, and took their places. Abruptly, almost in midnote, they commenced playing "Bye, Bye Blackbird."

Zelda's eyes widened excitedly. She swilled down her first drink in a few gulps, then lurched to her feet and pulled Bedford from his chair.

"*Dansant,*" she said, and came into his arms. "Let's get hot!"

Bedford had flown against some of the best pilots in the German Air Service's much-feared Jagdstaffel 28, barely escaping with his life. That now seemed less intimidating than accompanying this wild woman to the dance floor on a pitching, heaving, shifting ship, but he somehow found the courage.

It took a lot. The task of keeping their balance as they circled the floor made their dance an athletic endeavor of Olympic proportions, but for all that it was not unpleasant. Zelda clung to him tightly.

"I do know you, Bedford Green," she said, pulling back a little to look strangely into his eyes. "I do, I do. Where from? What do you do?"

"I told you. I own an art gallery in Greenwich Village."

"I never go to art galleries in Greenwich Village. Only go there to drink."

"I used to be a columnist for the *New York Day.*"

"Yes, that must be it. But I never read the *New York Day.* Were you one of those nasty gossips?"

"Of a sort."

"Were you witty?"

"Occasionally."

"That's all right then. Hold me tight, for I'm going to lead now, and we're going to go very fast."

Before he could object, or try to prevent her, she was off, moving him backwards around the floor much in the manner of a figure skater pushing a partner. Bedford managed to keep from falling, and help her stay upright as well, but then something caught her notice and distracted her attention and she stumbled. He shifted himself as they went over so that he would land first—a successful maneuver that caused him enormous pain and resulted in her coming down on his chest.

She appeared very happy, and kissed him.

"Zelda?" someone said.

Giving a shriek, she thrust herself up onto her knees, and twisted her head about to look behind her.

There stood a man, in long overcoat and knotted white

scarf, looking down upon them both with great detachment. He held a glass in his hand and sipped from it, pausing to contemplate the taste of its contents.

"This is Scott," said Zelda, to Bedford.

He was a very clean-cut and handsome man—a fitting match for her, except that she was such an untamed thing, and he looked like an illustration in an advertisement for Brooks Brothers shirts.

Bedford introduced himself from his awkward position and tried to explain the circumstance. Fitzgerald waved his hand to indicate his disinterest.

"Come along, Zelda," he said, turning away.

She got to her feet, unsteadily. "Mr. Green is an art dealer from Greenwich Village—traveling Second Class."

Fitzgerald kept walking.

"And he used to write a column for the *New York Day*."

The author paused, then turned about. "The columnist? Are you that Bedford Green?"

Bedford got up onto one knee, then struggled erect. He'd injured his right leg in an accident in the war, and it sometimes caused him difficulty.

"I am, for whatever it's worth—which isn't very much."

"Then you must join us for a drink."

He smiled, famously. Zelda grinned.

"And dinner," she said. "Oh, goody."

◆◆◆

EVENING clothes were a passport to many places, including the loftier levels of ocean liners. Black tie was not required for the Second Class dining salon, but Bedford had packed his tuxedo anyway, not knowing what situation he might encounter. Having encountered the Fitzgeralds, he was prepared. No one gave him so much as a glance as he ascended to First Class and its opulence.

The Fitzgeralds had made arrangements for him at their table, which was off to the side but agreeably distant from the too noisy orchestra, which was playing "You Were Made for

Me" as he entered. The room was almost as empty as it had been that afternoon.

His hosts had not stopped drinking in the interim. Zelda, incandescently lovely in a short, bare-shouldered, shimmering evening dress, was exceedingly restless, squirming in her chair as might a child on a too long train journey. She tried to follow and take part in the conversation but her attention constantly wandered, especially after Bedford declined a renewed invitation to dance.

Bedford had expected Fitzgerald to be as self-centered as most of the celebrated writers of his acquaintance, directing the conversation to himself. The fellow had been declared one of the most talented authors of the era on the strength of a first novel published when he was twenty-three.

But, quite to the contrary, Fitzgerald turned the discourse into an interrogation, quizzing Bedford for gossip about East Coast society and the New York demimonde as unrelentingly as a wartime intelligence officer with a prisoner of war. For his part, Bedford tried to be circumspect, especially about people who were his friends, but he tossed in enough tidbits to satisfy Fitzgerald, who seemed particularly interested in American heiresses who'd gone abroad in search of titles.

Eventually, after several glasses of champagne, he relented, allowing the conversation to drift to art and artists. Zelda contributed her posthumous and passionate remorse for the painter Amedeo Modigliani, whom she pronounced the handsomest man who ever lived. He had died five years before of influenza at the age of thirty-six, a tragedy that had prompted his beautiful mistress, Jeanne Herbuterne, to share his fate by throwing herself from a fifth-story window.

Bedford shuddered at this recollection. It put him in mind of Sloane's uncommon sadness—and Polly Swanscott's almost suicidal comment on the back of her postal card.

"We never met him, Zelda," said Scott, when his wife had reached the point of tears in her despair over the painter's end.

"I know," she said. "That's what makes it so sad."

"It's almost American, for him to drop dead like that,"

Fitzgerald said. "You know, there are no second acts in American life."

"Did you ever know a family named Swanscott?" Bedford asked. "From Michigan?"

Though he had gone to Princeton, the writer was from the Midwest.

"I'm from Minnesota, not Michigan," Fitzgerald said, a little indignant. "Are these people you know in Paris?"

"New York." Bedford kept the postal card in his pocket, but retold Polly's story.

"Man Ray, you say," Fitzgerald said. "I think I know of that fellow. He takes photographic portraits, and drives spectacular motor cars. Though he's not rich."

"But you know nothing of Polly?"

"Not acquainted, old sport. You say the family's in drugstores? In Michigan?"

"Yes."

"And they're very rich?"

"So it would seem."

"Interesting. I should think it would be hard to become very rich—just owning a few drugstores."

He began talking to Bedford about society folk, again. It became clear to Bedford that the Fitzgeralds were Right Bank people, who knew writers but few artists, and had little congress with their Montparnasse cafés.

But Zelda had not forgotten Polly.

"Do you know what, Bedford Green," she said. "Whatever else we're going to do in Paris, and what we do in Paris really isn't very interesting, except that we often do it in the middle of the night, but, no matter what, we're going to help you find this girl."

"That's very kind, but . . ."

"I can tell that you love her madly."

"Actually, I never met her."

"I know! It's like me and Amedeo Modigliani!"

"Zelda . . ." cautioned Fitzgerald.

"We'll help you find her. I swear it to you." Zelda leaned back. "Give me a cigarette, Goofo."

CHAPTER 6

THEY rode the boat train together to the Gare St. Lazare, and shared a taxi as far as the Champs-Élyssés and the Rue de Beri, where Bedford left them for the small, quiet hotel where he had stayed on his Paris furloughs during the war. The Fitzgeralds went on to their flat at 16 Rue de Tilsitt on the Right Bank, after extracting a promise from Bedford to meet them for cocktails at the Dingo American Bar in the Rue Delambre before dinner.

It was warm, so Bedford changed from his traveling suit into white duck trousers and white shoes and his blazer, adding a soft-collared shirt and red and blue striped tie. He'd left his straw boater back in America, and so went hatless to his first destination, which was not the Dingo Bar, though not far from it.

The taxi took him with some minor meandering through Montparnasse to the Rue Campagne Première, and an imposing, four-story building whose street-facing apartments boasted wide, floor-to-ceiling windows. Bedford presumed they were artists' studios. The concierge at No. 31 directed him up one flight to the first door on the left.

Jazz music was playing, a song he recognized as "Bootlegger Blues," though he couldn't identify the band. He knocked once, without result, then more loudly. Finally, the latch clicked and the door swung open, revealing a remarkable-looking woman utterly without clothing.

She was very full-figured, and magnificently so. Bedford decided if she was not an artist's model she should have become one—and a very high-priced one at that. She had dark, marcelled hair; very Gallic, heavily lashed eyes; a long, sharply pointed nose; and a mouth designed for smiling, though it was not disposed for such use at the moment.

"*Eh?*" she said.

"*Je cherche un homme—Monsieur* Man Ray."

"*Il n'est pas a' maison,*" she said.

"*Non? Je suis venu de les Etats Unis pour le trouver.*"

She shrugged, exposing some underarm hair. "*Pas ici.*"

From just behind the door she produced a cigarette, but no match. Her eyes demanded one from him. Bedford fumbled in his pocket and performed the required service. As his reward, she blew a long column of smoke in his face, followed by a low "*Merci.*"

Bedford took the opportunity of all that to glance beyond her at the room beyond. As its exterior promised, it was large, high-ceilinged, and filled with light. A small wooden staircase led up to a loft of some sort, but there was a bed on the main floor, set to the side of an arrangement of armchairs, large coffee table, and bookcases.

"*Ou peut-on trouver Monsieur* Ray?" Bedford said.

Another shrug, another exhalation of smoke. A sort of smile.

"*Je regrette, monsieur.*"

The door slowly closed.

Bedford was nearly a block away when a sudden thought struck him, swiftly followed by impulse. Hurriedly retracing his steps, he gave the concierge a nod and a smile once more, then ascended the stairs to Ray's door, rapping sharply.

This time, the door opened only a few inches. The naked woman had added a wineglass to the cigarette. The jazz music had stopped.

"*Quoi?*" she said.

"Polly Swanscott?"

The door slammed shut in his face.

◆◆

The Fitzgeralds were late. Bedford took a table just inside the Dingo's entrance, near a ruggedly handsome young man with a wide moustache who wore a rumpled wool suit that was too hot for the weather and might well have been his only one. He was writing in a composition notebook, so intent upon this work he showed no indication of discomfort.

Bedford turned away and watched the women passing on the Boulevard Montparnasse outside the window. Many were pretty. None resembled anyone he knew. None was six feet tall.

"They walk up the street. They walk down the street. But they're not streetwalkers."

The speaker was the young man at the table behind him. Bedford kept his eyes on the parade of ladies—some of whom were with men. His gaze followed a blondish woman in green dress, shoes, and hat as she approached and with a slight, careful smile, passed on.

"I think that one is," Bedford said. He gave the man a quick look. The fellow gave him a grin as wide as his moustache in return.

"*Es una mujer hermosa,*" he said. "That's Lady Duff Twysden. She'd argue with you on that point. But some here wouldn't."

He stuck out his hand. Bedford got the idea he was tired of his work and was looking for an excuse to put it away for the day—whatever it was.

"Ernest Hemingway," he said.

Bedford leaned to shake the man's hand. "Bedford Green."

"I know that name. Are you a newspaperman? Got a column somewhere? New York, right? The *New York Day.*"

"Past tense. Got the sack. Now I'm an art dealer."

"Past tense for me, too. I was with the *Kansas City Star.*

Toronto Star, too. Learned a lot. Saw a lot. But, newspapers?" He shrugged. "Now I have the work." He nodded to his notebook. "The work went fine today. It went very well." He closed the notebook.

"You're writing a book?"

"I am." Hemingway seemed very proud of the fact.

"A novel?"

"Of course."

"About the war?"

"No, I'm not ready for that."

Bedford fell silent. He'd presumed the young man had been a soldier. He had that air.

"It's about all this," said Hemingway, gesturing to the street.

A waiter was at Bedford's elbow. He ordered coffee, and nodded toward the young Hemingway's empty wineglass.

"Con mucho gusto," said Hemingway. *"Gracias."*

"I'm sorry," Bedford said. "I know no Spanish."

Another grin. "Sorry. I was thanking you. I was just down in Spain. Pamplona. We were. My wife Hadley and I. Ever been down to Spain?"

Bedford shook his head. "France and Belgium. England, and Berlin once."

"You were in the war?"

Bedford nodded.

"I was with the Italians," Hemingway said. "Lieutenant in the Red Cross ambulance corps." He thumped his backside. "Shell. Took more'n two hundred piece of shrapnel. Were you wounded?"

The Red Cross ambulance drivers were not really soldiers and their "rank" was merely honorary. Still, it took guts to take those slow, clumsy vehicles up to the front under enemy shellfire. Bedford shook his head.

"You served behind the lines, then."

"I did," Bedford said. "Sometimes ours. Sometimes theirs."

Hemingway's eyebrows rose.

"I was a flyer. First for the French. Then for the British."

"Not for the Americans?"

"I didn't like their hiring practices."

Hemingway nodded knowingly, though he could have no idea. He gestured to Bedford to move his chair to his own table just as the waiter returned with coffee and a clean glass, which he filled with a red Bordeaux. Hemingway motioned for him to leave the bottle and bring another glass.

"Goddamn good to meet you, Green. Honored to have a drink with you."

They lifted glasses. Bedford took a small sip. Hemingway swallowed half the wine in his, then leaned back and sighed happily.

"I'm looking for someone," said Bedford.

"Meet a lot of someones, in these cafés."

"Two someones, actually. A photographer from New York named Man Ray and a blond young woman—an artist of sorts—named Polly Swanscott."

"Ray's easy. Small guy. Frizzy hair. Big eyes. Always watching. Dresses well—not like you but as well as you. Always with good-looking women. Likes fast cars. Drives a Voisin roadster. Quiet, but kind of a tough little guy, sometimes. Has a bad temper. But a gent. Hangs out here a lot, and La Coupole."

"You seem very observant."

"When I'm not working, when it isn't going well, that's what I do. Observe."

And drink.

"I went to his studio," Bedford said. "He lives there. And not alone."

Bedford described his encounter with the naked woman. Hemingway leaned back in his chair, laughing.

"Don't you know who she is?"

"She's certainly unforgettable. But I've no idea who she might be."

"Have you ever met a queen, Bedford Green?"

Bedford thought back to the Russian Nobility Ball he'd attended with Tatty. "A Russian grand duchess once."

"Well, that woman you met was Kiki—Man Ray's model and mistress. And she's the closest thing to a queen I've ever seen or expect to. Kiki de Montparnasse. Half the artists in the quarter have painted her and it's anybody's guess how many have slept with her. But she rules Montparnasse, and she belongs to Man Ray."

"Yet you say there are others?"

"You bet. He has women around him all the time, but she's the only one who gets to live in his digs. When Kiki comes around, the others get scarce—fast. She's the belle of the ball around here, a good time gal—but you wouldn't want to get her mad at you. You wonder what it's like when she and Ray get mad at each other."

With great delicacy now, Bedford once again produced the postal card image.

"What about her?" he said.

Hemingway studied the picture carefully.

"Woman like that, she'd drive me crazy."

"She's Polly Swanscott, the young artist I'm looking for. Ever see her before?"

Now Hemingway held the card out at arm's length, squinting as though he were about to shoot it.

"You know, I think I have. If it's who I think it is, we used to see a lot of her—for a time. On the streets and in the cafés. She'd hang around like a stray cat. Didn't know her as Polly, though."

"What did she call herself?"

"Fou. As in crazy. And I guess she was. I remember seeing her with Ray. Couple times or more. Here at the Dingo, and at some party in Montmartre."

Bedford took back the card, hesitated, then looked at it anew. "Did you ever see her with bruises on her face?"

"Maybe."

"Maybe?"

"Hard to tell. She used a lot of rouge. Kinda looked like a puppet."

His attention wavered. He was looking over Bedford's shoulder.

Two men were approaching their table. One was Scott Fitzgerald, wearing a well-tailored suit and brandishing a silver-topped cane. The other was another well-dressed man who could have been F. Scott Fitzgerald, he so much resembled the other. Zelda was not with them.

"Bedford," Fitzgerald said, in great good humor. "Sorry to be late. Ran into an old friend from Princeton. And here he is. Dunc Chaplin. The greatest pitcher in the history of collegiate baseball, aren't you, Dunc?"

The greatest pitcher shook his head, smiling insincerely.

"This is Bedford Green—out-of-work newspaperman, art salesman, and New York Social Register."

"You sell the Social Register?" asked Dunc.

"I give them away," Bedford said. "To the needy."

Fitzgerald seemed irritated by this. Chaplin stared.

"This is Ernest Hemingway," said Bedford, avoiding further foolishness. "A writer. Mr. Hemingway, this is Scott Fitzgerald, also a writer."

Hemingway rose, shaking Fitzgerald's hand. "You wrote a very good book."

"Two of them," Fitzgerald replied. "And now a third. But I've heard of you, Hemingway. You write short stories. North Woods and all that."

He abruptly sat down, almost missing his chair. It had been obvious that the two had been drinking. Now Bedford noticed the sudden pallor that had come over Fitzgerald's face. He seemed a little uncertain as to where he was.

"Where is Zelda?" Bedford asked.

Fitzgerald refocused himself.

"She went her own way. Something about our Princeton stories boring her. Dunc, have I ever told a boring Princeton story? Is there such a thing as a boring Princeton story?"

Dunc shook his head, smiling now at the absurdity of the notion. Fitzgerald ordered champagne, demanding that the bottle be brought at once. When it arrived, he ordered another bottle—also to be brought at once.

"Ernest," he said. "May I call you Ernest?"

"Sure."

"I have to ask you something, Ernest, if I may," said Fitzgerald. "I have to ask you, did you sleep with your wife before you were married?"

Hemingway frowned, less from anger than from uncertainty about what to do. He decided finally to be amused about the insulting, tactless question.

"No, but I once took on six Chinese whores I won in a poker game."

He laughed. It was impossible not to join in. Fitzgerald leaned with his bottle to fill Hemingway's empty glass, and Hemingway became happier still.

Bedford consulted his wristwatch, then stood up.

"I'm going back there," he said. "Do you want to come with me, Mr. Hemingway?"

"To Man Ray's?"

"Yes, indeed."

"If you got ideas about Kiki, amigo, I'd . . ."

"I think Ray was there," Bedford said. "I think he was the one playing the jazz record. I want to go back and find out. I need to talk to this man."

Hemingway stuck his notebook in a side pocket of his suit jacket, then downed the champagne.

"You'll need my help," he said.

"What's this about, Green?" asked Fitzgerald. "Still playing detective?"

"Still trying to find that girl."

Fitzgerald exhaled sharply, as though frustrated at trying to get across a very obvious fact.

"She's rich, you say. And doubtless spoiled. Let her be, why don't you? You know how the very rich can be. They're so different from you and me."

"Yeah," said Hemingway, rising. "They've got more money."

❖

THE two of them hadn't progressed half a block up the boulevard when Bedford heard his name called out—the Southern accent unmistakable even over all the traffic noise.

A taxi had pulled to the curb just behind him. Half out of it, her foot on the running board, was Zelda. He was relieved she wasn't on the roof.

"Beddie!"

Bedford winced. No one in his entire life had ever called him that and he could scarce imagine what daft notion had prompted her to do so.

Zelda half leapt onto the sidewalk, and needed to be caught. Wherever she had been, liquor had been served.

"Beddie," she said, grinning oddly. "Where are you going? We were supposed to meet here. Isn't this the Dingo? It is. And I've just got here. How can you be going?"

Bedford refrained from noting the time. He patted her arm, stepping back from her.

"Your husband's inside, waiting for you. Mr. Hemingway here and I have to attend to a small errand in the vicinity, but will be right back."

Zelda looked upon Hemingway with shining eyes.

"Let's have a drink," she said.

"In a bit," Bedford said, then turned and started walking, giving her a friendly wave over his shoulder.

"I like him," said Hemingway, a few paces later. "He wrote a very good book. But I'm not sure about her."

"She's okay."

"Strange the way some men go for some women."

Bedford thought upon the photograph of Polly Swanscott on the postal card and the one on her family's piano.

"They change," he said.

◆

HEMINGWAY stayed beside him as they hurried along the narrow street. For a big man, he moved with great ease, accustomed to the out-of-doors and walking.

"Do you think he'll talk to us?" Bedford asked.

"Don't know. Never talked to me much. But I never had much interest in talking to him. Now Pascin—Jules Pascin. There's an artist to have for a friend. There's a man who knows the joys of life—and shares them."

They parted to move around an old woman who was carrying a sack. She ignored them, ignored all things except the movement of her feet before her. Crossing the next street, they had to dodge a high-roofed, noisy automobile that came swerving around the corner.

It was not a Voisin. The driver was not a small, dark man but a large fat one who appeared not to notice them.

Another block and they were at No. 31. Nothing seemed to have changed.

"Wait," said Hemingway.

"Why?"

"You've been there. The concierge will recognize you. Or was he drunk?"

"Who?"

"The concierge."

"It was a woman. And she was sober. Mostly so, at all events."

"He may have told her not to admit you. So I'd better go in first."

"And if she admits you and not me?"

"I'll bring him out. Invite him for a drink."

"And if he declines?"

"Then I'll ask him about this girl."

"In front of Kiki? You'd only stir up trouble."

"Maybe she's no longer there. She may have gone out."

"She wasn't wearing any clothes."

"Doesn't matter," Hemingway said. "I've seen her in the Dingo, eating dinner and naked as a jaybird."

Bedford imagined the scene, and found it agreeable.

"Is there some reason you want to go in there alone?"

Hemingway shook his head. "No. Just trying to help you out."

"Well, let's assault this position together."

The writer started up the entrance steps. "*L'audace! Toujours l'audace!*"

The French general who had said that had been responsible for many French deaths.

Their discourse had unfortunately delayed them too long. Before Bedford could take another step he sensed someone coming up quickly behind him. As he considered who it might be, he was struck by a thudding, numbing blow to the back and side of his head, and a lightning flash of pain that jolted down his neck and into his shoulders.

He sank to one knee, raising his left arm defensively as he tried to face his attacker, but another blow struck at his shoulder, making that arm drop. He made one more effort, pushing himself up with his right leg and twisting around left, trying to bring his right arm around in some kind of punch. He landed only a glancing blow, but he wore a square topaz ring on his right hand and it caused some damage to the man's flesh.

Before the third blow came, he took note of the thug's coal-hard eyes and business-like attitude. His only expression was one of annoyance, perhaps because this was taking so long. Then he struck once more. Bedford went down on both knees, hearing a lot of noise behind him. Then he heard nothing.

The first thing he saw through the bleary fog of regained consciousness was Hemingway's grinning face—with blood dripping down it.

CHAPTER 7

THE hospital treated Bedford for cuts about the head and neck and wrapped tape tightly around his chest for what was presumed to be a cracked or bruised rib. Hemingway, who claimed to have smashed the face, broken the jaw, ruptured the gut, and otherwise caused significant damage to his attacker, had a nasty gash above his left eyebrow and was rewarded with a bandage wound around his head in piratical fashion.

It was Hemingway's notion that they turn now to the cafés of Paris, using them as deer hunters in Northern Michigan used watering places. All the artists in the city were to be found at cafés at one time or another, he reasoned. All he and Bedford had to do to catch Man Ray was be in the right café at the right time.

Bedford had no wish to go looking for Ray or Polly down any more back streets. As he could think of no alternative course of action for the moment, he agreed to the writer's plan.

They started at the Closerie des Lilas, which was in Hemingway's neighborhood and his own favorite, as well as the place he came to most often for "the work." After nearly two hours of sitting there, sipping coffee, and then wine, Bedford suggested he go on alone, leaving Hemingway to attend to his writing. But the young man would have none of that. Dropping out of the search after they'd been attacked by those ruffians would be tantamount to deserting the front in wartime, he said. Nothing, not even his writing—which he valued above all things save his wife and child—could justify that, he declared.

So on they went—to the Dingo, the Dome, La Rotonde, La Coupole, Le Select, Deux Maggots, the Hotel Michaud, the Crillon, the Ritz, and others more. They talked to Marcel Duchamp, Paul Elouard, and many others said to be Ray's friends, but none admitted to having seen him recently. A few knew of Polly, describing her as a sort of pupil of Ray's, though they said the apprenticeship had been unsuccessful and comparatively brief.

A bartender acquainted with Ray said the photographer often seemed frustrated by the girl—sometimes enraged. One evening, when Ray had consumed far more than his usual single glass of white, he announced that he possessed a pistol "and was willing to use it," though he never made clear whether the object of this wrath was Polly, Kiki, or some unfortunate male who had dared dally with one of the women or the other.

Hemingway suggested they arm themselves. Bedford considered the idea, then dismissed it.

"We'd only end up in a French jail—or flirting with Madame Guillotine."

"Never saw a beheading," Hemingway said. "Never have. What that must be like."

"The worst view is looking up at the blade."

"They don't let you do that, do they?"

❖

AS they continued to make their rounds, they drank enough to quiet their fears and ease the pain of their injuries, and they ate very well, with Hemingway stuffing some of his food into his pockets to take home to his wife and child. Paris was said to be a place where poverty was of no consequence—at least to writers and artists—but Bedford began to wonder. Hemingway had told him of wringing the necks of pigeons he caught in the Luxembourg Gardens and taking them home for dinner. His child was still an infant.

"There is no point to writing just for money," he said, one afternoon at the bar of Harry's in the Rue Danou. "Your friend Scott does that, you know. He told me he writes short stories to please himself, then adds all kinds of plot twists and a surprise ending just to make sure they sell. Can you imagine Cezanne putting nudes into his paintings just to make them sell?"

"If you look at his bather pictures you'll see that he put in nudes to please himself."

"Anyway, I like Fitzgerald very much even though his wife is crazy as a goddamn loon. He writes very well, and I don't know if you have read it but he has written one damn fine hell of a good book. But sometimes I don't like what he has to say. So let's go somewhere else in case he comes here today."

Bedford nodded, without enthusiasm. It didn't seem to matter where they went. He feared he was going to accomplish nothing but the expenditure of Mrs. Swanscott's money.

"Where then?"

"The George V—if Mrs. Swanscott is still paying."

❖

BEDFORD finally got to meet Mrs. Hemingway—a happy, fresh-faced Midwestern girl with small nose, broad cheeks, and thick, dark brown hair. They were heading toward Montmartre when they ran into her walking along the quay near the Île de la Cité enroute to a music school where she was able to practice the piano.

It was a brief but pleasant encounter. The two Hemingways seemed very much in love with one another. After they'd parted and moved on, Bedford found himself a little disturbed, however. A man who killed pigeons in the park to survive could not well afford a nanny.

"Where's your baby Bumby?" Bedford asked. "He wasn't with your wife."

"He's with F. Puss."

"Who?"

"F. Puss is our baby-sitter," Hemingway explained. "They sleep together, Bumby and F. Puss, and F. Puss allows nothing to disturb them. I'd trust Bumby with F. Puss more than any nursemaid in Paris."

"Is she American?"

"She is a he. And he is a cat. A French cat, but a good one."

❖

T HE following day, much to the relief of Bedford's health and wallet, Hemingway broke off his participation in the search and went off with Fitzgerald to Lyon, where Scott and Zelda had left their car to be repaired weeks before, after driving up from Marseilles on their way back to Paris from Rome.

The two men were to be gone only briefly—a train ride down, a hotel stay overnight, and a leisurely drive to Paris the next day. Bedford would be free to pursue his quarry on his own, and was looking forward to that.

He'd sent cables upon arrival to Dayton Crosby and the Stieglitzes, informing them where he was staying and asking after his business and Sloane Smith.

There'd been only one reply: from Crosby. He had no word of Sloane or any new business. But said that a Mr. Swanscott was trying to reach Bedford and asked if he should give the man Bedford's Paris address.

Bedford cabled back that Crosby should not. He was becoming angry with himself over his lack of progress in all but the reduction of France's stock of wines and spirits. Meanwhile, his own business was being most abjectly neglected. He'd hardly looked at a painting since his arrival. He could himself end up strangling pigeons to survive.

He sent two more cables—both to Sloane, both telling her he had commenced his search for her friend Polly and both asking her to contact him in Paris if at all possible. If she had returned to New York, he asked that she look after the gallery until he returned. One cable he directed to her in New York and the other to her parents' in Lake Forest, Illinois. She sometimes returned home when the world at large became too much for her, as she had when her poet amour had died.

Finally, he dispatched one more cable, this to Detective D'Alessandro, asking him to keep a lookout for Sloane—adding, as not too much of an afterthought, that he keep an eye on Claire Pell as well. Rothstein and his friends sometimes went to great extremes to have their way—especially as concerned fiduciary matters—and they were well aware of his friendship with the Broadway belle.

◆◆

THERE was a bar in Paris that he and Hemingway had not yet visited—a jazz club in the Latin Quarter called Café Hirondelle Noir.

It meant "Café Black Swallow." During the war, when Bedford and the club's owner had flown together in the Escadrille Lafayette, the French had called his friend "The Black Swallow of Death," and had painted a deadly looking facsimile of such a bird on the side of his Spad.

His actual name was Eugene Bullard, and he was the first—and only— Negro to fly as a combat pilot, though it was for the French and not his fellow Americans. The others in the Lafayette squadron had been taken into the U.S. Air Service when the nation entered the conflict in April 1917. Bullard was ignored, though he had downed a German and flown twenty missions. Angry, he had remained with the French, and Bedford had done the same. Not long after, Bullard had gotten into a furious wrangle with his commander and been drummed out of the French military. Bedford had thought the commander had been in the right, but resigned as well. He had become weary of the French style of running a war, which was as high in casualties as it was low in tactical gains. He'd switched to British colors and joined the Royal Naval Air Service, patrolling the north end of the front along the Belgian coast.

Bullard had gone to Paris, and here he still was.

He was at a corner table of his bar, near a window, having coffee and reading a morning newspaper. As Bedford approached, he lowered it, then quickly, with a snap, returned it to the front of his face.

"Hello, Gene," Bedford said.

"Don't know you."

"Yes you do." Bedford pulled out a chair, but remained standing. "May I join you?"

"Heard you were in Paris; heard that days ago," Bullard said, from behind the paper.

"Yes."

"Why haven't you come by?"

"I was saving that. Seeing an old friend like you is a pleasure. I had business to attend to first."

"You've been in half the cafés in Paris."

"A few. On business."

The paper was lowered.

"You done now with your 'work'?" Bullard asked.

"No. It occurred to me you might be of some help, so I decided to mix business with pleasure."

With more exasperation than anger, Bullard folded the paper and set it aside.

"Business," Bullard said. "And what might that be?"

"You run the best jazz club in Paris."

"Yes, I do."

"I'm trying to find Man Ray, the photographer. I've been looking in cafés all over Paris, but it just now occurred to me he might come here—for the jazz. He's supposed to be crazy for jazz."

Bullard sipped his coffee. He was very well dressed, in a turtleneck sweater, expensive cashmere jacket, and gray flannels.

"He comes here," Bullard said. "But he hasn't in more than a week."

A waiter brought a fresh pot of coffee to the table, along with an extra cup.

"Do you know where he might be?"

"Maybe on a road trip. He likes to drive. What do you want him for?"

"I think he may have harmed a young woman. An American woman."

Bullard's brow furrowed.

"There was an American woman in here looking for him. A young woman. Just yesterday."

"Was she blond? A little wild-looking?"

"I wasn't here. She wore a hat. Might have been blond. She talked to one of my bartenders, and then ran out."

"Give her name?"

"No."

Bedford looked about the establishment. "Might I speak to your bartender?"

"That one? It's his day off. He'll be back tomorrow. I'll ask if she was a blond."

"She might have had bruises."

"I'll ask." Bullard set down his coffee. "You know, I ain't seen you for nearly two years, *Capitaine* Green. Why don't you join me in a drink and let's talk about something else. Music, maybe."

"Who recorded 'Bootlegger Blues'?"

"What?"

"The phonograph recording 'Bootlegger Blues.' Who made it?"

"The Mississippi Sheiks. Come around tonight and we'll include it in the set."

"*D'accord.* You'll have talked to your bartender by then, yes?"

Bullard shook his head, wearily. "Just what are you doing in Paris, Bedford?"

"Supposedly buying art. Mostly doing this."

"How'd you get so banged up?"

"Doing this. In the wrong place."

"Speaking of being in the wrong place, you know who else is in town?"

"Our old CO?"

"Worse. Liam O'Bannion."

Bedford stared at his hands. He'd scraped the knuckles on one of them in the fracas outside Ray's studio.

"I think I will take that drink."

Bullard snapped his fingers, and asked for scotch. "O'Bannion, as I recall, said something about wanting to kill you."

"That was during the war."

"When you were both flying for the British. On the same side. Never told me why he said that."

"It's between us, Gene."

"He has killed folks, you know."

"Shot down seven German aircraft. I saw one of them go down myself. He'd been on my tail."

The bartender brought over a bottle of excellent scotch and two glasses.

"That's good whiskey," Bedford said, after a sip.

"O'Bannion's in the business now. Bringing good whiskey to where it's appreciated. Especially New York."

"Then I wish him every success."

"I won't tell him you're in town, Bedford. But I'd make your business here brief."

THE remainder of the day was marked by two less than desirable discoveries. One was that he was being followed. Had it been dark, he would have run for the nearest gendarmes. In broad daylight, with the streets swarming with pedestrians, he felt brave enough to test the fellow.

He'd been walking down a broad avenue. At the next street, he rounded the corner, paused a few seconds, then turned about and went back onto the avenue.

His pursuer had vanished. He stood his ground a long moment, but the fellow failed to reappear. Returning to his original course, Bedford followed the avenue several more blocks, then crossed into a small park. The man was not far behind him. Tall, sallow-faced, in a shabby-looking double-breasted suit and wide brimmed hat, the miscreant would have been taken for a criminal type anywhere.

Bedford hailed a taxi. Whether his pursuer followed suit, he could not tell.

In his hotel lobby was the second surprise—a pretty woman with very nice legs perched on a wall table in the hotel's small lobby. She turned her head, and he saw that it was Zelda Fitzgerald.

"Beddie!"

Resigned to his fate, he went to her. She pushed herself off the table, landing just in front of him. Her eyes were wide with excitement. Bedford hoped that was all.

"I have a clue!" she said.

"A clue?"

"To the mystery. Scotty knows something!"

"Your daughter?"

"No, my husband. Goofo."

"What does he know?"

"I don't know. But he knows something about these Swanscotts of yours. I found it in his notes. Their name. It has something to do with his new book—the one that's just coming out."

"You've been rummaging in his notes?"

"He had them all out again. In a folder on the desk."

"Well then, I must ask what he knows about the Swanscotts—though I thought I'd asked that on the ship. As I recall, he said he didn't know them."

"You mustn't bring that up again, Beddie."

"Why on earth not?"

"If you do, he'll know I was rummaging in his notes. He'll be cross. It's awful when he's cross."

"Where's Scott now?"

"He telephoned from someplace called Mâcon. He says he's ill. Congestion of the lungs. From the rain. That's why they keep stopping. Goofo and Mr. Hemingway."

"Stopping?"

"The car has no top."

"Why not, Zelda?"

"It was damaged when they unloaded it from the ship so I had them cut it away. I don't like motorcars with tops."

"Is that all you came to tell me?"

"No. I'm lonely and bored and I want to go dancing."

Bedford looked at his watch. "Zelda, I'm afraid you'll have to settle for eating."

◆

T**HEY** went to La Coupole. It was crowded and raucous, with the *bal musette* downstairs in full swing, but they were able to get a table and have food put on it without much delay. There was an unusually large number of pretty women there. In equal abundance were handsome young men. Zelda's eyes flicked from one to another constantly, even as she drank her wine.

Then at once her eyes stopped their gadding about and fixed straight over Bedford's shoulder.

"What is it?" Bedford asked. "Not Man Ray?"

"No, no. It is a beautiful young Frenchman, and he keeps looking at us."

"At you."

"No, at you."

"At me?"

"He's coming this way."

Instead of turning, Bedford waited. In a moment, the gentleman was at their table, but instead of speaking to Zelda, he stopped before Green.

"*Excusez-moi, mais, est-ce-que vous êtes Capitaine Bedford Green?*"

Bedford found nothing at all about the young man familiar. He was handsome, very tanned, very French, and had dark, curly hair. He appeared the sort of man one saw depicted in book illustrations or on posters.

"I am. I was. In the war. No longer."

The other man switched to flawless English.

"You were pointed out to me—last year—in a café. La Hirondelle Noir. You are the American who fought with the French and British, but not the Americans."

"Yes."

"You shot down three Germans."

"Yes." Bedford was getting impatient.

The young man came to attention, and saluted, almost merrily.

"I wish to pay my respects, sir. You are still talked about in the Armee' de l'Air. Much celebrated."

"All exaggerations I'm sure. And you?"

"Lieutenant Edouard Jozan. A vôtre service. Un aviateur aussi."

He was too young to have been in the war. Bedford motioned for him to sit down.

He did so, accepting the offer of a drink, and asking for a Ricard. Then he turned his eyes fully on Zelda, who was looking at him as a hungry child might a large pastry.

"Monsieur," she said. "Dance with me."

Bedford was content to watch them for a while, then let his gaze drift about the room. There was a lot of movement in this capacious establishment, with people going from table to table in search of friends, conversation, or argument. He tried to tell the artists from the writers, but that proved as difficult and pointless as trying to determine which of the pretty females were prostitutes and which respectable ladies out for a good time.

An oddity attracted his attention—a man at the entrance. He was dark-skinned, wore a green jacket, and hesitated only briefly in the doorway, not looking to see who might be there but for a particular someone. Spotting his target, he made for a table at the other end of the wall from Bedford, ignoring all others and all else in the crowded room.

At that table, as Bedford hadn't noticed before, was the man who had been following him. Before Bedford could put down money to settle his bill and flee, before he could even extricate himself from his seat, they were on him.

They left no doubt that they were armed.

"*Allons!*" said the African. "*Venez avec nous, s'il vous plaît. Bien vite!*"

As they went out the door, Bedford looked helplessly to

Zelda and Jozan, who were still dancing and utterly oblivious to his departure—and fate.

◆◆

T HEY had a small, four-seater car, with side curtains in place. The tall man drove. The Negro man sat in front beside him, turned sideways in his seat to face Bedford. The other drove fast, weaving through the traffic with remarkable skill.

"You were in the war with Monsieur Bullard?" He spoke English, and his accent was American.

"Yes."

"I was in the war—in a labor battalion—until I deserted."

Bedford nodded, indicating his happy acceptance with whatever the gentleman might relate, no matter if it was beheading Belgian civilians.

"Do you work for Liam O'Bannion?" Bedford asked.

"Who's that?"

"A friend of Mr. Bullard's—but not, obviously, mine."

The Negro smiled. "We work for Monsieur Bullard."

He explained what should have been obvious to Bedford—as he was neither dead nor beaten up again. They had been following him for his own protection. And Bullard had put word out through the city seeking the names of the two who had worked over him and Hemingway, though nothing had yet been learned.

"Where are we going?" Bedford asked.

"We've found Man Ray. He has gone to a hotel with a woman. We are taking you there."

"Couldn't you just give me the address?"

"It is in a dangerous quarter. Would you go there without us?"

They were rumbling along now through a street so narrow it seemed Bedford could reach out through the side curtain and scrape his nails across the brick of the walls. It was a dark street as well, the headlamps picking out vague movements in the shadows, but little else.

"No, I suppose not. Will you be coming in with me?"

"There is only Man Ray—a small man—and the woman. Do you need us?"

"No. I guess not."

"Monsieur Bullard said to go in only if there is trouble."

"How do you know Ray's there?"

"We know."

◆◆◆

THE room was on the third floor. The hotel manager had had some sort of conversation with Bullard and had a pass key waiting for Bedford.

"*Rien de violence, s'il vous plaît, monsieur,*" he warned.

"*Ce ne serai pas nécessaire,*" Bedford replied. "*N'inquiet.*"

He mounted the stairs quietly. Given his height advantage, he had little doubt that he could handle Ray, should the photographer decide to get rough about matters. He was more worried about the girl. Would she be an ally in this? Or would she turn on him, causing who knew what misguided trouble, before he could make her understand he had come to help?

No matter. As he had reminded himself flying low-level reconnaissance at Ypres, the only way out of this mission was to do it.

He heard voices on the other side of the door to which he'd been directed. Slipping the key into the lock with the wariness of a cat burglar, he turned it with a click and swung the door open.

Man Ray sat on the lumpy-looking bed, his dark eyes rheumy and glowering, his hands folded in his lap, looking not only sad but a little ridiculous as he was wearing only sleeveless undershirt, cotton underdrawers, and dark socks with garters. Glancing to the right, Bedford saw a tall woman seated on the edge of a chair, still in her stockings but wearing only a slip. She was aiming a small pistol in the general direction of Ray's abdomen. At the sound of Bedford's entrance, she had turned her head. Bedford was struck at the calm, determined sanity evident in her eyes.

"Sloane?"

CHAPTER 8

THE cramped quarters of the small sedan required Sloane to
sit on Bedford's lap, which she agreed to without complaint though she had to bend forward to keep her head from
bumping against the roof. Beyond the occasional fox-trot or
Christmas hug, Bedford had never been in such close physical contact with her before. Her back muscles were tense and
hard with her anger, which was very focused and unrelent-
ing.

She still held the small pistol. Because of the confined
space, the barrel was thrust up against Ray's neck. The driver
was swerving on the rain-moistened streets. Bedford feared
more than one kind of accident.

The photographer was very stoic, ignoring the gun and
staring straight ahead, his view including Sloane's slender
bosom but his expression indicating he took no notice of it.
The little artist might be a brute, or not, but he was certainly
very brave.

"Did he tell you anything?" Bedford asked Sloane, as
though Ray was not present.

"Not much."

"Did he say anything about Polly?"

"That she's been staying with him."

"That's all?"

"Then you came in."

The car bumped over a curb taking a corner, tossing all of them in the backseat close together. Ray accepted the weight pressed against him as an annoyance that would pass, still exhibiting the same nonchalance toward the weapon that in an instant could take his life. Bedford was amazed that it hadn't gone off.

"Do we really need that gun?" he asked Sloane.

"Yes," she said.

"Where did you get it?"

"It's his."

Bedford's cramped right arm was beginning to hurt. He moved it to gain comfort, but his hand and forearm rested now on Sloane's thigh. She made no protest. He was the one who began to feel uncomfortable. Her mother had asked him to take care of her in big, bad New York City—as though he was a man her father's age, and not one just five years Sloane's elder. This automotive adventure was clearly not what she had in mind.

"Where are you taking me?" Ray said.

"To the Black Swallow."

"That's a jazz club."

"Yes. A very good one."

"Noisy. If you want me to talk to you, why go there?"

"I have friends there."

"I'll talk to you if we go to another place, a quiet place."

"Where you have friends."

"Yes. Le Bateau Ivre."

"The Drunken Boat," said Bedford. "I don't know it."

"*Par La Place L' Odeon,*" said the driver.

"All right," Bedford said. "But you must tell me one thing first."

"What?"

"Is Polly Swanscott alive?"

"That's a ridiculous question. Do you think I am a murderer?"

At the moment—weary, furtive, yet unconquered—he looked a bit like one. A professional, tiring of his work.

"She has vanished. And you told people you have a gun," Bedford said. "Which you do—or did."

"It's still a ridiculous question. We're civilized people. This is France."

"You haven't answered it."

"I'll tell you when we're there."

◆◆

BEDFORD dismissed Bullard's hired hands, with thanks. They departed with some reluctance, the black man giving Sloane a speculative glance, and then an appreciative one.

They took a corner table, Sloane and Bedford sitting to either side of Ray. The small man lighted a cigarette, then sat back, waiting with that same hardened sense of resignation. A moment later, a waiter arrived with an unrequested glass of white wine for the photographer, apparently his favorite. Taking note of Sloane's still rigid carriage and inflamed mood, Bedford ordered two large brandies in hope that the alcohol would have the same effect on the savage breast as music.

"You said you would answer my question once we were here," Bedford reminded.

Ray exhaled a long plume of smoke, then sipped.

"Of course she's alive," he said, in almost a mutter. "Women like her are indestructible—impervious, impenetrable, dense—incapable of nuance, insensitive to suggestion. In short, a brick."

Sloane had put the pistol in her purse. Bedford wished she had given it to him.

"I don't think that's a very accurate description of the lady," he said.

"You haven't lived with the lady," Ray said. "Or have you?"

"I have," said Sloane, her voice tremulous and strained.

Ray's dark eyebrows shot up, almost reaching his widow's peak.

"In college," Bedford said. "Where is she now?"

"That's not a question to ask of me."

"What should we ask you?"

"I'll tell you what I had to do with her—which wasn't all that much." Ray sipped and smoked, preparing himself.

"I met her in a café—Le Jockey," he began. "She had heard of me and came to my table and wouldn't leave. She went home with me."

"I thought you had someone at home."

"From time to time. Not then."

There was something engaging about Man Ray, a charm to his eyes, but he was not a handsome man. Polly was unusually pretty. Or had been. Was her taking up with him another dance in the moonlight?

"How long did she stay?"

"A century."

With those two words, Ray embarked on a long lament. He said the girl told him she had come to Paris to find herself as an artist, but exactly the opposite had happened. Her uncertainty about her talent had turned to confusion and then despair. People told her to put aside her painting and try something else. She had experimented with cameras in college, and wondered if photography might be her better course.

"She was brilliant," Sloane said, a statement uttered to defy any contradiction.

"She wanted to learn," Ray said. "She was very humble. I felt sorry for her. I took her in. She worked with me in my little darkroom. I taught what I could. It was hard. She was impatient. Irritatingly impatient."

"Then you must have been a poor teacher," Sloane said.

Ray sighed, and shook his head.

"I tried." He shrugged. "I did what I could. But she . . ."

Bedford took out the postal card, hoping it would be the last time he would have to do this.

"She learned this from you," he said.

Ray examined it, professionally.

"She stole it from me," he said. "The glass beads were an idea of mine. I made a number of images using them. Each different, but the same idea. My photographs are ideas." More smoke. "She had none. Nothing of her own. She stole this one from me, but executed it incompetently. This picture really isn't any good. And it isn't original. As I say, no ideas. Only her sorrows. Worthless."

"You told her that?" Sloane asked.

Ray saw the wisdom of not replying, but Bedford pressed the point.

"Is that why she left you?"

"I don't know why she left me."

"Perhaps your friend Kiki."

"Kiki is not mine. She's not anyone's. We all belong to her."

"But she would have resented Polly. She would have wanted Polly to go away."

"Polly might have irritated her, but she was no threat to her. Kiki wouldn't have done anything serious about her—if that's what you're suggesting."

Ray still had wine in his glass but kept lighting cigarettes. People in the room, doubtless friends, were watching the three of them closely. Ray's unhappiness was apparently fairly evident.

"And you have no idea where Polly might be?"

"No."

"Think. Maybe you'll get an idea."

More smoke. "She said she was going back to her art—to her painting. She had some nasty things to say about photography. I assume she took up with a painter. I heard she may have."

"Who?"

A shrug. "She was learning Spanish. I thought she was taking a trip. Maybe she wasn't."

Ray's glass was now empty. He stared at it. Bedford and Sloane stared at him, without speaking further. A waiter came toward them, hesitated, then turned around.

"If we let you go now," said Bedford finally, "what would you do?"

"Go home. Go back to work. Write Stieglitz a letter complaining about his taste in art dealer friends." His dark, haggard eyes turned to Sloane. "Maybe be more careful about whose acquaintance I make."

"Go home, then," Bedford said. "With my apologies for the inconvenience. And my thanks for your help."

Ray's eyes flicked back and forth over both their faces, as though searching for the legitimacy of Bedford's words. Then, taking them at face value, he rose, nodded, and walked slowly from the café, ignoring his friends.

Sloane hadn't shifted an inch in her chair. Her fair skin was now quite flushed.

"Why did you do that?" she said. It was a question uttered as by a prosecutor.

"Because I believe him."

"You were beaten up by his friends."

"I don't know who those people were."

The café had been remarkably quiet when they'd entered and now seemed quieter still. Bedford was conscious of being observed from several quarters in the room. Perhaps it was only Sloane's beauty—and unusual height.

"I wonder if the time hasn't come to make inquiries with the French police," he said.

"No."

"Why not?"

Her long, elegant fingers drummed softly on the table. She pondered her brandy glass a moment, then disregarded it.

"Good-bye, Bedford," she said, rising.

"What are you doing?"

"Leaving."

"Where will you be?"

"With Polly—if I can find her."

He stood, addressing her departing back.

"If you need me, I'm at the Hotel Californie."

"You would be."

He finished both their brandies, content that, with Sloane no longer on the premises, the other patrons were ignoring him. He was settling the bill when he heard someone come up behind him.

Turning around in expectation—certainly hope—that it was Sloane, he found himself looking again into the singular face of Man Ray.

"Something I forgot to tell you," he said.

Bedford sighed. "Polly's whereabouts?"

"No. There's someone else been looking for her. Someone came around my studio two days ago."

Bedford waited.

"His name was Oritzky," Ray said.

"Thank you."

Bedford got to his feet, as Ray was looking like he might sit down. He wasn't up to a conversation with this man—and certainly not up to any more to drink.

Ray seated himself anyway.

"Where's the beautiful girl?" he asked.

"I shouldn't think you'd want any more to do with her," Bedford said.

"She has my revolver."

"I would suggest that's a very good reason to leave her be."

CHAPTER 9

B EDFORD breakfasted the next morning on the *terrasse* of the Dome, ordering a bowl of Quaker Oats to calm his unhappy stomach and improve his state of mind. He was surprised by the number of Americans at the tables, most of whom seemed to be tourists. Their numbers explained the presence of American oatmeal on the menu—not a dish suited to the Gallic palate. No one there was anyone he knew.

He had two coffees, leafing through a French-language newspaper and then turning away from its superfluity of incomprehensible political stories to watch the passersby. He paid particular attention to pretty girls, telling himself the absurd lie that one of them might turn out to be Polly Swanscott. Finally, he prodded himself into leaving, walking to the Closerie des Lilas.

His feeling of futility was becoming oppressive. He was accomplishing no great good for his art gallery here in Paris, and not much more for Mrs. Swanscott. Certainly nothing for Sloane, wherever she might be.

Reaching the Lilas, he took a table by one of the trees out near the sidewalk. He kept his eyes on the pedestrian traffic again. Quite to his surprise, Hemingway came upon him from behind, punching him playfully but painfully in the shoulder.

"You come here to disturb me in my work, amigo?" The big man sat down in the chair opposite, smiling to show he was not really disturbed.

"I came here to find you," Bedford said. "Or ask where you might be."

"I was right inside."

Hemingway signaled to a waiter, who apparently knew what he wished.

"Got back last night," he said, returning his attention to Bedford. "Damnedest trip I ever made in a motor since I drove an ambulance through an Austrian barrage in the Italian goddamn Alps. I tell you the man is a raving lunatic."

"Which man?"

"Fitzgerald. There are times when I think he's no more sensible than his wife. At least when he's got some booze in him, and it doesn't take much. Champagne all the time. I tried to keep him company—glass for glass—and I got damn well sick of it. Took two whiskies to get rid of the taste."

He had a notebook with him but it remained closed.

"Is that why you took so long to get back?" Bedford asked. "Stops for refreshment?"

"Stops for the goddamn rain!" said Hemingway, thudding his fist on the table and laughing so loudly people turned to look from the next café. "The car had no top! It got damaged in transit so that crazy Zelda had it taken off. I lost count of how many times it rained. I know we stopped because of it at least ten times. Scott got the sniffles and was convinced it was pneumonia. Kept asking me if I was ever afraid to die—as though he wanted advice on how to go about it. We went to this hotel at Chalon-sur-Saone and he refused to get out of bed. Said he was dying of congestion of the lungs and asked that I take care of Zelda and little Scotty. Hell, I have trouble sometimes getting Hadley and our Bumby everything they need, but I said I would. Only thermometer we were able to get was the hotel's bathtub thermometer. Great big sonofabitch of a thing. But it showed his temperature normal. Every time. Didn't matter. He carried on as though he was in the midst of a fine, beautiful death—which he ruined by telling me over and over how much he hated the French. What's he doing here if he hates the French? Only Frenchmen he knows are hotel clerks and waiters, and he's always abusing them."

The Lilas waiter appeared with a brandy and water for Hemingway.

"*Merci bien,*" the writer said. He took a sip, noting Bedford's disapproving stare, then added, "Can't work this morning. Gone as far as I can today. Anyway, if Fitzgerald weren't such a beautiful goddamn writer I'd steer clear of him rest of my days."

"How did you get him out of there?"

"The drink wore off. Next day—yesterday—the sun was shining and it was very nice and we drove without stopping all the way here. I left him at his flat in the Rue de Tilsitt and got Hadley and came here and we had a very happy time for many hours into the night." He drank some brandy, ignoring the water. "Sonofabitch shouldn't drink. I told him that. No more than a half bottle of wine at a time."

They sat without speaking for a moment. The motor traffic in the street seemed irritatingly noisy, though there were no more vehicles than normal.

"Did you find the girl?" Hemingway asked.

"No, but I found Man Ray."

"Where? His studio? You didn't go back there?"

"Got a tip from a friend and found him in a cheap hotel with—with a woman he'd picked up. He talked with me. Said Polly Swanscott had been staying with him for a while, learning photography, but he didn't like her work so she left. Ray doesn't like women to leave him, so he made a lot of threatening talk about her, but I don't believe he did her any harm—or meant to. I think she gave him a beating—emotionally."

"So where is she?"

"According to Ray, she took up with some painter. Possibly a Spanish painter. Do you know any Spanish painters?"

"Sure. The best. Joe Goya."

"Joe Goya?"

"Francisco José de Goya y Lucientes. Big *cojones*, that one. Ever see his *Disasters of War*? Sonofabitch got it right."

"Joe Goya, as you call him—or, if you like, Frank Goya—he's been dead for a century."

"I know, but he's still the greatest. You want to go look at his pictures? The Louvre has . . ."

"She's supposed to have gone off with a *live* Spanish painter."

Hemingway stroked his moustache. "I think I know who it might be." He drank some brandy. "But he's too big a deal for a girl like that."

"A girl like what?"

"Anyway, I know someone who would know for certain. She knows all the painters in Paris—or claims to."

"An art dealer?"

"No. A writer. It's too early to go see her. Maybe this afternoon, but even then. Sometimes . . ."

"Sometimes . . ."

"Sometimes you don't want to go there in the afternoon. Tonight, though. Her flat will be filled with people. Writers, mostly. Great minds. We're bound to find out something."

"But we haven't been invited."

"I'm always invited." He drained his glass. "Now let's go look at Joe Goya's paintings."

◆◆◆

THE museum was not so far from the Rue de Tilsitt. Hemingway suggested stopping by to ask Scott and Zelda to accompany them.

"Too goddamn little art in their lives, those two. Parties, booze, and the rich. That's all they've got."

"The rich paid for most of those paintings we're about to see."

"Yeah, they did. But they didn't paint them."

They walked along the Seine. Waddling pigeons were underfoot, and Bedford hoped Hemingway would suppress any impulse to reach down and strangle one. But the big, bluff fellow was in great good cheer, and rather well fed of late. The notion, happily, seemed not to have occurred to him.

"Have you read Fitzgerald's latest book?" Bedford asked.

"The *Gatsby* thing? No. I don't think it's out yet. 'Least not here. But I want to. He told me about it, when he wasn't hurling abuse at the French."

"What's it about?"

"The rich. Just like the last one."

"Is there anyone like Polly Swanscott in it?"

"I don't think so. It's set out on Long Island. Why would you think that?"

"Something Zelda said."

"Well, amigo. That lady says some strange things."

"You sure there isn't a young girl like Polly in it?"

"The heroine's named Daisy Buchanan. She's from Chicago, and as far as I know, she doesn't even go to art museums, let alone become a painter. This Polly of yours reminds me of the girl in Somerset Maugham's *Of Human Bondage*. The one who couldn't paint? You ever hear of a good woman painter, Bedford?"

"Sure. Rosalba Carrierra, Cecilia Beaux, Tamara de Lempicka. But I also know a really good painter who also happens to be a woman. She'd sock you one good if you called her a woman painter."

"Who the hell's that?"

"Georgia O'Keeffe. Next time you're in New York, I'll introduce you."

"I'd like to meet her—go a few rounds." Hemingway laughed. Bedford thought the remark as strange as any of Zelda's.

THE Fitzgeralds' apartment was a carnival of disarray. Clothes and luggage were everywhere, along with champagne bottles, empty and partially filled glasses, and full ashtrays. Zelda, wearing a slip and loosely fastened dressing gown, stood barefoot in the midst of it all, smoking, and looking as though utterly dazed by the fact that it was now day. The maid, who had answered the door, was chasing back and forth after the little girl. Fitzgerald himself was not in view.

"Where are you going?" Hemingway asked Zelda, with a nod to an overflowing suitcase.

"To the South of France."

The reply came from her husband. Fitzgerald entered in pajamas and dressing gown as well, but every thread and hair of him was perfectly in place. Rubbing his forehead over and over again with his left hand, he went to Hemingway and Bedford in turn, shaking their hands without looking at their faces, finally ending up reclining on the sofa, the hand still in place on his head.

"We just came from the South of France, Scott," said Hemingway.

"I know, I know," said Fitzgerald. "I will never forget that miserable journey. But this is to the Murphys'. Gerald and Sara. You know them, don't you? They insist that we come down. We're not going to stay with them, though. There are always rows when we do."

"We have the rows," said Zelda, her hawkish eyes dancing about the room in search of something. "The Murphys never have rows." She went and stood before her husband. "Give me a cigarette, Goofo."

With his free hand, he reached into a pocket. "Sorry, darling. Haven't any."

Zelda growled, then scurried out of the room.

"I found Man Ray," Bedford said.

"Congratulations. What a fine thing to do." It sounded all the same to Fitzgerald as if he'd said he'd found a penny in the street. "Is the girl all right?"

"She wasn't with him."

"Oh. Sorry. Wish we could have been of more help to you."

"Did you say you knew the Swanscotts?" Bedford asked, as a thump came from the room into which Zelda had fled.

Fitzgerald ignored the sound. "No. Don't think so. Didn't I tell you I didn't? Should I know them? Is there anything at all interesting about those people?"

"Only their interesting daughter."

"She doesn't interest me—especially as I've never met her. Would you like to meet some interesting people?"

"Who do you mean?"

"Gerald and Sara Murphy—and their marvelous friends. They have the most marvelous friends in the world. Everything about them is perfectly marvelous. And marvelously perfect. You should come down with us."

"The merrier the merrier," said Zelda, reentering with a cigarette in her mouth. She went to a sideboard, taking a half-empty bottle of now flat champagne to hand. "Drink?"

"Yes," said Hemingway.

Bedford seated himself near Fitzgerald. He wondered what Sloane would think of this tableau vivant. He wondered more where she had gone—where she was at that moment. With luck, he might find her before he had to leave Paris. As he had realized upon awakening after a night of poor sleep, he was now far more concerned about Sloane than her unhappy friend from Smith College.

"Thank you for the invitation," he said to Scott. "But I want to keep looking for Polly Swanscott. I promised someone. If anything occurs to you, though—before you leave . . ."

"You really should meet the Murphys," Fitzgerald said, a touch of awe in his voice. "Gerald owns Mark Cross. Sara's family owns pretty much everything else."

"A gross exaggeration," said Hemingway, speaking over a very full glass.

"They have a very grand time being rich together," Fitzgerald said. "And they share it with others."

"They had Hadley and me to dinner once," said Hemingway. "They like writers. They like painters. Archie MacLeish is a pal of theirs. John Dos Passos, too. And Ferdinand Leger."

"Fernand," corrected Bedford, gently.

"Right."

"I hope they don't mind our coming," Zelda said.

"They invited us," her husband said, his hand resuming its therapeutic massage.

"No, I invited us. They agreed. But I feel badly about it. So we'll stay at our own place. After we find one."

"We came by to invite you to go with us to the Louvre," Hemingway said.

"To look at Joe Goya," Bedford added.

"No, no. I couldn't look at a painting now," Fitzgerald

said. "It would shatter my brain. Zelda, give me a glass of champagne. *Joe* Goya?"

"Get your own, Goofo."

When no one moved, and Fitzgerald only groaned, Bedford rose and performed the honors, bringing the author what remained of the wine. Then he stepped toward the door.

"It was very nice getting to know you," he said. "Sounds like you won't be back until after I leave, so perhaps I'll see you in New York."

Zelda took her cigarette from her mouth and ran up to kiss Bedford.

"Good-bye, Beddie." She stepped back. "I'm told you were very, very brave in the war. That you killed many Germans."

Hemingway looked up, his eyes widening a little.

"No," said Bedford. "Not many."

"Well, your fellow airmen certainly think well of you," she said. She looked about the room again for something, but it turned out to be a thought. "Oh, I just remembered! Another clue! Wait here."

She flew into the bedroom once more, and there was the sound of a drawer being opened and shut. When she returned, it was with a condom in her hand, removed from its package, and hanging loose.

He accepted it gingerly.

"A clue?" he asked.

"A reminder," she said. "I took it so I wouldn't forget. At this party last night—a sort of fancy dress ball only there wasn't much music. We came in our bedclothes, because we'd been in bed when they called. There was a man there dressed as the Queen of Romania, and a woman with him who came as a sea captain. What do you suppose that meant? Anyway, the host—he was a friend of Gerald and Sara's; said he was anyway. He had a skeleton strung up in the entrance hall of his flat and it had this thing hanging out of its mouth like a tongue. He said a girl had put it there and that she was crazy. When he said she was blond, I asked if she could be Polly Swanscott, and, do you know? I think he said yes."

"What was his name?" Bedford asked.

"I can't remember. Can you, Goofo?"

"No. And I shouldn't want to. Everything about that place was obscene and decadent."

"Do you remember the address?" Bedford asked.

"I did," said Zelda. "I remembered it twice. But now I forgot."

"When was this?"

"Last night. Wasn't it, Goofo?"

Fitzgerald groaned and sat up, not to reply, but to drink his champagne.

"When was the girl at this man's place?" Bedford asked, persistent.

"A few weeks ago. He couldn't remember."

◆◆◆

THEY walked to the river and turned toward the Louvre, with Hemingway continuing his unusual relish for the day. Taking a deep breath, he beat himself on the chest twice and then thrust out his arms and hit an imaginary foe with a series of punches. Perhaps it was the brandy at the Lilas.

"God, it's good to be alive," he exclaimed. For a moment, Bedford feared he was about to commence whooping and shouting.

"It is a nice day."

"How many did you kill?" Hemingway asked, ceasing his odd calisthenics and walking normally.

"Kill?"

"Germans."

Bedford bit down on his lip. "I'm not sure."

"Come on. How many German planes you shoot down?"

"Three. One went down burning. It was horrible. The Germans were issuing their pilots parachutes by then—unlike the American air service, which refused to give its flyers any for fear they'd bail out of all their fights—but this fellow's caught fire. I was ready to hang it all up there and then."

"But you didn't."

"No. But I had no more 'victories' after that. I stayed alive, which was victory enough. The war ended two months later."

"Three. That's pretty good."

Bedford had no response to that.

"So you killed three Germans then?" Hemingway was persistent.

"Four in the air. One of my kills was an observation plane with two aboard. But they had us doing strafing and bombing runs against the last big German offensive. I may have killed hundreds. I don't know. All I do know is that I don't want to do it again."

A barge was moving up the Seine, its blunt bow thrusting the water aside in two thick, churning waves. Bedford realized he was looking at it in the matter of fact way of someone who enjoyed but had become used to the sight. He had been here too long. New York seemed now very far away— as distant and unobtainable as the mysterious missing Polly.

He stopped. "Mr. Hemingway, if it's all the same to you, I think I'll forgo Joe Goya today and meet up with you this evening."

"Sure. We can see those paintings anytime. But what's wrong?"

"Nothing's wrong. I just think I'd better attend to my other business. My main reason for coming here is to buy pictures. I don't want to go home empty-handed on all accounts."

Hemingway looked disappointed. A child whose game had been cancelled.

"It's all right. I'll go back to the Lilas and the work."

"I envy you that."

"Meet me there at seven-thirty tonight." He hesitated. "You haven't given up on finding the girl?"

"No. Certainly not."

"Anything I can do on that score today?"

"If you come across a young man named Oritzky, find out where he's staying and let me know. I'd like to talk to him."

"Who the hell is Oritzky? A Russian?"

"A one-time swain. From New York. He's looking for her, too."

Hemingway gave thin air a couple more punches. "I'll find the sonofabitch."

"I don't believe he's a sonofabitch."

"Then I'll buy him a drink."

They took a step apart, but now Bedford hesitated. "It's too bad about Zelda."

"Yeah."

Hemingway could not have known what Bedford meant. He decided to leave it that way.

CHAPTER 10

A THIN, dark-haired, sharp-eyed woman in a Chinese print
silk dress opened the door part way, giving no indication
she would open it any further. She obviously knew Hemingway and just as obviously disliked him. The young author
and Bedford had arrived at 27 Rue de Fleurus more than an
hour later than intended—their tardiness entirely Bedford's
fault. He doubted it was much of a transgression in Montparnasse.

Clearly the sharp-eyed woman had other and deeper
grounds for her animosity. That she held it in reasonable
check, and that Hemingway so blithely ignored her feelings,
suggested to Bedford that she was not master of this house,
as she indicated when finally she deigned to speak to them.

"Gertrude Stein did not invite you," she said.

Hemingway took a step closer to the opening, but the
woman did not retreat.

The writer leaned close. "Alice, she told me to come
whenever I wished and now it's what I wish because I have
an important question to ask her."

"It's not what I wish, Ernest Hemingway. You were very
crude on your last visit. And you broke things."

Bedford could hear a mix of voices within—several conversations going on at once. There was laughter, starting and stopping abruptly, as though on someone's command. During this spasm of mirth, all other talk ceased. It resumed slowly.

"I'm sorry about last time," Hemingway said, sounding it. "Accident, Alice. And too much to drink."

She dropped the subject, looking to Bedford.

"Who is this gentleman?" she said. "And why has he come?"

Hemingway pulled Bedford closer, as though an inspection by this woman was a requirement.

"This is Bedford Green, a friend of mine. He's an art dealer from New York and he needs Miss Stein's help in locating an artist."

Still clinging tightly to the door, she squinted at Bedford.

"He is not an artist?" She turned back to Hemingway.

"No, Alice."

"Gertrude Stein no longer entertains artists here. Only writers. This is 1925."

"We didn't come here to talk to artists," Hemingway said, moving yet closer to threshold. "I want to ask her about one. A Spanish artist."

A flicker of nervousness passed across the woman's otherwise implacable face.

"You may come in, Ernest Hemingway. You, too, Mr. Green. But you may not interrupt Gertrude Stein. She will speak to you when it is time."

Stepping into the spacious, high-ceilinged apartment, Bedford found himself in an art and antique dealer's paradise. The furnishings, comfortable yet elegant, were an odd mix of French and Oriental—plush sofas, gold-lacquered Empire side tables, Persian rugs. The art was awesome and incandescently modern—advanced far beyond Bedford's concept of avant garde.

Chief among the works, dominating a far corner of the expansive living room, was a life-sized modernist portrait of the stout woman who sat just beneath it, instantly recogniz-

able as the ruler of these premises, and doubtless much of
Paris besides.

She wore a long, billowy, tent-like, dark blue dress; thick
woolen stockings; and sandals. Her hair was cut very short,
though somewhat longer on top. She had quick, intelligent
eyes and a large nose in a large face that at first glance
seemed the antithesis of beauty, yet was at the same time unusually agreeable. Bedford had talked to artists about this
phenomenon, how symmetry often counted for more than the
grace of features. The woman's face was arrestingly sym-
metrical. He felt drawn to her across the distance of the
room.

Sitting on her divan as though upon a throne, she was sur-
rounded by several men. Nearer to Bedford and Hemingway,
a clump of interestingly dressed women looked up as the
woman named Alice rejoined them.

"Wives," whispered Hemingway. "When Hadley comes
with me, she has to sit with them. Alice presides over the
wives. Miss Stein is the husband here. She talks to the likes
of us, and only to us."

There were others in the room, attached to neither circle.
A few chatted in small conversations. The rest looked at the
art, marveling at it.

Bedford did the same. Hemingway went for drink, returning with two large glasses of red wine.

One picture stood out among its fellows—the artist the
only one Bedford could recognize with any certainty.

"Henri Matisse," he said.

"Miss Stein is alleged to have discovered Matisse," said
Hemingway, after a large swallow. "I say Matisse discovered
Matisse, but I don't say that to her."

They were joined by a slim figure dressed in turn-of-the-
century gentleman's clothes, complete with a slightly dented
top hat and cape. The face was rather more beautiful than
handsome, and remarkably so. It occurred to Bedford that
this strange person was studying him just as assiduously as
he was her—or him.

"What have you written?"

The question startled Bedford. He thought upon the weeks

and years of meaningless newspaper columns he had churned out about the trivially famous.

"Nothing of note," he said. "Nothing at all."

"My favorite kind of writer," the "gentleman" said, and moved on.

Bedford and Hemingway moved closer to the wall, observing the others in the room and speaking so as not to be overheard.

"Who was that?" Bedford asked.

Hemingway grinned, as though Bedford was a provincial beyond hope. "That's Romaine Brooks."

"The artist?"

"The artist."

"I thought Romaine Brooks was a man."

"She is tonight. She is most nights. I'm just surprised to find her here. Her usual haunt is Natalie Barney's."

Bedford noticed that Miss Stein's all-seeing eyes were upon them.

"I'm not acquainted with Natalie Barney."

"Jesus, Green. Are you from New York, or Minne-god-damn-sota like Scott? Natalie Barney's the best-looking woman in Paris, and it's all a waste. She and Miss Stein run competing salons, if you want to call them that. Miss Stein here is the boss of everything modern. She decides what's modern—what counts and what doesn't. Natalie's queen of the past—all that decadent Oscar Wilde crap. But beautiful. Goddamn beautiful. I saw a photograph of her in the nude— Natalie in the woods wearing nothing but a pair of high-heeled shoes. I tell you it's enough to make you wish you were a woman, just to have a chance of getting into bed with her."

Bedford gave artist Brooks a lingering look, and found it returned, with a wisp of a smile. Then Brooks adjusted her cape and continued her leisurely traipse about the room.

"Hemingway!"

Both of them turned in the direction of Stein's commodious voice. She was summoning them.

There was no place to sit, so they stood before her, in the manner of suppliants.

"Good evening, Miss Stein," Hemingway said.   •

Her eyes remained fixed on Bedford.

"Evening." She made the word sound not a reply but a simple statement of fact. "Do you want to buy that Matisse?"

Bedford swallowed, sensing he was going to be ill-prepared for this conversation.

"I want to, very much, but I cannot."

"You're an art dealer, are you not? A dealer in art. A buyer and seller. One who turns art into money."

"Yes, but I haven't money to turn into art."

His response mildly pleased her. "Green is your name? Your name is Green? Bedford Green?"

"I didn't realize we'd been introduced, ma'am." It occurred to him in a rush that this was the very last woman in the world one would call "ma'am."

"What you do, what you have done—word of it precedes you, Green. You have been going around Montparnasse for days, looking for a Polly no one can remember—a Polly who is an artist whose art no one has seen. You have frightened poor Man Ray to death by making him think you were an angry brother of someone he may have wronged, but cannot remember wronging. In so doing you were attacked by gangsters who are not our gangsters, and therefore very dangerous. And you are having an affair with Zelda Fitzgerald." She leaned back, in great accomplishment.

Before he could speak, she did again.

"Yes? Isn't all this so? That is why I told Hemingway he should bring you."

"You are well informed, Miss Stein. Except in one respect."

"All of Paris comes to me here where I sit. Because I am who sits here. This is why here I sit."

"Yes," Bedford continued. "But, as I say, not perfectly informed in all respects. My acquaintance with Mrs. Fitzgerald is very recent and in no way intimate."

Except in his thoughts.

"Then you are a cad. Do you wear suede shoes?" She looked to see that he did not. "The Prince of Wales has angered his father by wearing suede shoes and is criticized for it because it is said they are the footwear of a cad."

"As I am not wearing suede shoes, perhaps I am not a cad." He wished he knew the rules of this game.

"But you are! You say you are not having an affair with Zelda Fitzgerald. And yet you say you are her friend. Someone must, don't you think? Don't you know? Her husband is a poor husband." She lifted her head. "Alice! Is not Fitzgerald a poor husband?"

The sharp-eyed woman at the other end of the room shushed the women around her, then tilted her head back as well. Bedford was reminded of birds in different trees, performing the rituals of the same species.

"He is. He is a very poor husband."

"And am I not a good husband?"

"Gertrude Stein is a very good husband."

Except for their immediate circle, the various conversations in the chamber resumed with increased volume. Bedford noticed that the Brooks woman had come floating by again, and was standing near the sofa, gazing up at the life-sized portrait of Gertrude Stein that looked down upon the real person.

"Were I married to Zelda," Bedford said. "I think I would be a good husband."

Stein nodded, again satisfied. She glanced to the man in the nearest chair. "Madox Ford. This man will need your chair. And you must need more wine, for you always do."

Bedford recognized the name, but not the appearance. The fellow was distinguished in the cut of his beard, yet shambling and disreputable in his clothing and demeanor. He rose, stoic and nonplussed, to retreat to the bar.

Stein gave a commanding nod of the head, and Bedford sat. Hemingway backed away slightly, rendering himself mere observer.

"I want you to tell me, Green," said Stein, "who is the best American painter who is not in Paris?"

Her invitation for him to sit was not for the sake of discreet conversation. She uttered her question loudly enough to be heard by everyone else. The performance was continuing.

Bedford struggled to assess the truth of his answer.

"Come, Green. All the best painters in America are now in Paris. So who would be the best one who is not in Paris?"

He had favorites: John Sloan, George Bellows, Joseph Stella. But he knew the answer.

"Georgia O'Keeffe."

"Georgia O'Keeffe!" Stein tossed back the name like something to be assessed and evaluated by the crowd.

"I know her work," said a man Bedford did not know standing by the wall. "It's wonderful. I suspect he's right."

"So, Green," said Stein. "You are a good art dealer, you are. A dealer in good art. You should have a Matisse to turn into money. But not mine. Not this one. One but not this." Her little smile faded. She was leaning back. She was done with him, interested now in someone else.

Bedford hesitated. She had put him in this seat to hold him—as in a trap—and now he was being released. He realized he now had her in the same position. As long as he sat there, she would have to deal with him.

"Do you know any Spanish painters?" he asked.

He supposed he had asked this question with too much urgency. She appeared wary now.

"I know all the Spanish painters in Paris. But there is really only one Spanish painter."

"Would he be someone who might be interested in a girl like Polly?"

Stein stiffened. "He would be interested in all women, in any woman, in Woman. He painted the painting you see above me. And it is my most prized painting. I would have it and no other."

Bedford studied it. He could in no way disagree with her.

"He is my friend," she said. "But what you see is not friendship. It is genius."

"Yes. Who is he?"

"Picasso," said Hemingway. "Pablo Picasso."

"You do not know of Pablo, Green?" said Stein.

"Of course. But I've not looked much at his work before."

"His work went to New York. It went to the Armory Exhibition. In 1913. Did you not see it?"

"I was in college."

"You would learn more from Pablo."

"What I'd like to learn from him most is whether he had any contact with this girl—Polly Swanscott."

"Why? What business is it of yours?"

"It is business. Her mother has paid me a fee to find her. She fears Polly may have come to some harm."

"From Pablo? From Picasso?"

"She seems to be attracted to men who treat her badly."

Stein was sitting bolt upright, eyes flicking back and forth, as though in search of axemen to come forward and dispatch Bedford.

"You accuse Pablo of abusing this girl?"

"I don't know."

"Then you should not speak, Bedford Green. And you will not speak to me anymore. You will not come here anymore. I am sorry."

Her need to have him gone was obviously very strong. She got up from her divan—her throne—and walked away, out of the room.

"We'd better go, Bedford,"

"You stay, Ernie. I need to take a long walk—and think."

"Come to the Lilas tomorrow."

"Yes, I will."

He was stopped at the door by Romaine Brooks.

"This girl is named Polly Swanscott?" she asked.

"Yes."

"If she is in Paris, I will let you know."

"Thank you."

Her hand came to his shoulder. She looked both ways, as though someone might be preparing to pounce on her, then leaned closer, whispering.

"Picasso," she said. "He is a fascinating man. But as far as women are concerned, he is a great brute."

Her cape brushed over Bedford as she turned away. The scent of her perfume lingered after.

H **E** walked all the way to the Black Swallow, thinking, but to no great conclusion. Bullard was enjoying a prosperous night. Had the place been less crowded, Bedford might have noticed that among those at Bullard's table was a thin, hatchet-faced, red-haired man who had also been a comrade in the skies over Flanders.

There was no retreat. In this city, it wouldn't have done much good.

"Captain O'Bannion," Bedford said, standing before them.

"Captain Green," said the Irishman, the twinkle in his eye rather like that of sun glinting on a gun barrel.

Two of Bullard's hangers-on swiftly vacated their chairs at the table.

"Sit down, Bedford," said Bullard. "We're all friends here. I insist upon it."

O'Bannion grinned.

"You make any progress in finding that girl?" Bullard asked.

Bedford sadly shook his head.

The band was playing "Diga Diga Do," with two Frenchmen doing for the Mills Brothers. Bullard poured Bedford a small whiskey, which he and his nerves appreciated greatly.

"Thank you," he said, after a sip.

"It's right off the boat," said O'Bannion. "One of my boats."

"You're becoming quite the international tycoon," Bedford said.

Whatever bonhomie O'Bannion might have been harboring swiftly vanished. "You know where we stand, Green."

"Something about a death threat," Bedford said.

"We have a score to settle, that's all."

"Why didn't you see to it when you had those thugs work me over in the Rue Campagne Première."

"I don't know what you're talking about."

Bedford pointed to his forehead, which still bore marks of bruise, cut, and scrape. "Two big lugs hit me and a friend of mine from behind. One of them had a lead billy. Might have killed me, if he'd been of a mind. Why didn't you have him do it?"

O'Bannion appeared indignant. "I sent no one to the Rue Campagne Première. I sent no one to get you."

"We don't know who that was," Bullard said. "I asked around. No one knows what that was about."

Bedford drank. The band had moved on to "Kater Street Rag." He evaded O'Bannion's steady, malevolent gaze and turned to Bullard.

"You once said this was a city of thieves and some of them run the government," Bedford said.

"Actually, it was Captain O'Bannion here who said that. But I was happy to repeat it."

Acknowledging this with a glance to the Irishman, Bedford continued.

"Because of your business dealings, you are well acquainted with the local police," Bedford said.

"The flics?" said Bullard. "*Bien sûr.* So I stay in business."

"I need a friendly flic."

"For what?"

"Corpses."

◆

THE late hour was no hindrance. In fact, it made matters easier. For twenty dollars in francs, Bedford received an escort to the central morgue, where he was first treated to a perusal of photographs of the last two months' worth of Paris murder victims. Each was a grotesque—unlike the beatific mourning photos that were in vogue in the previous century—but some more so than others. A few he gave no more than a second's consideration.

He used Polly's postal card for comparison, finding nothing near a match.

Finally, he was taken to the crypt, which contained the bodies of four young women recently made victims. One had been beaten to death, another had been strangled, another had drowned in the Seine, and the last had been shot through the heart. Two were blond, but in no way resembled Polly.

The beating victim was a little more difficult to determine. She had dark hair and her coloring was otherwise all wrong for the Swanscott girl, but it suddenly occurred to Bedford that he really hadn't come to this grisly place in search of Polly. His fears had been quite differently placed.

"How tall is this one?" Bedford asked, in French.

The man, who seemed grateful for this distraction from his usual dead-of-night routine, pulled back the sheet. Bedford wished he hadn't.

"*Presque deux mètres*," said the attendant.

"Looks about six feet," said Bullard, who had accompanied Bedford to assist in the arrangement.

Bedford rubbed his eyes, then looked again, relaxing finally with a long exhalation. The unfortunate woman had unusually large breasts. Sloane was not so endowed.

"*Bien*," Bedford said. "*Je vous remercie.*"

He turned to the police detective who was sharing in the twenty dollars. "*C'est tous?*"

"*Tous pour aujourd'hui. C'est assez.*"

Bedford agreed. It certainly was enough.

"As bad as the war in there," said Bullard.

"No," said Bedford. "Nothing's as bad as the war."

He had a nightcap at Bullard's, enjoying it more in the absence of O'Bannion, who had gone on to complete some business. Then he took a taxi to his hotel, finding both doorman and desk clerk asleep. He felt as weary.

There was no one to operate the lift, so he took the stairs. Opening his door, he was about to reach for the light switch, but halted.

He'd heard a sound. Thinking about it, he realized it was caused by a movement of the mattress springs.

Closing the door again, he pressed back against the wall. His inclination—rapidly becoming a desperate urge—was to make for the stairs and run. O'Bannion had been playing games with him for years. Most of the time, Bedford hadn't taken them seriously, but that was quite possibly a big mistake.

But why would a lurking assassin be on the bed? A lazy assassin, tired of waiting up for him? O'Bannion wouldn't hire such people. Or if he did, their employment wouldn't last long. Considering for a moment that it might be the same thugs who had attacked him and Hemingway near Man Ray's, he wondered why they hadn't moved as soon as he'd opened the door.

And if it was them, why weren't they bursting through that door that very instant, in pursuit?

It might be the mysterious boyfriend Oritzky, but that fellow's quarry was Polly, not Bedford. It was doubtful he would even know about Bedford. The Swanscotts would not have taken him into their confidence.

He'd been thinking in terms of men. That faint sound of someone moving on the bed wasn't all that had greeted his senses upon opening the door. There'd been a scent. Light, but sweet.

Suppressing his qualms and fears, he put hand to doorknob again and turned. The dim light from the hall illuminated a rectangle of carpet, but the bed remained in darkness. He held his breath a moment, listening. Breathing was what he heard, soft and gentle breathing.

Moving as quietly as he could manage, he reentered the room and closed the door behind him. Stepping sideways, he found the arm of the room's lone chair and lowered himself into it, realizing he was sitting on someone's clothes. He reached and touched silk.

The party on the bed rolled over. The rhythm of the breathing abruptly changed.

"Good evening," he said.

She sat up. "Bedford?"

"I've been looking for you," he said, "in some unpleasant places."

"This city has them."

"May I ask what you're doing here? And in my bed?"

"I was looking for you. All over. I gave up and came here—in the forlorn hope that you might return."

"But here I am."

She stirred, adjusting her position. He could see her outline now, faintly limned by the light from the opening in the window curtains.

"Sloane?"

There was a yawn. "Sorry. I was thinking."

"Are you all right?"

"Yes. Only sleepy."

"You were very upset."

"I was. Terribly upset. But now I know she's still alive. She's gone to the Côte d'Azur."

"With a Spanish artist?"

"No. In pursuit of a Spanish artist."

"Picasso?"

"Yes."

He leaned toward the table, then paused. "Shall I turn on the lamp?"

"No."

"Are you wearing any clothes?"

"A few. Not many. Hardly any."

He heard her pull up the sheet.

"Do you want to go to the South, Sloane?"

"Yes."

"With me?"

"Yes. That's why I'm here in your room."

"In the morning."

"Yes."

He yawned, then apologized.

"We should go to sleep."

She hesitated, but not long. "Will you be comfortable in that chair?"

"In all candor, no."

Another hesitation.

"Bedford, there is nothing more I would like right now than for you to give me a big hug and hold me in your arms for the rest of this awful night. I've been more scared and angry and sad in this city than I've ever been in my life. But

I made a vow to myself when I went to work for you that we would not become involved because there's a great deal I wish and need to do in the world before I let happen what would inevitably happen. Do you understand?"

"Yes."

"Does it make sense?"

"Of a sort."

"Are you sitting on my clothes?"

"I'm afraid so."

She sighed. "Come lie on the bed, then. But don't get undressed, and try not to touch me."

He doubted she could see his smile. "That's all right," he said, rising. "I'll move your clothes."

Returning to the chair, he stretched out his legs.

"Good night, Sloane. I'm so glad you're here."

"Tomorrow we'll go south." She said nothing more.

CHAPTER 11

SLOANE passed most of the train journey down to Nice either asleep or talking to Hadley Hemingway, who sat opposite her in their Second Class compartment. From time to time, she even took the baby Bumby on her lap, allowing the mother a respite.

Hadley was a warm, bluff, cheerful Midwestern person, much like her husband in that respect but lacking his bravura and penchant for center stage. Bedford knew she was the chief financial support of that marriage, having a small income from some trust fund, but she evidenced no unhappiness over the arrangement.

Husband Ernest had wired the Murphys that he and Hadley were taking them up on their standing invitation, apologizing for the lack of notice, and then following it with another belatedly informing them that he was bringing along Bedford and Sloane as well. There'd been no reply from the Côte d'Azur to either telegraph, but Hemingway insisted it wouldn't matter. The Murphys would take in a regiment of cavalry if it turned up on their doorstep, he insisted—as long they could provide amusement and worthy conversation. The Murphys were the most generous goddamn rich people on the planet, he said, tolerant even of the Fitzgeralds and their penchant for turning up dead drunk at six in the morning, seeking breakfast.

Hemingway was sure they could put Bedford in touch with Picasso, as they'd taken a great liking to the painter. Gerald Murphy was an artist himself, he said, though not so admired or talented as the Spaniard.

The young writer was in high spirits, his ebullience encouraged by a hamper full of food and wine he'd brought along from the Lilas. Bedford several times tried to ask him more about the artist Picasso and his connection with the Murphys, but Hemingway only wanted to talk about the war, and it was difficult to deflect him from his inclinations. He tended to dominate conversations the way a bull did a corrida.

Hemingway described his own war experience as remarkably limited in duration, but intense. Bad vision in his left eye had disqualified him for regular military service, so he'd signed up as a volunteer ambulance driver with the Red Cross. That was in April 1918, late in the war, but with more than six months of slaughter still left. As it turned out, he got to enjoy only a small portion of that.

Arriving in Milan in a military-style Red Cross uniform and the honorary rank of second lieutenant—just eighteen years of age—Hemingway had been thrust into service immediately, ordered to help remove the shattered and dismembered remains of a great many women munitions workers who'd been killed when an explosive plant there had blown up. Finally sent into the mountains and up to the front, he'd been assigned a vehicle and begun hauling out the Italian wounded, often under Austrian artillery fire. One night, while he was distributing candy and cigarettes to some troops in a forward position, a shell had nearly killed him, wounding many nearby. He'd been trying to carry one badly injured fellow to safety when he'd been hit by a machine-gun bullet in the leg. He'd somehow kept on and managed to save the man's life, an endeavor for which he'd received an Italian medal of valor. But his wound was serious and took him out of the war for good.

"They sent me home while I was still on crutches," he said. "By the time I was fully two-legged again, the goddamn thing was over."

"You saw as much as any man needs to," Bedford said.

Bedford's had been a much longer war, lasting nearly three years, each day both an amazement and a horror, though there was a strange, surreal beauty to dancing with death in the skies. He spoke of this only briefly, though, knowing how much Sloane hated the subject. She'd pretended to go back to sleep during Hemingway's retelling of his adventures, but at one point interjected a query as to how the man could have been hit by more than two hundred pieces of shrapnel when he'd been struck by only a single bullet.

"It was a shell," Hemingway said.

Bedford took advantage of the moment to redirect the conversation.

"Why would Fitzgerald have Polly Swanscott's name in his notes?" he asked.

"I don't know," Hemingway said. "Did he?"

"Yes. Zelda told me about it."

"Maybe, like me, he just wants to help you find this girl," Hemingway said. "He probably thinks this is a swell story, this missing rich girl. Scott's only written three novels, you know. But he grinds out those short stories like a Maxim gun spitting bullets. He must have had a hundred of them published already. He's got to get his material somewhere. And he never was in the war, you know. The army, but never the war. Spent all his time in Ala-goddamn-bama. That's how he ended up with Zelda. When we get there, why don't you ask him?"

"I already have—in a way. His answer wasn't very satisfactory."

"Look, amigo, all I can say is he's a pretty decent guy, despite his idiosyncrasies. I've done this book about Pamplona and the bulls. My best goddamn work. No crappola. Scott likes it and he's going to get his editor at Scribner's to look at it. I've sure as hell got no argument with the man, except his wife's crazy and he drinks too goddamn much."

Sloane stirred against Bedford, opening one eye and communicating some displeasure with it. Bedford patted her shoulder, then carefully got to his feet.

"Come on, Ernie," he said. "Let's go for a walk. Let the ladies get some rest."

"Swell idea."

Hemingway reached into the hamper for another bottle of wine. Before they returned to the compartment more than an hour later they'd managed to talk their way into the locomotive, at Hemingway's boisterous suggestion sharing their refreshment with the engineer and fireman. Hemingway got to sound the steam whistle and sit at the controls.

◆

BEDFORD rented a bright red Hispano-Suiza from a garage near the rail station in Nice. The car was an extravagance, but there was nothing else available. It was the sort of auto to impress the local gentry and gendarmes, however—which might prove useful.

Sloane certainly looked splendid in it. She'd changed clothes on the train and was wearing white gloves and hat and a pastel pink dress he'd not seen on her before. Sitting with her usual excellent posture, she looked a royal personage on tour.

Hemingway had been to the area before and claimed to know the roads, a knowledge that proved somewhat incomplete. It was late afternoon when they finally reached the estate called Villa America on a hill near the town of Cap d'Antibes. The sunlight was coming at an angle through the trees, in streaks and dapples and sudden flares when the breeze lifted branches. As Bedford turned the car through the gates into a graveled yard, a woman stepped from the shade, holding her hand above her eyes against the glare.

She seemed almost to glow with a soft, gentle, motherly beauty. Her features were very regular, small, and singularly patrician, but there was nothing in her countenance to suggest haughtiness or condescension. She smiled upon them all as a woman might at returning children. She was wearing a belted jacket over a bathing suit, and espadrilles. Bedford was curious to note a long pearl necklace looped about her graceful neck despite the casualness of her garb.

"Sara!" said Hemingway, vaulting over the side of the car and landing on the gravel with a mighty thump. "Meet my friends—Bedford Green and Sloane Smith."

Sloane got out the passenger side door without waiting for Bedford to open it for her. She seemed fascinated by Sara Murphy, but also wary, extending her hand a little tentatively.

Hands were shaken all around.

"I would sometimes read your column, Mr. Green, when we were in New York. You are very clever."

"Thank you. I'm no longer in the newspaper business, actually."

Mrs. Murphy's smile sweetened. "Then you should turn your talent to something better."

"He's an art dealer," said Hemingway. "You have any artists here at the moment?"

"Only two, and I'm afraid they're already well represented." She turned belatedly to Hadley, sensing the neglect. The two women embraced, and then Mrs. Murphy picked up Bumby and held him close.

"Everyone's still down at the beach," she said. "Your rooms are prepared." She gave Bedford and Sloane a cautious glance. "I'm afraid yours has no view of the sea."

"This is very kind of you," Bedford said. "But we thought we'd just find a hotel. We're strangers to you, and . . ."

"Pishtosh. Any friend of Ernest's and Hadley's can be no stranger to us. Not for long. And I believe you know the Fitzgeralds, too. *N'est ce pas?*"

"Yes, but . . ."

Sloane put her hand on his arm. "That will be fine. The room. Thank you very much."

"I'll let you settle in and freshen up. Perhaps you may want to go down to the beach. We'll have cocktails in about an hour."

"You know me, Sara," Hemingway interjected. "I'll have cocktails—and the beach."

HEMINGWAY made a small adventure out of their trek down to the water, replenishing the hamper with wine and spirits and setting out for the seashore below as though to rescue a party stranded in the wilderness. If there'd been a rifle at hand, Bedford had no doubt the man would have slung it over his shoulder.

Hadley and her child stayed behind with Mrs. Murphy; Sloane, after a brief pause in their guest quarters, decided to make the trip to the beach as well.

Parking was hazardous, as the road was narrow and there was only a small strip of ground to the side on which to leave the car, but there were other autos in the same situation. Bedford had left down the top, and looked unhappily to the skies over the mountains to the north, which had gone from haze to a threatening gray.

Hefting the hamper, Hemingway descended the narrow, rocky path down the bluff like a veteran mountaineer. Bedford, more cautious, lingered to assist Sloane, who was still wearing high heels. But she defiantly declined assistance.

Her eyes were on the people below. Her feline aspect was back in evidence, her concentration that of a predator.

The beach was very small and rocky, more a place of pebbles than sand. The people upon it, dressed mostly in bathing costumes, were variously disposed, but all seemed to belong to the same group. Bedford was surprised to find in these lush, foreign, and tranquil surroundings the writer Dorothy Parker—a habitué of many of his favorite New York speakeasies. She waved to him, but quickly shifted her attention to Hemingway, who had set down the hamper and was commanding all present to take their ration.

Most of them happily complied with the order. As they gathered around, Bedford was introduced one after the other to three men with thinning, slicked-back, well-groomed hair and aristocratic faces and manners. They might have been brothers. One was the host, Gerald Murphy, who in turn presented his Yale college chum Cole Porter, the composer, and another good friend, the writer John Dos Passos. Two little boys, running madly around Murphy's bare legs as they might a tree, proved to be Murphy's sons Baoth and Patrick. Two smiling and fluffy-haired women seated nearby on a blanket were Katy Dos Passos and Ada MacLeish, whose husband Archibald was at water's edge, talking to a very Russian-looking woman identified as Olga Picasso.

Bedford had been feeling sleepy, but now snapped fully awake. Introductions completed, he accepted the drink shoved into his hand by Hemingway and then stepped back to the periphery of the gathering. He studied Mrs. Picasso for a moment, sensing some disquiet there, then looked about the area for Sloane, confounded that someone with such presence could have vanished so quickly in so small a place.

But she hadn't. He finally noticed her just down the beach, standing under some trees and talking to a man much shorter than she. Moving toward them, Bedford took in a stocky build and sizable chest, a strong jaw and large nose, dark, staring eyes and a sweep of jet-black hair combed sleekly across his forehead. He looked in all a muscular peasant, but had remarkable posture—the cocky stance of swaggering gent.

Sloane was speaking very intensely to him. As Bedford came near, the artist appeared quite surprised by his sudden presence—and seemed to resent it. Sloane was the most attractive woman in all that gathering, and he apparently accepted it as a matter of course that she had gone directly to him immediately upon arriving at the beach, not bothering with anyone else.

He turned to Bedford as he might to an intruder, a frown gathering above his prominent brow. Sloane put her hand to Bedford's arm, keeping it there. Whatever this communicated, the other man suddenly became more civil.

"Picasso," he said, his voice as firm as the grip of his hand.

"This is Bedford Green," Sloane said. "My lover."

CHAPTER 12

"WHAT was the meaning of that?" Bedford asked, as he drove the Hispano-Suiza back onto the road.

They had left the others behind, ostensibly so they could complete their unpacking. More truthfully, Sloane wanted to get away from Picasso.

"Meaning of what?" she asked.

"Of your suggestive remark to Señor Picasso. About us."

"That wasn't a suggestive remark. That was a very obvious and direct remark—and it was directed at him, not you. He was trying to seduce me, having known me all of about sixty seconds. And with his wife just down the beach. I wanted to drop the gate on him. And damned fast."

A truck was careening down the hill toward them. The road had been built for carriages and there was barely room for a single vehicle. Bedford swerved their car up onto the sloping ground to the side, the sharp angle causing Sloane to slide across the seat against him. She didn't move until the truck had passed—its gape-mouthed driver smiling at them as though he had no control over the truck's movements, which seemed altogether possible.

Back fully on the roadway, Bedford proceeded slowly, his

eyes fixed upon the high horizon ahead. Sloane moved back to what she no doubt considered a more appropriate place.

"You know," Bedford said, "considering how you came at Señor Picasso in a rush like that, maneuvering him off into the trees, it's no wonder he thought you had amour in mind. This is France, after all. These are bohemians."

"I made it exceeding clear to him why I had come and why I was talking to him," Sloane said. "Her name was almost the first thing I said."

"Polly's?"

"Yes. I asked him about her. Where she might be. When he had last seen her."

"And what did he say?"

"He spoke in Spanish. I only know a little."

"And?"

"He said, 'So many girls.' And he shrugged."

"So Picasso claims no knowledge of her at all?"

"No memory of her, which is rot."

"I had mornings like that. During the war."

"Nonsense, Bedford. I'll wager you can recall every woman you ever slept with. All two."

Soldier's talk about women in war also displeased her.

"We could be misinformed. He might have had only the slightest acquaintance with her. She attaches herself to artists. Picasso may not have been receptive."

"He's receptive, all right."

"He said he couldn't remember."

"His eyes are unusually expressive. He looks at you so intently you feel you can see inside him through his eyes. Deep inside. He was lying to me. And I can tell you something else. He is a man capable of great cruelty."

"You can tell that?"

"In some cases. With him, it's very clear."

"He's supposed to be a very good artist."

"I think he is possibly a very great artist. Which makes what I say all the more probable."

"Modigliani was a great artist, and he was very kind."

She said nothing.

"When we get back to the house, I'm going to call the police in Nice."

"To come and arrest him?"

"Hardly. To ask if they might have found her. The police in Cannes, too."

"Found her dead?"

"Just going to ask."

As they rounded the sharp curve at the top, the scent of flowers enveloped them from the blossoming fruit trees to either side of the road. At the next turn, they were greeted with a view of a crescent sweep of sea and hazy mountains in the western distance, golden in the lowering sun.

"We're a ways from Grove Street," he said.

"I wish I were there. This is all very lovely, but . . ."

"Do you want to go back?"

"Can't. Not yet."

"We're not accomplishing much."

"Yes we are."

They passed a woman on a bicycle, its basket full of her marketing. A bit further, Bedford had to steer around an old man leading a cow. The animal looked at them as they went by but the man did not.

"I think it's time you told me," he said.

"Told you what, Mr. Green?"

"What this terrible thing is or was between you and Polly Swanscott."

She stared straight ahead for a very long time, not speaking, then suddenly stood up, holding onto the windshield post with one hand. With the other, she swept off her hat and flung it over the scrubby brush at the side of the road. The wind caught it and took it over the edge of the rise, down toward the sea.

"I'm tired of hats," she said, sitting down. "Hats are bourgeois."

"What?"

"That's what Polly used to say. She never wore hats."

They were at the gates to Villa America.

T⅟E room they had been given had a view north over trees toward the shoulder of a mountain, and there was a small balcony overlooking the gravel yard. These amenities were small compensation for the chamber's tiny size. It held one double bed, a chest of drawers, and a nightstand. Bedford guessed it had belonged to a servant before being converted for the use of guests.

She made him go out on the balcony while she changed for dinner, then did the same for him while he attended to his preparations. The sleeping arrangements she decreed were simple. They would alternate, one taking the bed while the other had the rug and a pillow.

He was not a man to put a lady to such discomfort.

"Whether you take the bed in your turn or not is up to you," she said. "But every other night I will be on the rug— as long as we're here."

"Shouldn't we just move to a hotel?"

"We need to be here, Bedford."

They heard the cars pull into the drive, the passengers disembarking with much chatter and laughter. Hemingway gave a great bellow and whoop, sounding like some North Woods moose in high excitement. Bedford stood just inside the balcony doors to watch them, observing how Hadley gave her husband a warm hug, as though he'd been weeks away in a place of some peril.

Looking to the other car, he saw a pretty young woman in bathing costume and flowered jacket hop from the running board.

"Zelda Fitzgerald's here," Bedford said. "I didn't see her on the beach, but here she is—in bathing suit and all."

"Is it blue? A dark blue?" Sloane was rummaging in her suitcase.

"Yes. Did you see her?"

"I saw a woman in the trees, a little bit down the shore. She was lying with a man on a blanket." Sloane stood beside him, peering down. "Yes. I believe that's her."

"But I don't see her husband."

"This is France. These are bohemians."

THE group gathered for cocktails on the villa's second-floor terrace. A few talked quietly, but most were content just to watch the last of the sunset. As the light faded, the distant mountains merged with the sea, and then with the night.

Gerald Murphy was bartender, and quite expert at it, working the cocktail shaker as though it were a rhythm instrument. His chum Cole Porter hung near him.

Picasso stayed close to his wife, and close to Sara Murphy, who sat near the railing in a chair that might have been a throne.

"Hello Beddie."

Zelda had crept up upon him. She was smoking.

"Good evening, Zelda. Where's Scott?"

"Writing. Still. Always. Have you found your little Molly yet?"

"Polly."

"Golly." She blew a cloud of smoke past his face.

"Were you on the beach today?"

"Of course I was on the beach. That's why we're here."

"Scott . . ."

She glanced quickly over her shoulder. "Where's Scott?"

"I mean, he wasn't on the beach."

She looked to either side of him. "No he wasn't, was he? Were you?"

"Briefly. Is he coming tonight?"

"Who?"

"Scott."

"I don't know. I haven't been to our place since this morning. He was writing."

"But shouldn't he be here now? It's the cocktail hour."

"Yes, yes it is. I need another cocktail, Beddie. A sidecar. No, a whiskey sour. Would you get me one?"

He bowed and went to the little bar. Murphy prepared the drink with grace and high efficiency, handing it to Bedford with a flourish.

"May I refresh yours, Mr. Green?"

"No thank you."

"Are you enjoying yourself here?"

"Very much."

Murphy was studying him. The man had painstakingly perfect manners, so Bedford presumed this small rudeness of a direct stare was calculated for effect.

"Were you able to get through to your party on the telephone?"

The question implied Bedford might have difficulty with the language. Murphy had no knowledge of Bedford's long war experience.

"Yes. I had to make two calls, actually. Nice and Cannes. But no problem. Thank you for the use of your telephone."

"Well of course," Murphy said. "I've forgotten. Why was it you've come to the South of France? A holiday?"

Bedford nodded to Sloane, who had joined Mrs. Murphy and the Picassos.

"Looking for a friend of Miss Sloane's."

"And that has brought you here?" He said this with a smile, but it was a restrained one.

"Ernest Hemingway brought us here. We only meant to come to the Côte d'Azur."

With that, Bedford excused himself and went to Sloane, drawing her away.

"The police have no knowledge of her—not in Nice, not in Cannes."

"That means little," Sloane said. "Go back to your Southern belle."

"Why?"

"She knows more than I do."

"That's certainly an incorrect statement."

But he did return to Zelda, who was at the railing with her back to him. Bedford couldn't tell if she was simply gazing into the night or looking down into the garden at something. Or at someone.

She gave a start when he reached to hand her the drink, then grinned foolishly and accepted the glass, taking a nervous gulp.

"Are you all right, Zelda?"

She was shaking a little. She took another swallow of her cocktail, then shuddered. "I'm fine. Swell."

They both turned to look over the terrace.

"Are you expecting Scott?"

"Why do you care about my husband? Why don't you care about me?"

"I do. We all do."

"You were on the beach today? I didn't see you."

"I believe you were under the trees. Further down the shoreline."

"You didn't want to pay me a visit?"

He sighed. "Not just then."

Zelda studied him intently, as though he were something she was about to buy—or eat. Then, of a sudden, holding drink and cigarette in one hand, she kissed him, very hard. The warmth of her lips set his head to swimming.

"I adore you aviators," she said.

She started to say something else, then took a swallow of her drink and darted away, going straight to Hemingway. In a moment, Bedford heard her talking loudly about God. Hemingway gave him a blameful look.

❖❖❖

T**HE** dinner was light—and late. There was too much drinking beforehand and it continued long into the night. Scott Fitzgerald arrived looking perfectly sober and within a few minutes was looking terribly drunk. He and Zelda began a row, which Dorothy Parker said was becoming a regular feature.

"As rummies go," said Parker. "I wish they would."

She had been knocking it back all night herself, but, as in New York, where she and Bedford had shared a few cocktail hours at the Algonquin or St. Regis, she showed not the slightest effect.

Bedford could stand no more. Excusing himself, he left the house to take a walk. He'd gone only a few paces down the road when he heard the sound of a woman's high heels clattering on the pavement.

It was Sloane.

"He has a studio," she said, catching up.

"Who does?"

"Señor Picasso. The Murphys have provided him with a studio. He paints there every morning. Sometimes at night."

"You find this of some import?"

"Certainly. Artists leave their whole lives lying about their studios. They're very sloppy."

"The studio is on the premises?"

"Yes. A shed at the back of the house."

They could hear laughter coming from the terrace.

"This is not the time."

"I'll arrange the time."

They walked along through the softness of the night, then stopped again, at a place where they could see the sea.

"Bedford, do you think Polly is still alive?"

His mind's eye went to the bodies he'd seen in the Paris morgue.

"I think that if she wasn't, we'd know," he said. "I think perhaps we've been a little overwrought."

"No. You're wrong." She turned, and started back toward the house and the laughter they could still hear.

CHAPTER 13

BEDFORD passed an uncomfortable night on the floor, with surreal images of Zelda, Picasso, and the weeping Polly flitting through his dreams and thoughts.

Sloane was not in these visions. He found her sleeping quietly when he awoke once and checked the bed, where she had taken first turn. When he looked again, the first pale light of dawn visible through the window, the bed was empty. He waited several minutes, and when she didn't reappear from wherever she had gone, he crawled onto the bed himself. The sun was well up when he awoke again—still alone.

The Murphys also rose early and were serving coffee and a strange drink of Hemingway's devise to what few guests were on the terrace. One of them was Sloane, decorously dressed in a long dressing gown and high heeled shoes and seated next to Picasso. The artist was wearing only swimming trunks and espadrilles. She did not avert her gaze from his bare, powerful chest, though Bedford did.

"Good morning," he said to her.

"Did you sleep well, Bedford?"

"I think better than you."

Hadley and her child were up, the latter clinging to his

mother's skirt so fixedly Bedford wondered if he harbored some fear of his father. The writer was present as well, standing at the edge of the terrace and looking toward the sea like a general on the morning of a battle.

Hemingway was drinking from a cup of coffee in large, hasty swallows. Done, he set it down and went to the bar, where he poured himself a glass of the concoction he had invented from a full pitcher Gerald Murphy had made.

"Not invented, discovered," Hemingway corrected, "by the bartender at the Ritz and me."

He held his glass aloft, as though it were some marvel of science—or God. It looked to contain tomato juice.

"Tomato juice," he confirmed. "And vodka, though it's better with gin. Worcestershire sauce, peppers. Cayenne peppers." He took a large sip, smacking his lip and wiping his moustache. "Puts a man back on his feet. Warms the *cojones*."

"I'll have one," said Sloane.

Picasso simply stared—at the entire scene. It occurred to Bedford he might see everything—understand everything—in terms of pictures.

Bedford took a chair just near the artist.

"I'd like very much to see some of your paintings," he said, wondering how well the man spoke English.

He was suprised. The Spaniard was fluent.

"So would your girlfriend," he said, nodding toward Sloane. "But it is not possible."

"She's an expert," Bedford said. "She works in my art gallery."

Picasso's eyes narrowed, almost squinting, though the sun was behind him. "You are a dealer?"

"Yes."

The artist thought a moment, then shook his head. "I already have one. I am well represented."

"In New York?"

"Everywhere. I am known everywhere." He paused, lowering his voice. "If you are a dealer, here to buy art, why are you and she bothering me about this girl?"

"Polly Swanscott is Sloane's friend. And she's disappeared."

Picasso shook his head, scratching his chest idly while he did so. "I cannot help you. Europe is full of young girls—American girls. More and more of them. Some of them think they are artists. One should not give them brushes."

Bedford looked to Sloane, who was pretending not to have heard. She accepted her drink from Hemingway with a nod of thanks. It was the first time Bedford had ever seen her take alcohol this early in the day.

The tranquil sounds of quiet talk, the light breeze, and the morning birds were of a sudden overcome by the clattering chug of an automobile engine, and the louder noise of its horn, sounded three times in quick succession. Then came Zelda's voice, exclaiming, "Good morning all! Good morning everybody! We're back!"

"I thought they'd just left," said Hemingway.

Zelda was again dressed for the beach, though this time in a swimming costume of a much lighter and brighter shade of blue. Her eyes were vague and hazy, though not so bleary as her husband's. Scott went for one of Hemingway's tomato juice concoctions before speaking a word.

The rest of the guests began appearing on the terrace one by one, like forest creatures coming out from cover after a passing danger. The MacLeishes and the Dos Passos were friendly and cheerful, but far from as quick witted and intellectually engaged as they'd been the day before. Olga Picasso joined the gathering with a look in her eyes so dark she might have just come from a murder. The previous late night had taken its toll on everyone—except of course the host and hostess. As always, the Murphys were in perfect spirits. Anything less would have been bad manners.

"People call them the world's happiest couple," Hemingway said, joining Bedford at the railing. "They're going to pay for that one day. We all do."

Zelda moved close to her husband. They looked incongruous—she in her bathing suit; he, lacking only a tie to have stepped from a haberdasher's catalogue.

"What you've got *there* is the world's unhappiest couple," Hemingway said, quietly.

"They enjoy themselves."

"No they don't. Maybe that Polly girl got to look the way she does in your photo because she spent some time with those two."

Bedford disagreed, but didn't want to turn idle morning chatter into something else.

"Have you heard from Fitzgerald's editor at Scribner's? About your Pamplona book?"

"Yeah. I did. Things are going great, Bedford. I just have to get out of my contract with my old publisher. And maybe out of this place. Maybe go back to Italy. You ever thought of writing a book about the war?"

"No. I tend to shy away from unpleasantness," Bedford said.

"Then what are you doing here?"

"This may well be the most pleasant place on earth."

Hemingway grinned. "And what does that tell you?"

Dorothy Parker emerged from the house looking like a participant in a scientific experiment gone terribly wrong. She blinked at the sun as though it were an intruder.

"We have medicine for what ails you, Dotty," Gerald Murphy said to her. "Compliments of Dr. Hemingway." He poured her the last of the tomato juice cocktail into a large glass, then set to work making another pitcher.

Hemingway moved back over to the bar, positioning himself to accept Parker's homage after she took a large swallow of his elixir. She was not timid with it.

"The Nobel Prize has been wasted on all those others," she said.

Scott Fitzgerald came up to Bedford, then drew him away, to the far end of the terrace.

"I have a great, great favor to ask of you," he said. "Very great. Very important."

Bedford was familiar enough with the man now to know this could mean anything from a request for the exact time to the loan of a thousand dollars.

"You are our friend," Fitzgerald continued. "You have become Zelda's very good friend. I think that's very nice. I am grateful for that."

"As am I," Bedford said. He meant it as more than a pleasantry.

"She has been having spells," Fitzgerald said.

"Spells? Fainting spells?"

"Spells when she is not quite herself. Or perhaps when she most particularly is. They are becoming more frequent. I am quite distressed."

"I'm sorry to hear."

"I would appreciate it if you could look out for her, today on the beach. Keep her, keep her out of trouble. Not let anyone bother her. Stay with her at all times. I'll drive you down myself."

This was hardly the way Bedford planned to spend the day.

"Aren't you coming with her?"

"Can't, old sport. Must write. I came down here to write, not drink. All we all do is drink. And Zelda . . ." He shook his head in dismay, then began to walk back to the others. "The day advances," he announced, loudly. "The sun also rises. Everyone to the beach."

Gerald frowned. It was his duty to make such pronouncements.

Picasso rose, grunting. "I am going to paint."

Olga's eyebrows shot up. She apparently trusted her husband as she might a poisonous snake.

"Yes, you must paint," said Sara. "You must always paint. I'm sending everyone off to the beach so that you won't be disturbed."

"I'm going home to write," said Fitzgerald. "All day. But I'll take a carload down to La Garoupe. Bedford and Sloane. Anyone else?"

"Why do we have to go to the goddamn beach?" said Parker. "Just because it's there?"

"Don't worry, Dotty," said Gerald Murphy. "We'll come amply armed with refreshment. And I will personally guarantee you an amusing day."

Hemingway was at the refilled pitcher. He refreshed

Parker's glass, and made another for himself. His wife, Hadley, looked at him very sadly.

◆

BEDFORD was uncertain as to how much Fitzgerald had had to drink that morning, but the writer was driving very fast along the narrow road, making little or no allowance for any vehicle that might by chance be coming the other way. Scott slowed, and not by much, only when approaching the very sharp curve at the top of the bluff where the road began its descent to the shore.

"Give me a cigarette, Goofo," said Zelda, with a particularly maniacal smile.

Bedford and Sloane sat speechless in the back seat as Fitzgerald nonchalantly produced a package of smokes, shook one out for her, then brought forth a lighter and clicked it into flame as she leaned over it—all the while steering the automobile through the sharp sweeping curve and two more turns below it.

Exhaling a wispy plume of smoke that was quickly snatched by the wind, Zelda turned in her seat and looked over its back at Bedford and Sloane.

"Goofo is magnificent, isn't he?" she said. "Too bad he couldn't have been an aviator, too."

At that, Fitzgerald erred at the wheel, causing the car to slip leftward toward the abyss. He quickly corrected. The muscles of the back of his neck were visibly tight.

When they arrived at the bottom of the bluff, Sloane announced she was feeling ill and couldn't possibly abide an entire day at the beach.

"Do you want me to come back with you?" Bedford asked.

She shook her head. "Leave this to me."

As she and Fitzgerald drove away, Sloane, still in the back seat, gave Bedford one quick wave, but without looking back.

G **ERALD** Murphy first set about raking the beach, scowling with marked disapproval at the damage done to his neatness during the night, as though the tide was some vandal. When that was accomplished, he organized another of the Murphys' endless games, this time commanding his guests to costume themselves as exotically as possible, using only things they could find there at the beach.

The Hemingways and Dorothy Parker wanted nothing to do with that, and moved off by themselves. Everyone else took up the challenge with enthusiasm, especially Cole Porter, who went to a tree and began plucking blossoms for his hair. Zelda made a half-hearted effort to do the same, but when one of the flowers fell off, she wandered away, pausing only for a quick glance at Bedford.

"Excuse me," Bedford said, rising.

He followed Zelda along the curve of the beach to a point marked by a clump of trees, catching up with her before she got past them. She turned angrily when he took her arm. He'd been very gentle, but she acted as though he'd caused pain.

"Scott sent you to do this? To follow me? To hound me like some Alabama coon dog? Leave me alone!"

Bedford maintained his grip, but spoke softly.

"I just want to talk to you about this."

"About what?"

"About what you're doing?"

"I'm having a good time. A damn good time. I deserve it. He's always writing. Always. Even when he's not writing. Why can't I be writing? Why is it him?"

"I'm sure you'd have some marvelous things to say, Zelda. And I would love to read them." He put his hands on her shoulders, leaning close. "This man you were with yesterday—and I believe other days—he has dark, curly hair."

"Yes."

"And he is French? And an aviator?"

"Yes."

"Edouard Jozan?"

"Yes. *Oui.*"

"What is he doing here?"

"He's stationed here. Near here. Many French aviators here. He told us both that, when we met in Paris."

"When you were dancing."

"He's a good dancer."

"Is this why you're down here? Did you ask Scott to bring you down here to meet Jozan?"

"No, but when he said we were coming here I was happy. I like being happy."

He felt her shoulder muscles trembling beneath his hands. He lowered his arms to his side. "Where is Jozan now?"

"Probably around the point. He and his friends go to the beach there."

"And you've been joining him."

"Yes. Scott doesn't mind."

"I believe he does. At least today. Zelda, I'd rather you didn't go to Jozan today."

"Why not? Who are you to be telling me that? I hardly know you. Who are you?"

"I need to talk to him. You can see him tomorrow."

"But, Beddie!"

He started to walk away.

"You have to do something nice for me," she said.

"I will." He kept walking.

"Promise."

"I promise."

He didn't stop until he reached the point. As she had suggested, he saw a group of young men down the beach, throwing a very large ball from one to the other. Behind him, Zelda hadn't moved. He waited until she finally turned and headed back to the Murphys', then continued on.

THE athletic Frenchmen were tossing a medicine ball that doubtless weighed more than Bedford cared to lift that morning, let alone throw. He stood at the edge of their group for a moment, until Jozan at last noticed him.

"*Capitaine* Green!"

Flinging the ball to a comrade, he left the circle and bounded over.

"*Comment ça va?*" he asked.

Bedford was not up to French. He began moving away, nodding for Jozan to accompany him—which with noticeable curiosity, he did.

"It needs to go better," he said. "I'm staying with a party—with Gerald and Sara Murphy."

"*Très élégant.*"

"That they are. The Fitzgeralds are part of the group. You know the Fitzgeralds? Yes? I believe you do."

"*Bien sûr. La belle madame.*"

He could see how the feeling might be mutual. In a bathing costume, the muscular French pilot doubtless could have embarked upon a friendship with any woman in the Murphys' circle—excepting Sara Murphy, whose devotion to her husband seemed part of her considerable allure.

"*Un peu fou.*" Bedford turned so he could see back in the direction from which he had come, not wanting to be taken by surprise by Zelda, should she take it in mind to join them. "She and her husband, there is trouble between them."

"I know this. I try to make her happy. To cheer her up."

"Well, you're not cheering him up." Bedford looked out to sea, where a two-masted sailing boat was gliding by. "Lieutenant Jozan, I need a favor."

"*Bien sûr, Capitaine.*"

"I am looking for a woman, a friend of a friend. Her name is Polly Swanscott, and I'm told she came down here."

"Is she pretty?"

"Yes. Blond. Slender. *Un peu fou, aussi.* If you should see her, I should like to know."

"*D'accord.*"

"Immediately."

"Of course."

"She's missing. *Disparu.*"

"*Quelle tristesse.*"

"I think Scott Fitzgerald knows something about her. I've been trying to get him to tell me, but he won't. *Il est évasif.*"

"*Entendu.*"

"Jozan. If there's trouble over Zelda, he may take her away. They may leave. He would be very angry with me, because I think he knows you are my friend."

Jozan's fellow officers were following this conversation with great curiosity. It occurred to Bedford they took him for Jozan's cuckold.

"But if you stay away from her today—for the first time in many days—he may be grateful to me, enough perhaps to tell me what I need to know. *Comprennez?*"

The French officer smiled broadly. At last he had what he would consider a logical, acceptable reason for refraining from an otherwise innocent dalliance.

"Okay." Jozan gave him a friendly punch to the arm, then started to move away. "Okay. Good luck, *Capitaine.*"

"Jozan?"

He stopped, waiting.

"What will you do today? Without Zelda?"

Another beaming grin. "We will look for pretty girls. Maybe we find this Polly for you."

◆◆

RETURNING to the Murphy beach encampment, Bedford found everyone looking perfectly ridiculous. Gerald had made himself into a sort of Roman emperor, fashioning a toga out of towels and a laurel wreath from pine branches.

Hemingway, Bedford was pleased to see, was having none of this. He had removed his shirt and sat on the ground next to Dotty Parker, bare-chested. As best as Bedford could determine, he was telling her about his work.

Or the war.

Murphy handed him a drink, which he politely accepted. After a sip, he looked around.

"Where's Zelda?"

"She went for a walk."

Bedford turned toward the point, wondering if she had slipped through the trees to get by him without him noticing.

"Not that way," said Gerald. "In the other direction."

"There are rocks down that way."

"She seemed fine. Do you know the Fitzgeralds well?"

"Not long, but too well, perhaps."

"We are very fond of them."

"Not everyone is."

"We are."

Bedford excused himself and went to sit beneath a palm tree to wait for Zelda to return. In deference to the increasing heat, he removed his jacket, recalling his grandfather's admonition that a gentleman never did that in public, but happily doing so anyway.

He had seen his grandfather in public once without his suitcoat—in an old photograph. The straight-backed old man was posed standing with a croquet mallet, obviously in the midst of a game, and wearing high-collared shirt and tie. And vest.

Bedford rolled up his sleeves, set down his drink, lay down upon the sand, and fell instantly and perfectly asleep. He slept so long that when he awakened and saw the sun low on the horizon, he thought at first it was still rising.

Hemingway was shaking him. "Time to go, chum. We're all going to a restaurant tonight."

Bedford squinted at his wristwatch. "It's hours before the Murphys like to take their dinner."

"The restaurant's up on a mountain above Nice. The view's worth the trip, or so he says. Anyway, they need you to drive your car. Scott's not up to it."

Bedford stood up. "He's been writing all day."

"Yeah. He probably finished one whole goddamn page."

◆◆◆

T HERE was a large rock beside the road at the entrance to the Murphys' Villa America. Sitting on it as Murphy's car came up the road was Sloane, looking like a mermaid out of water. Bedford asked Murphy to stop and departed the car by vaulting over the side. The rest of them drove on.

"Are you a welcoming party?" he asked.

Sloane barely stirred in response. Her sad eyes were on a

lone flower in the weeds. "Quite the contrary. I believe I've all but worn out our welcome here."

The rock was big enough for two, if one didn't mind touching. Bedford didn't. If Sloane did, she said nothing about it. After a moment, she put her hand in his.

"I feel very, very stupid," she said.

"Something to do with Picasso?" he asked.

She nodded. "I went to his studio."

The possibilities this raised were unpleasant to contemplate.

"Were you welcome?"

"He didn't notice at first. I went around to the window and watched him awhile. He's working on a painting of a beach. I think it's the beach here. There are three figures in it. Two are men and one is a woman. She's naked."

"Polly Swanscott?"

"I'm not sure. His style, you know. Those Roman noses and all that soft abundant flesh. And I wasn't very close. But whoever the woman is, I think he's fond of her. He was very attentive to her image. Very, very attentive."

"If he was that attentive to Polly, we'd be seeing some sign of her about the place."

Her head lowered. "Unless something awful has happened to her. I'm beginning to think that again."

"We should ask him."

She scuffed at the dirt with her shoe. "I tried to. I left the window and went to the door. He was furious at being disturbed—and even angrier at the reason."

"You should have tried seduction again. He seemed to like you well enough at the beach."

"That's precisely what I tried—very openly. I just wanted to get into the shed and see that painting. See whatever else there was to see. But he would have none of it. He began shouting and swearing in Spanish, and chased me away. I think he's now complained to the Murphys."

"We still seem to be invited to dinner. It's some wonderful place on the cliffs above Nice."

"Oh what fun." She spoke the words mournfully.

THERE wasn't transport for all and not everyone wanted to come. The Dos Passos and MacLeishes stayed behind, as did Dorothy Parker, who said she didn't want to interrupt her drinking for the time it would take to get to Nice.

The Picassos stayed behind, too—without explanation.

Two automobiles sufficed for the party. The Hemingways and Cole Porter went with the Murphys. The Fitzgeralds, at Zelda's insistence, traveled with Bedford and Sloane in the Hispano-Suiza.

Scott was barely awake, though Bedford could not tell whether his state was due to fatigue or alcohol. He sat collapsed in the rear seat, his head lolling back against the folded top, looking like he might have been one of the wounded in Hemingway's wartime ambulance. Zelda was full of energy and sat far forward, leaning on the back of the front seat and chattering continuously.

They took a different road north than that which went to La Garoupe, but eventually it, too, turned toward the edge of the cliff.

"Give me a cigarette, Goofo."

Leaning hard on the brake as they went into a wrenchingly sharp turn, Bedford realized Zelda was addressing him.

"Don't smoke, Zelda," he said.

"I do," she said. He sensed an impish smile.

The road switched back of a sudden. Bedford yanked around the wheel sharply, causing the car to skid a little. When they were straightened out again, he shifted down to a lower gear.

Sloane produced a cigarette, lighted it, and handed it to Zelda. Mrs. Fitzgerald looked at it a moment, then flicked it into the night and leaned back in her seat, tilting back her head to stare straight up at the sky.

"God," she said.

"Are we far?" Sloane asked.

"*Patientez, mademoiselle.*"

THE restaurant was in the village of St.-Paul-de-Vence, oc-
cupying the larger part of a clifftop some two hundred feet
above a verdant valley. There were tables set out on the terrace, which had a nighttime view of twinkling lights leading
to the sea. There was a moon, shimmering the water at the far
distance. Two tables had been pushed together for them, both
near the terrace railing and stone steps that led down the
steepness to the valley floor.

A light breeze was blowing, and the moonlight limned the
mountain ridges above them. The menu looked interesting.
Once again, the Murphys had chosen well—chosen perfectly.

Murphy arranged their places, Bedford finding himself
between Sara Murphy and Hadley Hemingway. Across from
him was Zelda, smoking furiously.

Sara and Hadley talked about children, but at length Mrs.
Murphy turned her attention to Bedford.

"Have you bought any interesting paintings since you've
come to France, Mr. Green?"

"Not yet."

"You seem to be taking quite an interest in Pablo's work."

"I can't afford Señor Picasso's work, but I'd like to see
some of it."

No one was attending to Zelda. She was blowing streams
of smoke in all directions, drinking wine thirstily, and drumming her fingers on the table between sips. She shot a dark
look at Bedford, as though her problem, whatever it might
be, was his fault.

"That is up to Pablo," said Sara.

"Of course."

Hadley started to speak, then thought better of it, turning
to the view.

Sara continued doing her duty to the conversation.

"Have you a favorite painter, Mr. Green?"

He thought upon it. "The closest to that would be George
Bellows."

"Do I know him? Is he here in France?"

"He prefers New York—or did."

"Did?"

"I believe he just died. It's very sad."

"It's always sad. I truly hate death."

A large woman at a nearby table attracted Bedford's attention with her hearty laugh. She wore a long billowy dress and was barefoot. There were three effeminate-looking men at the table with her, who seemed to be vying to see who could amuse her most. When she looked Bedford's way, he realized who she was.

"There's Isadora Duncan," he said.

Sara and Hadley looked to the dancer, and then Zelda did, too. Scott leaned across the table at the other end. "Who'd you say that is, old sport?"

Bedford raised his voice, but only slightly. "Isadora Duncan."

Fitzgerald stared, then slowly, with uncertain step, got up and went over to the woman's table. He introduced himself, bowing ornately, and seated himself on the floor. He apparently intended a long stay, for he crossed his legs Indian-fashion, gazing up at her raptly.

"I think Scott had a similar interview with Edith Wharton," Sara said.

Hadley giggled. Zelda took a long drag on her cigarette, then rose and walked around the table. Bedford thought she might be wanting to say something to him. When she did not, he turned around just in time to see her put both hands on the top of the marble railing and fling herself over the side.

CHAPTER 14

BEDFORD, dreading the sight that must await them on the other side of the terrace wall, could not make himself move. Sloane leapt to her feet, but then succumbed to the same indecision as Bedford. Scott remained at Isadora Duncan's feet, oblivious to what his wife had done, as though it was a common occurrence that no longer merited his concern.

Hemingway, though, always in character, resolutely pushed back his chair and moved to the grim business that awaited below. But he was held back by Sara Murphy, who had reached the stairs by the railing before him, and put her hand against his great chest.

"Let me," she said, softly, and then started with no further hesitation toward the stone steps that led below.

Bedford sat a few seconds more, curious than he'd heard no outcry from Zelda and fearful as to what that might portend. Then he willed himself to rise and go to the railing.

Zelda had not sailed over the precipice to her doom hundreds of feet below, as he and doubtless everyone else there had feared. She had dropped perhaps seven feet onto a landing of the steps, a bruising fall, but not a fatal one. As he looked down at her, she rose onto hands and knees. Sara has-

tened to her side and took the injured woman into her arms.
Now Bedford could hear Zelda's moaning. He turned sadly
away, waiting for Mrs. Murphy's call for assistance—when
she was ready for it.

No one at the table was speaking, or moving. Gerald Murphy appeared still perfectly poised, but in his eyes Bedford
could see he was stricken.

"Is she all right?" Hemingway called loudly to Sara.

There was no response, and then there was. Zelda, in
ghostly fashion, appeared at the top of the stairs. Her knees,
arms, and hands were bloodied, and there were crimson
smears on her dress. She smiled, as though this was all great
fun somehow.

Sara appeared behind her, holding her a moment, then
going to the table for a napkin, with which she began to dab
at Zelda's scrapes and wounds. It seemed more a grooming
measure than medical treatment. In either case, it was doing
no good.

Scott, in company with everyone on the terrace, was observing the bizarre tableau. But it was with the gaze of a man
indeed interested, but disconnected.

"Scott!" said Gerald Murphy.

This was uttered as admonition, but it had no effect.
Fitzgerald resumed talking to Isadora Duncan, perhaps offering explanation of his wife's bizarre action.

No one else except Sara was moving at all. The appalling
scene seemed to have no end to it. They were all frozen in
their state of anguish and dismay.

Bedford and Sloane came forward in the same instant—
Bedford putting his arm around Zelda, supporting her. It was
beginning to dawn upon her that she had done something
wrong—something very strange.

"Are you dizzy, Zelda?" he asked. "Did you hurt your
head?"

She put a hand to her hair, then looked at him wonder-
ingly with those weird eyes.

"No. My head is fine. I am fine. Are you fine, Beddie?"

"No, I'm not. I'm worried about you. We all are. I want to
take you to a doctor."

"I think she should stay with us," Sara said.

"We brought her," Bedford said. "We'll take her to the hospital in Nice." He began to steer Zelda away from the table and toward the restaurant's parking area on the other side of the terrace. As they came to Isadora Duncan's table, Bedford hesitated.

"Fitzgerald," Bedford said. "Do you realize what's happened?"

The writer, terribly pale, ridiculous in his supplicant position at the feet of the great dancer, replied almost casually.

"Yes. Thank you, Bedford."

"Aren't you coming?"

"She's in safe hands, I'm sure."

Zelda paid her husband no attention whatsoever.

◆

THE young doctor at the hospital in Nice seemed happy for the diversion from his routine night's work, which amounted largely to dealing with the results of sailors' and fishermen's nightly brawls. Zelda was now in considerable pain, but attempted to hide and ignore it, as though anxious to please. Her scraped knees and one of her hands required extensive bandaging, and a cut along her arm took a half dozen stitches. Happily for her vanity, she had only a slight bruise on her face.

"I can't believe that man wouldn't come with us," said Sloane, as the doctor and a nurse went about their labors.

"What man?" said the doctor. "Was she attacked?"

"No," Bedford said. "She had an accident. Slipped and fell on some stairs—at the restaurant at St.-Paul-de-Vence."

"*Elle a de la bonne chance,*" said the doctor, finishing up the stitches. "That's a dangerous height."

"It's her husband we're talking about," Sloane said, testily. "He just sat and watched. Didn't even come with us."

"But no attack?" the doctor asked. "*Rien des coups?*"

He smiled at Zelda, who smiled back, wincing.

"No," said Bedford. "Why do you ask?"

"It happens. Too much, nowadays."

"It was an accident."

The hurt and stiffness were beginning to encroach upon Zelda's spirits. She cried out a little as she slipped off the examining table and put her full weight to the floor.

"Give me a cigarette, Goofo," she said.

"I'm not Goofo, Zelda," Bedford replied.

"Madame," said the doctor. "Would you like some morphine? The pain will become worse, I think."

"No," said Bedford. "I don't think that will be a good idea."

"Are you sure?" Sloane asked.

"She needs to sleep," the doctor said. "And . . ."

"She's been drinking a lot," Bedford said, putting his arm around Zelda. "And there are other reasons."

The doctor cleared his throat. "Uh, there is a bill."

"I'll take care of it," said Sloane. "Where do I pay?"

"At the reception."

Sloane started in that direction, but Bedford, still holding Zelda, lingered.

"Have you had any other cases like this?" he asked. "Women being attacked?"

"*Oui.* Three or four this month."

"Was one of them a young American woman? Very blond?"

The younger man nodded. "*Oui, c'est vrai.*"

"Was her name Polly Swanscott? An artist?"

The doctor went to a desk and took up a clipboard. "No, not Polly Swanscott. She said her name was—yes, *voilà.* 'Fou. Mademoiselle Fou.' That's all the name she gave."

"Was there a man with her?"

"Someone brought her here, but did not come in. She left on her own."

"Did she say where she was staying? Was it here in Nice?"

The doctor shrugged. "Don't know. There was no address."

"Come on, Goofo," Zelda said. "I have to have a drink."

She stumbled twice walking to the car.

❖

THEY drove on to the Fitzgerald apartment at the Hotel du Cap with Zelda curled up in the rear seat, presumably asleep. Bedford had a lingering fear she might leap over the side, as she had done at the restaurant, but she seemed content now—or at least unwilling to stir herself much.

"You're driving very slowly, Bedford," Sloane said.

"A bit."

"Why?"

"In the probably forlorn hope that, the longer we take, the more likely it will be that Scott will be waiting for her."

"Why do you wish that?"

He drove a while longer without speaking, the headlamps burrowing a tunnel in the darkness beneath the overhanging branches of the trees to either side.

"Actually," Bedford said. "That's not at all what I want."

He pushed the accelerator hard against the floor.

◆◆◆

THE hotel staff was most attentive and helpful, despite the very late hour, but none of them seemed at all surprised at Zelda's state. She smiled at the night manager weakly, but was otherwise quite obviously fighting pain.

Once they had her in the Fitzgeralds' suite of rooms, Bedford tipped the night porter and the manager as generously as he could manage, and hurried them back outside. Sloane took Zelda into the bedroom, removing her dress, stockings, and shoes and getting her under the covers.

Zelda sat up. "Where's Scott?"

Sloane sat on the edge of the bed. "He'll be along soon. Can I get you something?" She looked to Bedford. "Should she have a drink?"

Bedford thought upon it. "Yes. She needs sleep more than anything. I'll make her one."

There was a bar in the sitting room, amply stocked. He prepared her a strong gin fizz. She drank it greedily.

"Rest," he said. "Things will be better tomorrow."

"It almost is tomorrow, Beddie."

"Rest."

Sloane stayed with her, talking quietly. Bedford opened

the doors to the balcony, admitting a summery breeze. Then he left the room.

Scott had turned the suite's other bedchamber into his writing room. Much of it was in the same chaotic disorder as the rest of the Fitzgerald quarters, but the area around the desk was neat and tidy, as was the desk itself—notebooks and manuscript pages stacked in very orderly fashion. There was a small portmanteau on the floor to the side of the desk, its lid unlocked and ajar.

Bedford turned to the notebooks first.

◆◆

WHEN he was finished, he went into the sitting room, finding Sloane stretched out on a chaise longue with her head tilted back over its curving back. The door to the bedroom where Zelda reposed was open a crack, the interior dark.

"Are you asleep?" he asked.

"No."

"Is she?"

"She'd better be—for everyone's sake."

He seated himself in a chair opposite her. She had the most beautiful legs.

"You've been on a rummage," she said.

"Afraid so."

"Make you feel a little shabby?"

"Of course."

"Did you find what you were looking for?"

"No."

"No? You said Zelda . . ."

"Zelda said there was something in his book notes about Polly, but I can't find a single reference. Nothing at all that would pertain to her. There's a lot of material, but it seems mostly to do with his next book. There are many entries about psychiatry. He seems well aware of Zelda's condition."

"Condition?"

"She's been diagnosed as schizophrenic."

Sloane's expression twisted a little. He guessed his

revelation put her in mind of her friend, who had given herself the nickname "Crazy."

"Scott just doesn't know what to do about it," Bedford
said, "except use it as material for a book."

Sloane sat up, smoothing down her skirt. "But this has
nothing to do with Polly."

"No. There's a beautiful young woman, but I think he's
making her a Hollywood movie star. She seems a lot like you."

"Me?"

"Yes, but the girl seems to be in love with a character
based on Gerald Murphy."

"I've hardly talked to the man. I don't think they approve
of me."

"There's lots of stuff on the Murphys. I think Scott's a bit
in love with Sara. He seems to have a curious opinion of Gerald's role as a husband."

"Do you feel guilty, going through his papers?"

"I would have—before that dreadful scene at the restaurant. He's the one who should feel guilty. These notebooks
are full of the most minute details about people, how they
look, what they say, what they might think. I don't think he
found me very interesting, but he has pages on our friend
Hemingway—and he's only known him a couple of weeks."

"But nothing about Polly."

Bedford shook his head.

"Once again, we've been wasting our time."

She turned toward the bedroom door. Zelda was calling to
them.

Bedford went to the doorway.

"Zelda?"

"Is Scott here yet?" Her voice was very faint.

"Not yet. Soon."

"Come here, Beddie."

He entered, seating himself where Sloane had been at the
edge of the bed. He took her hand—gently—but it was the
injured one, and she pulled it away. With the other, she began
rubbing at her forehead. Then she turned her head to look at
him quite directly, her eyes oddly illuminated. There was a
soft light coming from the window.

"He goes to Cannes."

"What? Who goes to Cannes?"

"Picasso goes to Cannes. I just remembered. Olga told me. She's unhappy about it. He won't tell her where he goes there, but he goes."

"Cannes?"

"Yes. But he hasn't gone there since you and Sloane have come."

"Cannes."

"I thought you should know, because you're still looking for that girl Polly. You should go to Cannes."

"Then we probably shall. Thank you."

"Kiss me, Goofo."

Rather than protest, he did, as decorously as he could.

"Now I can go to sleep, because I remembered, and I told you."

"Good night, Zelda. Thank you."

"Good night, Goofo."

Bedford closed the door behind him.

"I think we should go now," he said to Sloane.

"Can we leave her alone?"

"Probably not. I'll pay the night manager to have someone sit up here with her until Scott comes back."

"Will she be all right?"

"Sloane, she's exhausted."

"Me, too."

❖

THERE were only two or three lights on at Villa America as they approached along the blufftop road. It was close to dawn, but there was no telling whether anyone was still up.

"Park the car on the road, away from the house," Sloane said. "Quietly, if you would."

"What is it you want to do?"

"Visit Señor Picasso's little studio. We'll hold an exhibition. Just for us."

"It will be locked."

"I know."

◆◆

BEDFORD tried opening the lock with his penknife, employing a trick taught him by his detective friend, Joey D'Alessandro. But it didn't work. After several fruitless attempts, he broke a pane of glass at a side window and reached inside to open the latch.

"Wait," he whispered, putting a finger to his lips.

They listened for sounds of human stirring, standing close to one another. For all their long night, Sloane still smelled sweet.

"They're still asleep," she said, and gently pushed past him, entering the studio.

In the gloom, Bedford located a lamp, and switched it on. The room seemed neither neat nor disorderly; simply a place of work. There were a number of canvasses stacked in two groups against a wall. On an easel was the painting Sloane had described—only with a difference. She had said there were three figures depicted there—two men and a woman. Now there were just two—men standing on the shore. The woman she'd said Picasso had painted standing in the water had vanished, painted out with wide flat brush strokes of white.

"I swear that was Polly," she said. "Now he's trying to hide the evidence."

Bedford leaned close, trying to make out the outlines of the eradicated figure through the fresh paint. He tilted up the lampshade to cast more light on the work.

"The woman you saw here was naked?" he said.

"Yes."

"Did she have large breasts? From what I can see, I think this one does."

"Possibly—and also a sort of Roman nose. But that's how Picasso is doing all his women now."

"Did Polly have large breasts?"

"No. She was rather flat-chested—a perfect model of the New Woman. But that doesn't matter with Picasso. Where I think it looked like her was in the face. The nose was wrong, but there were the same large beautiful eyes. A lot of sadness. Just like Polly's. I remember that particularly."

Bedford stood straight, looking about the room. There were cupboards and shelves and a chest of drawers.

"You go through those," Bedford said. "I want to look at the rest of the paintings."

"What do you expect to find?"

He shrugged. "I don't know."

At the rear of the second stack, he came upon a small canvas—perhaps 11 by 14 inches. He took it to the lamp.

"Actually, I have found something," he said.

"So have I," said Sloane.

"Come here a moment, please," he asked.

She closed a drawer she'd been looking through, and came to stand by his side. He showed her the small painting he'd come upon.

"I found a scrap of canvas—a piece of a painting—in the closet of her flat in Little Italy," he said. "I feel quite certain it was done by the same artist who did this."

Sloane took it, transfixed, her mouth slightly open.

"Sloane?"

"It's her. It's Polly."

"I shouldn't think anyone could be as unhappy as she looks."

"It's devastating."

"Do you think it's a self-portrait?"

She held the work at arm's length, hesitated, then shook her head.

"No. She could never have produced anything like this."

"Do you mean this good or this crazy?"

"Both."

The light in the studio suddenly increased. They turned to the door to see a woman standing there, mostly in silhouette against the pale pink sky.

"What are you doing in here?" said Sara Murphy.

There was no point attempting excuses. Bedford stepped forward, exhibiting the small painting to Mrs. Murphy.

"This is the woman we're looking for," he said, solemnly.

Sara was as polite a lady as Bedford had ever encountered and she manifested that gracious comity with her gentle voice. But there was no masking the anger in her large, soft, sad eyes.

"I believe that canvas belongs to Mr. Picasso," she said.

"Yes," said Sloane. "That's the point."

Mrs. Murphy was wearing only a nightgown and light dressing gown, which had fallen open slightly. She must have noticed their break-in from her bedchamber.

"Has this something to do with the unpleasant young man who came by last night?"

"What unpleasant young man?" asked Bedford. The name that leapt to mind was Jozan, but no one would ever call the French aviator unpleasant. Pleasantness was his great talent.

"He didn't give his name. He said he was looking for this Swanscott girl of yours. He said he'd been told in Paris she was down here."

"Was he French?" Bedford asked.

"Not at all. American."

"What did he look like?" Sloane asked.

"Dark hair. Young. Rather brusque, and forceful."

"Oritzky? Norman Oritzky?"

"I told you. He didn't give his name."

"Where is he?" said Sloane.

"I don't know. I sent him away."

"Did he say where he was staying?"

"No!" Sara was very close to losing her temper, which she would have found unforgivable.

"Did he say anything more than that he was looking for Polly?"

"I don't think so."

"Please. Try to remember. It's important."

Sloane was pressing in on Mrs. Murphy like a predator. Sara stepped back, and stood very straight.

"Mr. Green. Miss Smith. We have been delighted to have you as our guests. But I think at this juncture it would be best for all concerned if you were to move on and pursue your interest in that young woman elsewhere. If you don't mind."

"On that point," said Bedford, "I think we all agree."

CHAPTER 15

"**W**HERE shall we go?" Sloane asked.

They had thrown their things together and departed the premises within a quarter hour, without waking anyone. Bedford was driving south now toward the curving coast and Cap d'Antibes.

"I mean to stop at the very first hovel that resembles an inn, or quite possibly any place with a bed. Actually, at this point, I'd settle for a cow barn, or a chicken coop. Or a soft place in a ditch."

"They don't seem to have chicken coops here. They let them wander about."

"Which reminds me. I'm hungry as well."

Sloane stretched, raising her hands to the onrushing breeze before finally folding them in her lap.

"When we reach the sea, we will have to turn left or right," she said.

"I'm not sure I'm up to such a complicated decision. I wonder if we shouldn't just drive straight on into the water and end this absurdity."

"Don't talk that way." She rubbed her eyes, then looked

forward again, blinking. "Turn left, and the road goes round to Antibes and then back to Nice."

"Yes."

"Right goes to Cannes."

He slowed, pulling cautiously around a farmer on a flat, donkey-drawn cart with several milk containers on it. Reaching into a pocket, Sloane took out a slip of paper. "I found this in the shed. It's an address. In the Rue Saissy."

"The Rue Saissy in what town?"

"Doesn't say. This is all there was."

After a few more descending turns they could see the coast road ahead. When they reached it, he without hesitation took the turn toward Cannes.

"You meant to do this from the beginning," Sloane said.

"Curiosity," he said, "and something about cats."

◆◆

THE street they sought was high up on a hill overlooking the harbor and the long point beyond that jutted out into the sea. Rue Saissy was short and narrow, with small, cramped buildings huddled close together. The address Sloane had found was that of a small wine shop with apartments above. Bedford inquired of a friendly old man behind the wine shop counter, describing Polly as accurately as possible.

The fellow shook his head and shrugged, all at the same time.

Bedford showed him the postal card, but this produced the same result. Finally, he showed the man the paper with the address on it, asking if this was the same. The shopkeeper assured him that it was. Bedford started to leave, but Sloane stopped him.

"Wait," she said, and began describing Picasso.

The description proved unnecessary. As soon as she said the name "Picasso," the wine man's face indicated recognition.

"Picasso, *ici?*" Bedford asked.

"*Oui. Il vient plusiers de fois.*"

"*Au dessus?*"

"*Oui.*"

"*Une mademoiselle?*"

He smiled broadly. "*Oui. Très belle. Le deuxième étage.*"

"*Merci bien.*"

◆◆◆

DON'T understand why she's using an alias," Sloane said.

"She doesn't want her parents to find her."

"At the moment, that means us."

They reached the landing and stopped. There were two doors. Bedford looked from one to the other.

"I forgot to ask which," he said.

"Bedford—we'll just knock on both."

She tried the left. There was no response. He rapped sharply twice on the one to the right. Hearing nothing, he tried again.

"*Momentito.*"

Italian?

It was a young woman's voice.

"*Nous sommes amis de Monsieur Picasso,*" Bedford said.

"*Il n'est pas ici.*"

"*Je sais.*"

Bedford said nothing more. They waited, Sloane moving closest to the door in hopes the sight of another female might be reassuring should the occupant of the apartment ever open it.

Finally, she did—only a few inches, but revealing dark hair and a dusky, beautiful face.

"*Comment?*" she asked.

With French, English, and a small bit of Italian, they were able to explain they were looking for a lady friend of Picasso's. The girl replied that she had only met the artist a few weeks before in the market; that he had come to visit twice since to talk to her about posing for him; that she had declined; that she was by no means his girlfriend; and that, though she would enjoy very much talking to two such nice Americans, she was late for her job.

She smiled and closed the door.

"Are you sure that's what she said?" Bedford asked.

"Yes."

The door opened again. The girl said she remembered something that might be helpful. Picasso had complained about some woman across the bay in Napoule who had made his life difficult. He had stopped visiting that woman. He had asked the Italian miss to pose for him in the nude, but as a good Catholic, she had declined. He continued to press her to do so.

"I'll bet," Sloane said.

They thanked her, and returned to their car.

"No Napoule. Not now," said Bedford. "Now hotel. Bed."

"I saw one up the street. Where we turned at the top of the hill. But it looked very small. Do you want to share a room with me again?"

"Sloane, that is a remarkably rhetorical question."

◆◆◆

WITHIN five minutes of registering, they were both sprawled on the tiny room's only but commodious bed— not touching, but secure and comfortable in each other's company. He felt almost married to her.

◆◆◆

THIS time, he was the first to awaken. Sloane lay with her face buried in her pillow, her breathing even and slow. He expected it might be hours before she rose.

Amazingly, his wristwatch showed nearly half past two o'clock in the afternoon. Leaving Sloane to her slumber, he rose, washed and shaved, and dressed in clean clothes. Descending the narrow stairs, he walked down the hill to Cannes town center, turning onto the broad, waterfront boulevard called La Croisette and walking along it until he came to a café.

He ordered a Pernod, and sat sipping it sparingly, observing the passersby. There were many young women out on this fine day, and among them were a few slim blonds. One or two mistook his intent stare for something more amorous and responded with amiable glances. This cheered him, but only a little. He wished Sloane was with him.

Taking note of an artist who'd set up an easel on the promenade across the boulevard, he at long last had an actual useful idea. After paying for his drink, he went over to the man, who was middle-aged and not terribly accomplished, but was going about his work very seriously. Bedford waited for him to finish a small detail of sea before intruding.

The man said he hadn't noticed any young woman of Polly's description painting a picture around Cannes. All he could provide Bedford with was the location of an art supply shop only a few streets away.

The shopkeeper there was uncertain at hearing Polly's description and became perplexed when Bedford showed him the picture postal card. He asked whether Polly might be an inmate of a lunatic asylum. Bedford wasn't sure whether that might now be the truth of it.

More helpfully, the shopkeeper did give Bedford the address of the only other art supply store in the little city—a smaller place over on the west end of town. There was none in Napoule, he said.

The proprietor of the second establishment was a woman, suspicious and unfriendly. She looked at the postal card carefully but was unwilling to say a word in useful response until Bedford identified himself to her satisfaction, which was to say, as an American art dealer interested in buying paintings in France. She said such a young woman had been a customer, though she hadn't been in for more than a week. She had no address for the girl and did not know the name. Bedford's saying "Polly Swanscott" produced no reaction.

"*Cette mademoiselle*," she said. "*Elle marche.*"

"*Quoi?*"

"*Elle marche—se promener—partout. Rien des voitures. Rien des bicyclettes.*"

"*Elle habite près d'ici?*"

The woman shrugged.

❖

WALKING as briskly as he could manage, Bedford followed the seafront Boulevard du Midi west out of Cannes to a point abreast of a high hill that came close to the water. Look-ing across the bay, he realized he still had another three or more miles to go to reach Napoule, and decided to turn back and get the car. By the time he trudged up the hill to their hotel, he'd decided to wait until that evening, or the next day.

Sloane awoke as he sat down on the bed.

"Any luck?"

He lay down beside her. "I think she is staying in a town called Napoule just down the coast. I found a paint shop where she's bought things, but she hasn't been there recently. Picasso appears to have broken with her. At all events, he hasn't gone to that shop."

"Shouldn't we go there?"

"Napoule? Now?"

"Yes."

Bedford closed his eyes. "It will be dark soon. Let's wait until after dinner."

◆◆◆

THEY ate in a small restaurant on the waterfront not far from the café where Bedford had earlier watched the informa-tive artist. He was gone, and the sea was very dark under an overcast sky.

He looked to his meal unhappily. He had ordered a seafood platter made of a variety of creatures and they had arrived with their heads still attached to their edible parts. He averted his eyes from the baleful gaze of a large, cold, dead shrimp, deciding finally to settle for a bit of bread and the good, cool white wine.

"If we don't find her there," he said, "how much longer do you want to keep on with this?"

Sloane, still weary, gave this some serious thought. "How much money have you left?"

"Of mine? Or of Mrs. Swanscott's?"

"Both."

"Probably enough for another week or two of this—and then passage home in steerage."

"I won't let that happen." She had ordered a seafood pasta and was devouring every morsel. "I want to keep looking."

"We could be very close."

"Not close enough. Not yet."

She reached and touched his hand.

"Bear up, Bedford. You've no idea how grateful I am to you for this."

He was staring over her shoulder as she talked, a discourtesy that irritated her a little. She looked around in that direction.

"Don't tell me you saw her," she said, turning back.

"No. I wish that were the case." He sipped more wine. "Someone is following us."

"Who would be doing that?"

"Don't know. A man. He was following me this afternoon—all the way back to the hotel."

She turned her head toward the supposed intruder once again.

"Where is he?"

"He's out there. Further along the promenade."

"Bedford. I think the lack of sleep is getting to you. What do you know about people following people?"

"I learned a little in my time as a police reporter."

A taxi went by, slowly, its driver looking at them speculatively. The cab's headlights revealed nothing of the man he'd seen on the promenade.

"Is he there?" she asked.

"Not that I can tell."

"I'm just now remembering what happened to you and Hemingway when those bully boys jumped you outside Man Ray's place in Montparnasse."

"We survived."

"That time. The hotel room door has a good lock. Come on."

She took money from her purse to cover *l'addition*, then pulled him by the hand to his feet.

CHAPTER 16

BEDFORD awoke to the boisterous sound of male voices, seemingly right there in his hotel room. As he progressed to full consciousness, it was with the numbing fear that they might be associated with the mysterious figure who'd been shadowing him the previous day. He opened his eyes cautiously, looking to where Sloane had lain beside him, finding the place empty. Then he rolled over, discovering that he was safe.

Before him stood a grinning Hemingway and a curious Jozan.

"*Pourquoi dormez-vous en vêtements?*" Jozan asked.

Bedford had indeed slept in his clothes. It was something he and Sloane had agreed upon as a condition of sharing the bed.

Bedford sat up, swinging his legs over the side. "I was tired," he said. "Where's Sloane?"

"Down the hall, taking a bath," Hemingway said. He had a bottle of wine and took a swig from it, then offered it to Bedford.

"No thank you," he said, blinking. "What are you two doing here? How did you find us?"

"Sloane telephoned last night," Hemingway said. "Told us you'd been followed and there was need for a boxer."

With his free hand, he shot out a jab, causing Jozan to duck. As the Frenchman cautiously straightened, Hemingway put his arm around him, and took another drink of wine.

"Good man here, this Jozan," Hemingway said. "Was in the war."

The French pilot was far too young for that, but neither he nor Bedford bothered to disabuse Hemingway of the notion.

Sloane entered, wearing a robe but barefoot, her hair wet and her skin bright. She looked oddly exhilarated.

"All of you out," she said. "I must get dressed."

"Sloaney," said Hemingway, turning to the door. "You ask too much of a man."

◆

THE day was gray with a warm dampness to the air. They elected to go in one car, leaving Jozan's behind at the hotel. Bedford put up the top of the Hispano-Suiza, but not the side curtains, preferring whatever rain might fall to an obstruction of their view. They passed a number of people on the beach as they prowled along the oceanfront, and Bedford drove slowly to make sure they had a good look at all of them.

In this manner, they passed along through Cannes and on past Font de Veyre and the harbor at Mandeliu, pulling up finally at the docks at Napoule. The town was small—little more than a village—though the marine facilities were extensive. Fishermen and yacht crews could be seen along the quay, returning from or preparing for voyages.

"If she's as fond of men as you say," Hemingway said, "there are some prime specimens here."

"She liked artists," said Bedford. "Not sailors."

He'd used the past tense again. Sloane appeared not to notice.

"No artists here," said Jozan. "The scenery not quite so good as Cannes—or Juan les Pins."

"She's here," Bedford pronounced.

"It's no good the four of us riding around together in the

car," said Hemingway, once again the general in command. "Waste of manpower. Jozan and I will start from here on foot, work our way up the hill on the left. You guys take the right side. We'll meet at that café across the road for lunch."

"We'll walk too," said Sloane, opening the car door.

"It's going to be hot—and probably wet," Bedford said.

"We'll go from house to house on foot," Sloane said. "It's the only way to be sure."

◆

IT was a trudge. They knocked only at a few places, wanting to cover as much ground as possible and preferring to conduct their search by carefully examining the buildings they passed, guessing whether they might be places where an artist might wish to reside. They looked most closely at the shabbiest structures—ratty lofts above shops, run-down two- and three-story apartment buildings, dilapidated houses, even sheds, like Picasso's. Polly had made a point of not being easy to find.

They encountered mostly children and old people in the streets, neither of much help. One grocer recognized Polly from the photo, saying she was an occasional customer. But he knew nothing more about her, except that when she left his store she usually headed up the hill.

Further on, they encountered a woman leading a small goat. She looked at the postal card picture of Polly and nodded recognition, briefly erasing Sloane's frown. But her response to all other questions was a shrug. Near the top of the hill was a small house, perched at the edge of the bluff, that seemed an ideal situation for an artist—or would have, had there not been a large family living in it.

"Almost to the top," Bedford said.

"Then what?"

"Go back down again."

At the crest, the road came to an end. There was a field of sorts just beyond and they made their way to it, seating themselves in the high grass.

"Napoule's a bit larger than I thought," Bedford said.

"She's got to be here. Two people recognized her."

"Nothing up here but trees."

The view was to the east—grayish water disappearing into haze behind Île Saint Marguerite and Île Saint Honorat. Sailboats dotted the wide channel called Rade de Cannes. In the wider seas beyond, a small freighter was crossing toward the south.

They could see the entire town. The only vehicular traffic that seemed to be moving was on the shore road.

Sloane was looking elsewhere.

"That house just down there," she said. "Isn't that the one we passed?"

"I think we passed all the houses in France."

"I mean, the one with all the little children." She leaned forward. "You see, it has a small building just behind it—a shed or barn or something."

"I see it."

"There's a bit of laundry on the line. Why would someone leave laundry out when it's going to rain? And do you see what's on that line? A blue dress. And a blue blouse."

"You have remarkable powers of observation."

"You don't understand. Polly was very partial to that shade of blue."

Putting her hand to his shoulder, she got to her feet.

"Come on, Bedford. I think we've found her at last."

He pondered the possibility, as he might those of eternity.

"Bedford!"

"I don't mind doing all this for your friend Polly, but I think it's Zelda who's in the most trouble."

"Zelda can take care of herself—and if she can't, she has her husband, and people who are better friends to her than we've been."

"The latter part is what's been nagging at me. She could have killed herself at that restaurant."

"Bedford, please."

"I feel as guilty about Zelda as you do, for whatever mysterious reason, about Polly."

"Bedford. You have an obligation here. If not to me, certainly to Mrs. Swanscott."

"Very well."

The breeze ruffled her dress and she smoothed it. Then she started down toward the house as resolute as he'd ever seen her.

❖

SLOANE went to the front door of the landlord's house and rapped on it sharply. Children appeared, then a weary-looking French woman who'd been disturbed from some domestic labor. Sloane asked for Polly, and when the woman frowned and said she'd been gone for days, Sloane reached for her purse and began taking out money.

"I'm her sister," she said. "*Sa soeur.* I'm here to pay her rent." She thrust forth some franc notes. "*Pour a' louer.*"

Surprised, the woman stared at the money, then stuffed it into a pocket of her dress. "*Cette assez pour deux mois.*"

"Yes," said Sloane, urging the woman outside. "Two months. Fine. Now we need to go into the house. *C'est bien?*"

The other shrugged. "*Mais, oui.*"

❖

THE door was unlocked. The interior was two rooms—the larger serving as bedroom, sitting room, and artist's studio; the other, a rude kitchen and storeroom. Both were in disarray, and had not recently been cleaned. There was old fruit in a bowl, with insects crawling on it.

The work area was littered with the necessities of the painter's craft, emptied tubes of oil paint lying wherever they'd been cast off, a roll of canvas lying atop a pile of wooden frame pieces, rags, and cups of turpentine with brushes in them left in several places. Whatever she'd been doing, it looked as though she'd thought of little else.

The iron-frame bed was old-fashioned, and fairly large. The sheets were thoroughly rumpled and had not been changed in some time. There was a wineglass on the paint-stained nightstand, and empty bottles on the floor to either side of the bed. Cigarettes, too. On a shelf near the grimy window was a small bottle of Irish whiskey, half full.

"Is that something she'd drink?"

"Not at Smith College."

"Where are her paintings?"

Sloane put her hands on her hips, turning slowly about the room, making a face at a mouse that crept out from under a chair and sat quietly observing them.

"In there?"

They went into the small kitchen, ignoring the clutter and old food. Sloane poked through the cupboards, gingerly. Bedford noticed a trapdoor in the ceiling. Pulling up a rickety wooden chair, he climbed atop it and pushed on one end of the door, without success. Shifting, he put pressure against the other end. It lifted. Pushing it up altogether, he extended to his full height and peered into the space above.

It was small, no more than half his height. But it did for her purposes. Within reach of him was a stack of seven or eight canvases.

"I have found art," he said.

"Let's see it," said Sloane, moving near him.

One by one, he handed down the paintings, warning her that the first one seemed still wet. He had little chance to look at them, except to note that they seemed to be portraits. With the last, he stepped down.

Sloane had set them all about the room.

"They're all the same," she said.

They were all self-portraits. Vincent Van Gogh, in poverty and madness, had turned to self-portraits. He'd died, by his own hand, in a countryside not far over these mountains.

Bedford looked from painting to painting. "They're not all the same," he said. "They're just all of her."

In half the portraits, her eyes were open and wild and witness to some kind of horror. In one the expression was so deranged it seemed a visual representation of a scream.

But the others were more subdued; her eyes downcast or closed. In the last he looked at, she was almost serene. A Madonna. Or at least, a Madonna inspired by Edvard Munch's idea of a Madonna.

"I wish I knew what order they were done in," Sloane said.

"The one with wet paint would have to be the last," Bedford said.

Sloane looked at her fingers, wiping them off with a rag. Then she pointed to the painted scream.

"That tells us something," said Bedford.

A light tapping could be heard. Bedford looked to the window, and saw that it had begun to rain—gently, and sadly.

"Is that all you found up there?" Sloane asked.

"I'll look again."

He climbed back on the chair, running his hand around the edge of the opening, stopping about three-fourths of the way around. He pulled what he found toward him—a much smaller canvas—then completed his search. That was all there was.

Taking the small painting in hand, he returned to the floor and displayed his find for them both to examine.

"It's not by her," he said.

"No, of course not," said Sloane. She leaned close, staring at the signature.

"Picasso," she said.

◆◆◆

THEY wrapped the pictures in some oilcloth they'd found for protection, leaving out only the one by the Spaniard. Then Bedford returned them to the tiny attic.

"Do you think they'll be safe here?" he asked.

"I've paid two months' rent. We ought to get something for that."

Sloane found a rain hat among Polly's belongings, and pulled it low over her head.

"Won't she need that?" Bedford asked.

Sloane was tight-lipped. "We don't know where she is. If we find her, I'll gladly return it. Or better, buy her something new."

They stopped at the landlord's on the way out. They'd wrapped the Picasso in oilcloth as well.

"*Ce peinture est pour nous,*" said Sloane, to the French

woman. "*Nous vennons ici pour ça. Comprennez? Dites ma soeur que nous l'avons, s'il vous plaît. C'est bien.*"

The woman shrugged. Having paid two months' rent, they could take all the paintings if they wished.

❧

HEMINGWAY and Jozan were in the dockside restaurant as promised. They'd not begun lunch, though the hour was late, but Hemingway had started on some oysters—served with two cold bottles of white wine.

He poured all around. "Any luck, comrades?"

Sloane unwrapped the small painting, and set it down upright on the table. Her grin was no more than bared teeth. "We've got him."

"Who?" said Hemingway, squinting at the picture.

Sloane's finger shot to the bottom right-hand corner. "Picasso!"

"You bought one of his paintings?" Hemingway looked more closely. "I thought they were expensive. And what is it of?"

"This is a woman—a painting of a woman," said Sloane, turning it slightly to the side so Jozan could see it fully.

The aviator shook his head. "*Je ne le comprends pas.*"

"It's Polly Swanscott," Sloane said. "See? The yellow hair."

"You know, I understand Matisse," Hemingway said. "I got Cezanne figured out—especially those bather pictures. Modigliani, and those women of his—hell, you can see he knows women. But this?"

"*C'est très moderne,*" said Jozan.

Sloane sat down, a frown coming Bedford's way as he tried to help with her chair. He sat down.

"We found her place," said Bedford. "It's a sort of shack behind a house almost at the top of the hill."

Hemingway looked around the room, turning his head sharply. Bedford reminded himself that the writer had a problem with his left eye.

"She's not here—not with us," Bedford said. "We don't

know where she is. The landlady said she left several days ago. Maybe more than a week. We found some paintings she'd done and the oil was still wet on one of them. I estimate it was no more than four or five days old."

"And Picasso was here." Sloane said, her words like a verdict.

"Not in the last four or five days," Hemingway said. "He's been at Villa America. Either down at the beach or up at the house. Freeloading and painting. You were there."

"Some days he was painting when we were at the beach," Sloane said. "Who knows where he went."

"He has no car," Hemingway said.

"Perhaps Polly does."

Bedford frowned. They'd failed to ask the landlady that.

After they ordered food, and more drink, Sloane left the table to repair her rained-upon appearance in the ladies' room. Hemingway watched her walk away appreciatively, then moved his chair a bit closer to Bedford's.

"There's something else about Picasso," he said. "Some woman trouble up there at Villa America. Serious stuff. I should have seen it. Right in front of us, all the goddamn time."

"What do you mean? Polly wasn't at Villa America."

"I said 'serious stuff.' Sara Murphy."

Jozan was paying scant attention, looking off through the open front of the restaurant toward the sea. A dumpy fishing boat was approaching the quay.

"Sara Murphy and Picasso—having an affair?" Bedford said, keeping his voice low as well.

"No, no. The sonofabitch ain't that lucky. He's just in love with her—maybe even more than the rest of us are. Even you—right, Green?"

During the night, Sloane had come against him, and stayed there, with her head on his shoulder and her arm across his chest. Bedford had carried the memory of that around with him all day, along with uncomfortable thoughts of his feelings for Claire and Tatty.

"She's a remarkable woman, and a damned attractive one—but my affections are directed elsewhere."

"Suit yourself, but with our pal Pablo, she's *un idée fixe*. Obsession. She caught him doing a painting with her in it—*très au naturel*. Hot stuff. In her quiet, well-bred goddamn way, she hit the roof. Gave him the skidoo by telling him how much she loved her husband. Gerald, you know, is not exactly Pablo's kind of guy. He struck back by painting her out of the picture. It makes no sense now, but, hell . . ."

"I saw the picture. I thought it was Polly."

Hemingway laughed. "I once asked a guy what French women had that other women didn't. He said they had exactly what other women had—only a lot more of it." More laughter. "Sara Murphy has a hell of a lot more of it. This Polly may be some pumpkins, but nobody's going to write a great book about her. Fitzgerald's already latched onto Sara. Picasso's wiping her out of his painting—that's one big goddamn grand gesture."

Jozan had wandered out onto the quay, and was talking to sailors there. The rain had lightened.

"He gave Polly this painting," Bedford said.

"It may just mean he didn't like it. I sure don't, though they say he's a genius."

Sloane returned, her fury cooled and hardened.

"You're just sitting here, eating and drinking," she said. "A lovely lunch by the sea."

"We have to eat—if we're going to keep at this," Bedford said. "I suggest you do the same."

"I'm not hungry," Sloane said. She took a glass of wine.

"We have two choices," said Hemingway. "One, we keep on looking for her."

"Or two, we go back to Juan les Pins and confront Señor Picasso with the evidence of his criminality," Sloane said.

She took a large sip of wine, then sat staring straight forward, her hands on the table. She looked almost as though she were preparing to vault over it.

"We've had confrontations with Señor Picasso, without accomplishing much," said Bedford.

"He can tell us where she is," Sloane said.

It was wishful thinking.

"I don't think so," Bedford said.

"But we have to do something."

"Lunch," said Hemingway. "It will help us think."

He poured more wine. Sloane fidgeted, then asked Bedford for the keys to the trunk of the Hispano-Suiza.

"I'm going to lock up the Picasso," she said. "It belongs to her. I don't want it stolen."

Bedford handed her the keys, half afraid the next sound they'd hear would be of her driving away—destination unknown.

But she returned, standing before them in a gathering fret.

"Lunch," said Hemingway, eating more oysters.

Her eyes ignored him, flitting elsewhere about the room. "Where's Jozan?"

Bedford looked out onto the quay. The aviator was no longer in view.

THEY found the lieutenant out by the end of a pier, speaking with a man in a sort of uniform. Bedford assumed him to be with the French Coast Guard, which Jozan confirmed.

"She has gone on a voyage," he said.

"Voyage?" Sloane asked, incredulous. "Where?"

"To Toulon. With some sailors. A few days ago."

"What sort of sailors?" Bedford asked. "French navy?"

"*Pas militaire,*" said Jozan. "Roughnecks."

"What kind of boat?"

"Some kind of small coastal steamer. The *Ariadne.* It goes from Nice to Toulon and Marseilles but stops here a lot. He said he knows it because it is very rusty and its crew is drunk a lot. The girl has been on the waterfront with them many times—also drunk—but this time she went off with them."

"That's all he knows?" asked Sloane.

"*Malheureusement, c'est vrai.*"

Sloane started walking back toward the restaurant—and the car.

"That's a long drive," said Hemingway. "Toulon."

It began to rain in earnest.

CHAPTER 17

THEY took an inland route through the mountains to save time, bypassing Saint Tropez and Cap Benat. But it was slow going in the recurring downpours. Twice Bedford had to stop and wait for the rain to relent, just to be able to see the road.

It was well into the night when they finally descended into Toulon, curving this way and that through the narrow, twisting streets until they came to the harbor and pulled up by a large pier.

"What do we do now?" Hemingway said. "Go boat by boat until we find this *Ariadne*?"

"Let us find a place to stay tonight and then look in the·morning," Jozan suggested.

"You do that if you like," said Sloane. "I'm going to look now."

"Mademoiselle . . ."

"If the vessel's here," Bedford said, "I doubt they'd be aboard her. I think they'd be in the bars."

"Toulon is full of bars—and this hour, they'll all be full of trouble," said Jozan.

"The worst'll be on the waterfront," Hemingway said. He appeared to be unhappy, but doubtless they all did.

"Still, that's likely where they'd be," Bedford said. "The sailors, anyway. There's no telling where Polly might have gone. She could be back at her place by now."

"She's been gone for days, Bedford." Sloane's voice was leaden.

"All right," said Jozan. "*Allons.*"

"You stay here, Sloane," Bedford said. "If those bars mean trouble, a woman'll mean ten times more." He paused. "Any woman."

She didn't argue.

"Will you be all right?" he asked.

"I still have Man Ray's gun." Her eyes were on the rain.

◆◆◆

HAD they thought to change into rougher clothing, they might have had an easier time of it. As it was, entering the first place they came upon, they attracted much the same kind of fiercely speculative attention they might have encountered strolling into the bears' quarters at the Paris zoo.

The smoky room was as crowded with noise as it was with sweaty half-drunk and thoroughly drunk seamen. A prostitute or two could be glimpsed along the bar—a peal of feminine laughter piercing the din of grunting, bellowing, animal-like male discourse.

One henna-haired creature withdrew from a circle of muscular louts and snaked her way toward them. Jozan was by any measure the handsomest of the three of them and Hemingway easily the most fun. But she targeted Bedford— doubtless because she assumed he had the most money.

"You look like money," Fitzgerald had said to him at the Murphys'.

"Either you've had too much to drink or I should become a con man," Bedford had said. "Because I'm the poorest person here."

"That's beside the point," Fitzgerald had said.

"*Bon soir, mademoiselle,*" Bedford said to the woman,

who was desperately in need of a bath. "*Nous cherchons les hommes du bateau* Ariadne. *Est-ce-que ils sont ici?*"

Her face went blank, then she scowled.

"*Ne désirez pas moi?*"

"*Je regrette, mademoiselle. Un autre soir, peut-être.*"

Her scowl deepened, and she turned away. A smile at Jozan produced only the same line of questioning. Finally, she left them, though her odor lingered.

After buying a round of drinks, they asked after the *Ariadne* crew with the bartender, receiving only shrugs. Bedford searched among the crowd for someone—anyone—who might be more responsive, but they all seemed equally unpromising. He debated whether to show the postal card photo of Polly around, deciding against it. These men would likely take him for some sort of pimp, and Polly for a product he was offering.

Jozan, as befitted the youngest and most military of them, bravely went up to a table where four large men were sober enough at least to be playing cards. Smiling politely, he made his inquiry, saying that he and his friends were looking for the crew of the *Ariadne*.

One of the men began making what Bedford gathered were highly idiomatic derisive comments. Another pushed back his chair and rose, indicating with a few extremely communicative gestures that Jozan and company had only a few seconds to live.

They hastily withdrew toward the door—and then, at Hemingway's sage urging, back out onto the street.

"He took me for a man who does not enjoy women," said Jozan. "How can this be?"

THE second place they visited was worst than the first, and the next worse than that. The fourth establishment they entered, very dark and lit by candles, was blissfully quiet and free of patrons, but a gathering of several malevolent-looking men and an unfriendly woman around a table at the rear

made them feel decidedly unwelcome. Hemingway departed
without even trying to order a drink.

They had left the Hispano-Suiza parked in a circle of light
beneath a street lamp at the near end of the pier. Looking
down that way, Bedford discovered unhappily that the space
was now empty.

"Maybe she moved it to a safer place," Hemingway suggested.

"That was the safest place."

"Maybe the waterfront got to her and she drove back up
into town."

"She wouldn't do that."

Bedford realized the folly of that statement. Sloane might
do anything, whatever the situation.

"Let's try one more of these dives," said Hemingway.

"Aren't you a little apprehensive about these places?"
Bedford asked.

The writer grinned. "Hell, this is the most fun I've had
since the war."

There were no more bars or cafés facing the harbor, but
one of the side streets leading down to it looked promising,
boisterous laughter beckoning further along the narrow way.
The rain had stopped and Bedford felt his spirits improving,
if only a little.

They'd try one more bar, then head for the first decent
hotel, where he was sure they'd find Sloane. With the
Hispano-Suiza as a landmark, the search should be easy.

Hemingway led the way, ascending the dark street in a
rapid trudge, heading for the sounds of bacchanal as though
he knew their source. Jozan, very sleepy now, followed along
amiably, his mind obviously on his next mattress. Bedford
was the rear guard, and a poor one, for he kept his attention
to the fore, and thus failed to notice the small group of rep-
resentatives of the cult of thugee who fell on them just after
they had passed a small alley.

He had no idea of their exact number but there were several of them—very deliberate in what they were about and
very good at it, attacking like wild animals interested only in
making quick work of their kill. Hemingway held up the best

of the three of them, bellowing loudly and punching with fists and elbows. Jozan, a much smaller man, tried valiantly but was having a hard time of it. Bedford was getting blows on the back. He tried to turn to face his assailant, but a whack on the muscle between his shoulder and neck numbed his arm and sent him sprawling. Looking up from the ground, he saw the roofline of the building opposite and an odd shaft of moonlight illuminating a patch of thick cloud. Rolling over, he noticed that Jozan was down as well. Hemingway was somehow still on his feet, though grappling with three men.

With one great lunge, Bedford got halfway to standing, then received a kick to the back of his knee, and then two stabs of pain—to his head and to his side. Then he lost consciousness.

When he came to, it had begun to rain again. Oddly, he welcomed the wetness against his face. Hearing voices, he lifted his head. There were several men standing there, holding electric lamps and talking volubly. Happily, they were in uniform. *Les gendarmes.*

"*Monsieur* . . ." Bedford began.

Two of them came over. Without speaking, they took hold of Bedford's arms and lifted him to his feet. He could barely stand but struggled to do so.

"*Je vous remercie.*"

Still holding his arms, the policemen pulled them around his back. The next he knew, there was a metallic click and handcuffs were locked around his wrists.

"You bastards!" shouted Hemingway, but strangely, he said nothing more.

CHAPTER 18

IT puzzled Bedford that there could be so many cockroaches crawling over the walls of their cell when there was demonstrably so little for them to eat. The three of them had been in the lockup for the remainder of the night and well into the morning, and there'd not been the slightest suggestion that they might be fed.

His head hurt from pains within and without and his ears recurringly filled with noise of their own making. His side burned when he moved and, pulling up his shirt and probing the area just above his waist, his hand came away with a bit of blood on it. There was blood on his shirt as well.

Their request to call the Murphys, Jozan's commanding officer, or a lawyer went ignored, as did their protests over their treatment. Hemingway's complaint that he and Bedford had fought the Hun in the Great War made small impression. The least of the jailors had the small ribbon of the Medale Militaire on his uniform. These jobs seemed to be sinecures for veterans.

A half dozen or so drunks had been lying in heaps upon the floor when they'd been brought in. With the coming of morning, they'd been released, though their aroma remained behind.

"The Germans treated their prisoners of goddamn war better than this," Hemingway said, rubbing his chin.

"*Je ne comprends pas,*" Jozan said. "*Je suis un officier. Cela, c'est incroyable.*"

"I'm getting worried about Sloane," Bedford said.

"Don't worry, amigo," said Hemingway. "I'll bet she just got smart and moved her lovely self the hell out of there," Hemingway said.

"That thought will be in my prayers when they take us to the guillotine."

"Why would they do that?" Hemingway asked.

"We've not been kept here all this time because they think we're tourists who have lost our way," Bedford said.

Jozan's good humor was entirely spent.

"If you were truly worried about your friend Sloane you wouldn't have brought her to this place," he said.

"What're you talking about?" Hemingway said. "She brought us."

Footsteps were sounding along the corridor, two sets of them, approaching with some swiftness. In a moment, a pair of uniformed gendarmes were standing outside the bars. They studied Bedford with unpleasant directness, glanced at the other two, then unlocked the door, swinging it open with a loud clang.

"*Venez,*" one of them said.

❖

THEY were taken to the office of a portly but well-dressed senior police official who introduced himself politely as Inspector Roche. With his small round spectacles, large, thick moustache, and meerschaum pipe, he seemed more professor than cop. But there was that telltale weariness about the eyes, and the calm and repose that come from having witnessed too much to any longer be surprised by the extremes of human conduct. He was courteous, gesturing them to wooden chairs against the wall, but not friendly. He looked through papers while they waited—the two gendarmes now standing as though sentries.

Finally, Roche turned to Jozan. "*Votre commandant n'est pas heureux.*"

"*Je le regrette,*" Jozan replied. He switched to English. "None of this is our fault."

The inspector switched, too, without hesitation.

"I have here your explanation for being in such a very bad place at such an hour," Roche said, in English as flawless as Jozan's. "I have heard many ridiculous tales but this one is of a high order of absurdity."

They made no response.

The inspector opened a desk drawer, removing gingerly a long clasp knife, which he held up for all to see. Then he returned his attention to Bedford.

"This was found in your coat pocket, Monsieur," he said. "Is it yours?"

Dumbfounded, Bedford could only shake his head.

"Can you explain how it came to be in your pocket?"

Bedford looked down at his blazer. There was a tear at the side of the right-hand pocket he hadn't noticed in the cell. He shrugged.

"The curious thing is that the blade was partially opened," said the inspector. "Now what kind of cretin carries a knife around like that?"

No one answered.

"Are you that kind of cretin, monsieur?"

"I don't think so."

Roche leaned forward, elbows on his desk, pointing at Jozan with the blade, which he had fully opened. "You vouch for this man, Lieutenant?"

"Yes. *Certainment.* He is *Capitaine* Green. He flew with our air arm in the war."

"Your commandant says you have an excellent record, Jozan," Roche said. "No history of brawling."

"This brawl here last night was most involuntary, Monsieur Roche."

The inspector turned now to Hemingway. "I think that you, monsieur, are no stranger to brawling."

"I also fought in the war," the writer said. "*Avec les Italiens.*"

Roche paused to relight his pipe, puffing billows of smoke. "We were about to charge you all with murder."

"Murder?" said Hemingway. "We must have been outnumbered ten to one. I held my own for as long as I could, but the bastards attacked us from behind."

Jozan muttered something. Bedford suspected he was losing his fondness for Americans—except for a certain married lady from Alabama.

"Was someone killed?" Bedford asked.

"*Mais, oui.*" Roche pulled forth a piece of notepaper. "His name was Robert Milhaud. A sailor, on a vessel called *Ariadne*. I believe you were asking after this *bateau*, and its crew."

"Without success," Bedford said. "No one would tell us anything."

"This Milhaud was found in an alley—not far from where you were found," Roche said. "He'd been stabbed and had his throat cut. Quite possibly by this weapon."

"We didn't go into any alley," Hemingway said.

"Did your men find those people who attacked us?" Bedford asked.

Roche put his pipe to his mouth again, reaching for another match. "No. They were gone. Only you three and the unfortunate Monsieur Milhaud."

"If we'd cut him up, we'd be covered with blood," said Hemingway. "Look at us."

Roche did. "You are not so tidy. And *Capitaine* Green has blood on his shirt and jacket."

He studied Bedford again, taking his time.

"But I do not think that is his own doing."

Their sudden feeling of relief and impending liberation was palpable—and audible.

"Are we free to go?" Jozan asked.

The inspector shook his head, a bit sadly. "No. Not just yet. The case of sailor Milhaud is not closed. And there is something else."

He reached into the desk drawer again, removing a ribbon with a piece of jewelry hanging on it—a gold medal.

"Have any of you seen this before?"

Hemingway reached to take it, examining the medal with a squint, then passed it on to Jozan. Bedford had no need of it.

"Yes," he said. "I've seen it."

"You have not looked at it, monsieur," said the inspector.

"I don't need to." Bedford reached into his coat pocket and took out the postal card of Polly. There was a ribbon around her neck. The medal on it was a gleam at the base of her throat.

"It's this." He handed the card to Roche.

The inspector studied it with some concentration.

"*Bien,*" he said. "There it is."

"Where did you find it?" Bedford said.

"It was in the pocket of this Milhaud."

"She sailed down here with him on the *Ariadne,*" said Jozan. "That's what they told us on the dock at Napoule."

"Where is she?" Bedford asked. "Polly Swanscott. Where is she?"

"Is that her name? Polly Swanscott?"

"Yes."

The inspector drummed his fingers on his desk top briefly, then nodded. "*D'accord.*"

A dart of a look at one of the gendarmes sent the subordinate to a different door than that through which they had entered.

A moment later, Sloane came into the room.

Bedford rose, feeling a bit wobbly, and started to go to her. Her eyes went to his shirt, which had blood on it, then to his face.

"My God, Bedford," she said. "You look half dead."

"I'm fine. But are you . . . ?"

He wanted to throw his arms around her, but she edged away from him, her somber eyes aimed at the inspector.

"*Voulez-vous s'asseoir, mademoiselle?*"

"No thank you. I'll stand."

"This lady came in earlier and told a similar story to

yours," Roche said to Bedford. "I thought it unbelievable at first. But now, as other things come to light, I think there is a certain *vérité*." He paused, his attention returning to Sloane. "This woman you have been seeking, her name is Polly Swanscott?"

"Yes."

He held up the ribboned medal.

"And is this hers?"

"Yes," said Sloane. "She always wore it. The medal is for winning an art competition in college. She said it was the first time in her life she ever felt any pride in herself."

Roche frowned, then rose and pushed back his chair.

"If you would come with me, please," he said. "All of you."

Sloane's hand came into Bedford's. Her fingers closed around his tightly.

◆

BEDFORD had bribed the flics in Paris twenty dollars in francs for a view of their corpse collection. He would have paid ten times that amount to avoid this descent into the official catacombs of Toulon. Hemingway and Jozan, following behind, were as somber and silent as he. Sloane had let go his hand and moved ahead of him, following along behind the inspector as erect and graceful as always. Bedford was glad he did not have to look her in the eye—just yet.

At the bottom of the steps was a set of iron-studded wooden doors, adding to the feel of the Dark Ages in this place. Roche pushed one of them open with little effort, then led them through a long, gloomy tunnel. At the other end, past another set of doors, were stairs leading upwards, eventually taking them into the back chambers of some sort of hospital.

"*Par ici*," said Roche, taking a turn to the right.

When they at last reached their destination, the inspector went directly to the rear of the room, where a shrouded human figure lay on a long table.

He coughed, glanced at each one of them, then slowly

pulled back the gray-green covering, halting when he had revealed no more than the top of the woman's head, brow, and eyes.

Though he had never met her, Bedford could recognize Polly from the other side of the room. The tangled hair appeared less golden than he would have expected from the two photos he had seen, and she was surprisingly small. But the eyes were unmistakable. She had died with them open—as wide and wild as on the postal card—as though she had seen through the awesome maw of eternity, and the horror of it had frozen her stare.

Bedford nodded to Roche and started to turn away.

"*Non*," said Sloane.

"*Mademoiselle?*"

"*Tout sa visage, s'il vout plaît*," Sloane said. "I want to see it all."

Roche gave a quiet sigh, then slowly pulled the covering down to the girl's chin, revealing a mouth opened in mid-scream. It was uncanny how much her contorted expression resembled that of the photo. If there had been tears, the sameness would have been exact.

But there had been tears—dried now—but detectable in runnels across the dirt upon her cheeks.

"Where did you find her?" Bedford asked.

"On the docks," said the inspector. "Where we often find them, when not in the sea."

Sloane had not moved an inch.

"*De plus*," she said.

"*Mais, mademoiselle. Vous avez vu . . .*"

"*De plus!*"

Reluctantly, Roche tugged the covering until it revealed the poor woman's shoulders, whereupon Sloane fainted. Bedford was barely able to catch her in time.

CHAPTER 19

"**T**HAT goddamn sailor is lucky some sonofabitch murdered him," Hemingway said. "Because I'd happily kill the bastard myself—only I'd take ten times as long."

They were at a café near the police station—the first they could find. All four of them had ordered brandy, not to numb their senses, but to revive them. Bedford was drained of all feeling—emotional and sensory. Except to lift his glass, he had no wish to move. The others were in as bad a way. Sloane appeared as dead to the world as the unfortunate young woman they'd come to find.

"He all but cut off her head!" Hemingway continued. "He must have used a Bowie knife. Ever see the like of that? All my time in the war, all those poor bastards blown to *merde*. Never anything . . ."

"The inspector said it was a razor," said Bedford, quietly. "The razor they found in Milhaud's pocket."

"We have two killers here," said Jozan.

"I didn't say that," said Bedford.

Hemingway fell silent. An old man came along the cobbled street, trundling a wheelbarrow full of wood, with a decrepit dog following along behind. Bedford's art gallery might as well have been on another planet, it seemed so remote.

"Do you think Inspector Roche is going to bother with us anymore?" Jozan asked. "I must get back to my aerodrome."

"I think he may let you go, and probably soon," Bedford said.

Unshaven, untidy, and unslept, Jozan looked infinitely less the poster picture of a dashing French aviator than he had upon their initial meeting. Bedford supposed that at this point they all could have taken up residence in the waterfront quarter without anyone thinking them out of place, including Sloane, whose customary perfect grooming was now marred by runs in her stockings and smudges on her face.

"But why keep us at all?" said the Frenchman. "It's obvious we had nothing to do with the sailor's death. We were attacked as well."

"Roche wants to wait until he gets a cable back from Polly's parents, verifying that Sloane was Polly's friend and that I was here on their behalf," Bedford said. "It's not unreasonable. And he probably has some other questions."

"Such as?" Hemingway said, interested.

Bedford wondered if the writer was planning some short story or novel out of this. It didn't seem quite his métier, the sordid death of an American blueblood.

"Sailors turning up with their throats cut in that district are doubtless a regular occurrence," Bedford said. "But how many are found with money or an expensive gold medal still in their pockets? That fellow had both."

"If that gang who came after us killed him, maybe we scared them off before they could rob him," Hemingway suggested.

"I would not describe our encounter with that bunch as 'scaring them off,'" said Jozan.

"And if it was them," Bedford continued, "why didn't they use knives or a razor on us? We certainly got the worst of that scrap. There wasn't much we could have done if they wanted to kill us."

"The police came along pretty quick," Hemingway said. "They would have been enough to scare off those thugs."

"Not quick enough to catch any of them," observed Jozan. "Every one of them disappeared—rats into the sewer."

"Maybe those guys killed both Polly Swanscott and the sailor," Hemingway said, "for reasons we shall never know—except that this is how life often ends on the docks of Toulon."

Sloane hit the table hard with both fists, causing the glasses to rattle and brandy to slosh and spill.

"Stop it! All of you!"

"Sorry," said Bedford.

"It doesn't matter who wielded the blade," she said. "The sailor, those thugs, some other miscreants. Ernest is right. That is what the beasts do in this jungle. But who and what drove her to this terrible place?"

Her eyes flashed at Bedford.

"You," she said. "You and me. We are the murderers. Everyone of us who dismissed her paintings or told her she was no good. May Ray, Picasso. Who knows how many other bastards? Cruel people who told her she could not and should not paint. Not to bother. Go back home and become somebody's wife."

"Sloane," said Bedford. "I think you could do with some sleep."

"I mean it—every word. Her mother is going to ask you who is guilty of this and I want you to be honest and tell her who it was—us. Her, too."

Hemingway began pouring more brandy around.

"The world is full of disappointed and frustrated artists," he said. "They don't all end up slashed and stabbed on the Toulon docks. I feel damn sorry about the kid, but she . . ."

"I'm not concerned with anyone else. She was my friend. She asked for my help."

"Had she told us where to find her . . ." Bedford began.

Sloane put her hands over her eyes.

"But she did not," said Jozan. "And do you know why? Whoever wielded the weapon, this was suicide. I see what Sloane means. When she sent those postal cards, she wasn't telling you where to find her. She was telling you what she was going to do. And now she has done it."

"Come to think of it," said Hemingway, after taking a

long swallow, "there was a short story like that, by that English guy, Bill Maugham."

"Somerset Maugham?" Bedford asked.

"Yeah. William Somerset Maugham. I met him once.
Down here somewhere. Called him Bill. Anyway, the story
was about a rich kid who wanted to become a pianist—instead of just being a rich kid. His family gave him a year to
study, and if at the end of that time he didn't pass muster as
someone of talent, then he'd have to give up. And that's how
it went. They had a respected musician listen to him play. He
said, no dice, so the kid goes and blows his brains out. His
family couldn't understand why someone would kill himself
just because he couldn't play the piano."

"Life isn't always like books!" said Sloane. "Polly wanted
to live. She was in a terrible state, but she came here to es-
cape, to paint—not to kill herself."

And once again—for only the second time in their years
of friendship—Sloane began to weep. Bedford moved his
chair and put his arm around her. He feared she'd pull away,
but she turned and wept against his shoulder.

Jozan and Hemingway were looking in a different direction—down the street. A uniformed gendarme was approaching.

"Inspector Roche says you may go," he said.

Hemingway, beaming, pushed back his chair.

"You may go back to Cannes," said the policeman. "But
no farther."

◆◆◆

THEY took an overland route again, driving hard straight
through the mountains to Cannes. It was deep into the
night when they came over the crest of the last hill and began
the descent into the town. Still, lights were sparkling and
glowing throughout, giving the place a festive air in contra-
vention to their stricken mood.

Pulling the Hispano-Suiza up behind Jozan's car, which
appeared to have been unmolested during their absence, Bedford noted a change in Sloane's demeanor, a return to the so-

cial grace that was her most natural state. He hoped it might be a sign that she was beginning to put the tragedy of Polly Swanscott behind her—or at the least, recognizing that this was something she now would have to do.

"A strange time, we've had," said Hemingway, lingering by the car door. "Strange." He put his hand on Sloane's shoulder. "I'm really sorry the way things worked out for you, Sloaney."

"Thank you. I appreciate your help, both of you. It was wonderfully kind, and I won't forget it."

"Well, you're aces with me, kid. You went through some tough stuff there. Took it like a man. You've got *cojones*, Sloane. You are very brave."

Bedford abruptly restarted the Hispano-Suiza's engine.

"Should I tell them anything?" Hemingway said. "Picasso? Scott? The Murphys?"

"No," said Sloane. "Leave the matter be."

Bedford waved, then put the car in gear and started up the street, the engine resonating loudly against the night-quiet walls.

"A good night's sleep," Bedford said. "Then tomorrow we can take the afternoon train back to Paris. In a day or two, we can be on a boat for New York."

"Stop the car, please."

He did so. "Yes?"

"I want to go back to Polly's place."

He sighed. "What will that accomplish?"

"I want to get her paintings. They're all she's left behind, really—all she's had to show for her time here. All that's left of her life. I don't want to leave them to the mercies of the gendarmes. Or her landlord."

"Shouldn't they go to her parents?"

"Yes, they should. But do you honestly think they'll want them?"

❖

BEDFORD pulled the car to a stop just down from the top of the hill. There were no lights on in the house.

"Why don't you turn the car around and wait?" Sloane said. "I'll go get the canvases and be right out."

"You want to go in there alone?"

She opened the door. "I'm not afraid of a few rats and mice. There'll be less disturbance this way. And if there is trouble with these people, we'll be able to get away fast. But I mean to have those paintings."

"All right. Don't tarry."

There were stars out, but the moon was below the horizon. Bedford waited until Sloane had reached the path beside the house, then killed the headlights. A moment later, he eased the car into gear and drove slowly to the top of the hill and the end of the road, turning around with some difficulty. Headed downhill once more, he cut the engine and coasted to a halt just opposite the house, slipping the shift back into gear and pulling on the hand brake.

There was no sound or light coming from the main house, but down the narrow lane beside it he saw a yellow glow from a window of Polly's cottage.

All at once he heard loud voices, and then the bark of the damnable dog. Vaulting over the car door in Hemingway fashion, he sprinted past the house and the yapping animal, tripping once over some wood but keeping his balance. Drawing up at the cottage door, he hesitated, listening. The voices were more subdued now—Sloane's and a man's. Bedford turned the knob and stepped in, recalling his encounter in the Paris hotel room with Man Ray, Sloane, and Ray's pistol.

She was standing in the center of the main room. The little pistol was in her hand again, but held barrel down, not threatening anyone.

In the kitchen doorway was a dark-haired man—young, but looking frazzled and beaten and wary. He had darkish circles under his eyes and, like Bedford, needed a shave. Otherwise, though simply dressed, he appeared perfectly respectable, though doubtless Mrs. Swanscott would not have thought him so.

"This is Norman Oritzky," Sloane said.

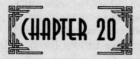

CHAPTER 20

YOU'RE sure it's him?" Bedford asked, shutting the door behind him.

The young man's eyes flitted back and forth between them, reminding Bedford of a wild animal caught in a bright light.

"It's him," said Sloane. "I remember him from the Village. I saw him on Bleecker Street once. Outside Polly's."

"What are you doing here?" Bedford asked.

The young man was not intimidated.

"I'm looking for Polly. I've been looking all over France." He turned to Sloane. "The woman who owns this place said you were Polly's sister?"

"We were here before," said Sloane. "We've come back for some of her things."

"Her things?"

"Her paintings," Sloane said.

"What paintings?" He took a step toward Sloane. "Where is she? Where's Polly?"

Bedford moved closer, drawing the man's attention away from Sloane. "She's in Toulon."

"Where's that?" The words, spoken urgently, came out

almost as one. Oritzky had a decided accent, but Bedford couldn't place it. It was not quite New York, more likely some other city.

The man's clothes were a mixture of American and French—corduroy trousers, espadrilles, a sailor's open-necked jersey. He had a very masculine, heavy-featured face, with large nose and ears and a pointed chin. His image would have sold no shirts for Brooks Brothers. If Mrs. Swanscott had met him, she would not have approved.

"It's a seaport two hundred kilometers or so down the coast," Bedford said. "Sailor town."

"For God's sake," Sloane said. "Tell him."

She turned aside, looking elsewhere in the room.

"Polly's dead," Bedford said. "She was murdered."

The young man stood dumbly, waiting for more words—either rejecting or not comprehending those Bedford had spoken.

"You seem very calm," Bedford said.

"Calm," Oritzky said, flatly.

"I'm afraid it's true," Sloane said. "We've just come from there. It's horrible."

Oritzky began to tremble, starting with his hands. He was slim but muscular, and had initially struck Bedford as very self-possessed. Now all that was rapidly disintegrating.

"Why don't you sit down?" Bedford asked.

A rickety chair was near. The young man lowered himself into it wearily, then put his face into his hands.

"Would you like something to drink?" Sloane asked. "There was some wine."

Oritzky made no reply. After an impatient moment, she went into the kitchen anyway.

"What happened to her?" said Oritzky, hoarsely, from behind his hands.

"A waterfront murder," Bedford said. "What you might expect. She got caught in the company of the wrong kind of man."

"Did they get him?"

Bedford considered his reply carefully before making it.

"Somebody did. He's dead, too. Also murdered. Lovely place, Toulon."

Sloane returned with a glass and a dusty bottle of *vin rouge ordinaire*. She poured the glass half full. After a long moment, Oritzky finally reached to take it.

"I've been searching for her," he said, after taking a substantial swallow. "All over France. Cost me all the money I had to get over here."

"But she left you," Sloane said. "Why make things worse?"

"That's what her mother said. But it isn't true. She left New York. We weren't quits."

"Did you inquire after her at the Murphys?" Bedford asked. "Was that you?"

"Those rich people at Juan les Pins? Yeah, I talked to them. They weren't much help. Sent me away. Just like her parents."

"How did you find them—the Murphys? How did you find this place?"

"I got to Paris, and just started asking. Artists, mostly."

"Are you an artist?"

"Bedford," scolded Sloane. "Stop interrogating him. Think what he's going through."

Oritzky drank more wine, then set down the glass, his head going into his hands again. He rubbed his eyes. "I'm an artist. I do constructions."

"Constructions? Buildings?"

The head came up, eyes full of resentment and malice. "Sculptures. Wood and metal. Other stuff."

Bedford had no notion of what that might be. Oritzky took his blank expression for disapproval, and responded accordingly.

"Just who the hell are you?" he said.

"A friend."

"Of Polly's? Or her goddamned parents?"

His dark look was now being matched by Sloane's. Bedford was getting impatient with this.

"I'm a friend of Sloane's." He nodded toward her.

The young man got to his feet. "Where's Polly? Where do they have her? In Toulon?"

Bedford nodded. "In a morgue. The police are contacting her family."

Oritzky turned back and forth, uncertainly. He looked at his wristwatch.

"I'm going down there. I came here to find her, and I'm going to do that. No matter what."

He went to a corner and picked up a rucksack Bedford hadn't noticed before.

"Do you want us to drive you to the railroad station?" Sloane asked.

Oritzky shook his head, glanced around the room, then was out the door, leaving it ajar. They heard the dog recommence its barking. Then all was silent. Bedford listened for the sound of a car engine, but there was none.

"I'll get the paintings," he said.

Sloane turned to the chest of drawers, pulling out the top one. "I don't want to leave anything behind—nothing she thought enough of to bring here."

"I doubt very much there's anything her family will want."

"Her art medal."

"I have that," Bedford said.

"Roche let you take that?"

"He didn't notice that I didn't give it back." Bedford took it from his pocket. The ribbon was soiled and wrinkled. "There's blood on it."

"You keep it. I don't want to look at it."

RETURNING to Cannes, they slept late in their hotel room, and took a long while bathing and dressing. Lunchtime passed with no call from Roche. After coffee, Bedford returned to the hotel and phoned Toulon, but the inspector was not in.

"We'll have to wait," Bedford said.

"Let's pack the car. If he says we can go, I want to be ready."

With that accomplished, Bedford tried phoning Toulon once more.

Roche had returned.

W₤ can go," he said, getting into the car.

Sloane was in the passenger seat, where she had been waiting. "I was going to leave, whatever he said."

"He says we can go to Paris, but not leave the country. Mrs. Swanscott vouched for us, but I don't think the inspector is quite done with us yet."

He started the engine.

"Why is that?" she said.

"They matched the razor to the cut on Polly's throat and the knife to the sailor's wounds. But that doesn't go very far toward explaining everything. I think Roche wants to keep us on ice until they find one or more of those thugs."

"How likely is that?"

He pulled out into the street. "Not very."

"Paris is nice ice. Why is he being so generous?"

"They have gendarmes in Paris, too. I think they're going to watch us a while."

Bedford headed down the hill, toward the coast road.

"Are the Swanscotts coming here?" Sloane asked.

"Roche says they aren't. Oritzky hasn't shown up in Toulon, but I suppose he will."

"It's a long walk to Toulon."

"Did you want to give him a ride?"

"Not to Toulon. What about Polly?"

"She's to be cremated—and the ashes shipped home. Parents' wishes. I guess they can't face up to that face."

"That's horrible."

"There's little about this tale that isn't."

STOPPING at the Murphys' to return Picasso's painting, they found that the Fitzgeralds had already gone back to Paris, taking the Hemingways with them. Everyone else was still in residence, and, thanks to the now departed Hemingway, fully informed of the dreadful happenings in Toulon.

Sloane remained in the car, not wishing to speak to any of them. Bedford took the Picasso canvas into the house and presented it to Sara Murphy, as the artist was nowhere in view.

"If this belonged to her," said Sara, "surely her family . . ."

"No. It's his," Bedford said. "He should have it."

"He may not want it now."

"I'll leave that up to him. Thank you for everything." He stepped back, gave a wave to Dorothy Parker before she could come nearer, then returned to the gravel yard and the Hispano-Suiza.

Sara followed him, leaning on the car door after Bedford had settled into the driver's seat. Sloane kept her eyes fixed straight ahead.

"I just want you to know how terribly sorry we all are about what's happened," Sara said, her emotion obvious and sincere. "I had no idea the situation was so monstrous."

"Thank you. Neither had I."

"Ernest told us about the wretched time you had. Why don't you spend the night with us and go on in the morning?"

"That's very kind," Sloane said, "but we're taking the afternoon train."

She looked at Bedford's watch. "By the time you reach Nice, you'll have missed it. Please stay for dinner at least. There's a night train."

Sloane sent him no signal—either way.

If nothing else, the company at the Murphys' offered a brief respite and diversion. They both were aware of their need for that.

"Thank you," he said. "We'll be happy to accept your invitation. You're very kind."

THERE had been no friendship with the Murphys during their initial stay, but the tragic conclusion of their quest had created an odd, unforeseen bond. The conversation at dinner was about art and fashion, much as it might have been before, but Bedford and Sloane felt themselves central in a circle of intimates—not the peripheral interlopers they had been initially.

Only Dotty Parker tried to turn the talk to Polly, raising Bedford's fears of another predatory writer circling a prospective subject like carrion over a carcass.

Sara came to the rescue, changing the subject to the rampant nudity evident at that year's carnival in Nice. By evening's end, Bedford fully understood the woman's extraordinary ability to so effortlessly make men fall in love with her.

"It's a pity Singer Sargent has died," he said to her, later. "I think you might have been his greatest portrait, had he the chance."

Her sweet smile in reply was endearing.

"His death is to be regretted for many reasons," she said. "But not that."

"In artistic terms, it probably came too late," said her husband Gerald, rather coldly. "A brilliant and painterly technician, but he was not modern."

"His art collided with the war," said Dos Passos. "And lost. Even his war paintings seem trivial."

And so the conversation turned again.

They left just after sunset, hands shaken all around, Sloane and Sara Murphy, at the latter's unspoken insistence, embracing warmly.

"You will always be welcome, wherever we are," said Sara.

"New York, perhaps," said Sloane.

THEY continued on along the coast road, the sky above the mountains to the west smoldering with the last light of the vanishing day.

"I used to love France," Sloane said.

"You will again. It's a lifelong addiction. Can't be broken. Not even by this."

"Maybe a lifelong curse."

"You begin to sound like Fitzgerald."

"Then forgive me."

A pair of headlights, two tiny pinpricks in the distance, appeared in the car's round rearview mirror, then vanished as they went around a curve.

"Do you want to take a private compartment on the train?" Bedford asked. "I have a little money left."

"It doesn't matter."

"What about the ship? Do you mind Second Class?

She didn't answer.

"I for one will be happy to get back to normalcy," he said, "to borrow a phrase from the late Mr. Harding."

The headlights appeared again, only much closer. The other car was moving very fast. He presumed it was a Frenchman, with a very thorough knowledge of the local roads.

"Everything's different now," Sloane said.

"Not as much as you think," he said.

"Did Mrs. Swanscott want anything more from you?" Sloane asked. "Did she pass on any instructions?"

"Apparently not. She hired me to find her daughter. And so I did. I guess that's that. I shouldn't blame her if she never wanted to hear from me again."

"I trust the feeling's mutual."

The road was twisting back and forth in sharp curves now—ascending. Bedford shifted to a lower gear, pressing the gas pedal harder.

"Bedford?"

"Yes?"

"I may want to leave your art gallery."

The words struck a silent, thudding blow.

"That's not necessary. And it's *our* gallery."

"I may want to do something else. Art—it's not a happy business."

"I'm happy."

"I'm serious."

"Time enough to think about that."

They reached the top of the rise. The road wound on before them, following the edge of the bluff—a glimmering sea with a wine-dark horizon stretching off to the right.

"I have been thinking about it," she said. "Every night, when I go to sleep."

The other car emerged from its climb behind them. It had fallen farther back, but now proceeded to gather speed, rapidly diminishing the distance between them.

"Damned Frenchmen," said Bedford. "They show no mercy to anyone who doesn't know the roads as well as they do."

"New Yorkers drive the same way."

The other car's headlights were making a glaring incandescence in the rearview mirror. Bedford tilted it upwards, eliminating the distraction, but making it difficult to follow the other vehicle's movements.

"Why don't you pull over and let him by?" Sloane asked.

"I don't know where I can do that. If I try to pull over along this stretch we'll end up down on the rocks."

Sloane turned around in her seat.

"Try slowing down," she said. "He'll have to do the same."

"I'm not sure I want him to. I'd like him to just go whizzing by."

"Just try it!"

He didn't want to brake, for fear the other would just pile into him, sending them both over the side. Instead, Bedford merely took his foot off the accelerator. The Hispano-Suiza began to slow.

"It's working," she said.

Bedford readjusted the mirror, and saw his pursuer begin to drift back a car length or two. He thought he might begin to use his brakes—ultimately coming to a complete stop and letting this madman have all the road ahead to himself.

The madman appeared to have other intentions. Abruptly, he increased his speed again, roaring up at Bedford like some fiend from Hell.

There was a clang and a jolt, as Bedford realized they'd been struck from behind—steel bumper against steel bumper. The rear of the Hispano-Suiza slid out to the right. Yanking the wheel around in that direction, Bedford regained control, but barely.

They swept into a long, shallow curve, carved along the top of a high cliff, which rose from the left. At the end was a much sharper turn. Bedford put the gas pedal to the floor, guessing from the other's slower rate of ascent that his rented car might have the faster engine and could outrun the other in the straighter stretches.

And so it proved. But he soon had the fiend on his tail again, as the road twisted back into curves.

Angry, Bedford slammed the brakes hard, hoping he might catch the other by surprise and gain a little respect. The Hispano-Suiza raised violent objection to this, its rear wheels skidding right, and then left as he tried to correct. The other car followed, move for move. This was a dogfight.

"I'm just going to have to ignore him until we get to the bottom of this bluff," Bedford said. "There's nothing else I can do."

But the other was having none of that. He roared up and took another whack at Bedford's bumper. This time, Bedford kept control, and the other man faltered, recovering just at the brink of flying off the cliff.

He was quickly back in place, hanging there, curve after curve. Then all at once he vanished from the mirror. Confused, Bedford wondered if he could have turned off somewhere.

Then he saw the other's right front fender from the corner of his eye. The damned fool was pulling up alongside from the left. There was barely room for one of them.

"Can you see the driver?" Bedford shouted to Sloane. He

could not look himself, if he was to keep his car on the pavement.

She said nothing, and then, unhelpfully, she grabbed his arm. "Bedford! Duck!"

Duck?

A gunshot rang out, the sound echoing off the mountain slope to their left and resounding as though across the entire Mediterranean.

Now Bedford did take the time to steal a look at his adversary. The man's face was barely visible in the pale light from the dashboard. The flash that came with the next gunshot produced a flare of brilliance that briefly took away much of Bedford's night vision. His steering became guesswork—lucky rolls of dice. The tires of both cars were squealing now, kicking up dust and rocks.

The other car came up fully alongside. Bedford reached to pull Sloane down out of the way, but she shoved him back.

There was another, much brighter flash, blue and orange, and very close. A sharp, stinging, enveloping sound deafened his right ear. His nostrils filled with gunsmoke.

Sloane, kneeling on the seat, was holding a pistol with both hands. It was a little gun. Man Ray's.

Bedford returned his attention to the other car, which had disappeared once more, this time behind him. Its headlights were dancing weirdly in the mirror, swinging from side to side. As the automobile fell further back, the swings became more violent. Suddenly the headlights shot up in the air and the machine vanished again, this time for good.

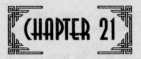

CHAPTER 21

BEDFORD had no wish to back up on this precipice of a road at night—and wasn't so sure he'd try it even in bright daylight. He pulled the Hispano-Suiza over as far to the right as he could manage, then turned off the engine.

"You'd best stay here," he said, getting out.

Sloane ignored the suggestion, climbing out on his side and then hurrying on down the road ahead of him in her clattering pumps.

It was difficult to determine just where the other car had gone over the edge. The two of them moved backward and forward along the roadway until at last Bedford noticed the broken place in the shrubs where the automobile had torn loose branches and a wheel had dug a little trench. Climbing atop the mounded earth, he peered down the escarpment.

It wasn't so far to the sea as he had imagined—perhaps fifty feet, if that. He looked over the area below for several minutes before finally noticing the car. It lay on its back, smashed against a large rock outcropping, just shy of the pebbled beach and breaking waves.

"How will we get down there?" Sloane asked.

"We won't. We can't. Not in the dark."

"But he needs help."

"Whoever that was, he's beyond help."

"That was Norman Oritzky."

"So he said."

"I've killed him."

"He killed him, trying to kill us."

"Bedford, I shot him."

He put his arm around her, leaning close.

"Sloane, you shot at him—to scare him off. That little pistol of Man Ray's might hit someone standing a foot or two away. But not anyone in a careening car at night. You startled him, that's all. It threw him off. He lost control and went over the side. And he damned sure had it coming."

"He somehow blamed us for Polly's murder."

"You're absolutely sure it was Norman Oritzky?"

"Aren't you? That face. He looked maniacal. All that fury and sadness. Polly used to say he was a gentle young man."

They stared at the wreck below as though something was about to happen, or about to change. But nothing did. The waves broke, and fell away. A night bird called from someplace near. The breeze blew softly against their faces. Sloane was trembling slightly. Bedford pulled her closer to him.

"Why would someone like Norman Oritzky have a gun?" she said.

"Mr. Ray had one. Perhaps it's a new fashion among artists."

"Bedford, this is no time to try to be amusing."

"Sorry."

She shivered.

"Let's go," he said, "or we'll miss the train."

There were no other cars on the road they could see or hear.

"What will we tell the police?" she asked.

"As little as possible."

She gestured toward the wreck at the bottom of the cliff. "We just can't leave him? What about his family?"

"I'll take care of things. I don't want you to even think about it anymore."

"Bedford . . ."

He held her by both shoulders. "That could have been us. Thanks to you, it wasn't. Now let's move on."

Somewhere on a long straight stretch between Antibes and Nice, where the road descended from the bluff and ran along the sea, Bedford pulled over to the side by a small promontory and walked out onto it. Looking both ways for oncoming autos, he threw Man Ray's little pistol as far as he could into the sea. The weapon, spinning, flew so far he never heard the splash.

They reached Nice with nearly an hour left before the train.

◆

HEMINGWAY insisted on a party for them at the Dome, celebrating both their return to Paris and their pending departure for the United States. His notion was that they might be leaving in a hurry, so best that the party was arranged swiftly.

It was a small affair—the Fitzgeralds, the Hemingways, Bedford and Sloane, and an odd couple, the writer Harold Stearns and the magazine correspondent Janet Flanner, who as "Genet" wrote the "Letter from Paris" column for the *New Yorker*.

Stearns had been at the Enghien racetrack that morning with Hemingway. Flanner had come along to the café looking for material for her column, of which Bedford was a regular reader in New York. They sat around some tables pushed together outside on the sidewalk, and Flanner had taken a place between Bedford and Sloane.

The events in Cannes and Toulon had achieved great currency in the cafés of Montparnasse, in large part because of the peripheral involvement of Picasso, Man Ray, and the Murphys, but mostly because the tragic heroine of the tale was a rich American heiress. The species was becoming as numerous as flower vendors in Paris, and the murder of one had produced as much titillation as horror in the expatriate American community. Accounts of it were appearing in the Paris newspapers, though details were limited.

None of these articles were quite so colorful as Hemingway's account of events. He cast himself, Bedford, and Jozan as veteran warriors taking on an enemy army of waterfront lowlifes, failing to save the fair maiden's life but coming close.

If the gathering at the café was meant to be a festive occasion, it was a struggle to keep it so. The Hemingways were cheerful enough—especially Ernest—and Zelda carried on like a child at her own birthday party. But Scott was scowly and morose, and Stearns rather reticent.

Flanner appeared interested only in the Polly Swanscott story. Finding Sloane uncommunicative, she pestered Bedford relentlessly, apparently seeking some political angle to the tale, or evidence of French–American animosity. Bedford tried to disabuse her of both notions as best he could.

"There's nothing more to this than what you already know," he said. "I don't understand how it could be of much interest to the readers of the *New Yorker.*"

"A beautiful, blond, disgustingly rich New York heiress comes to the Left Bank, attaches herself to some of Paris' most brilliant artists, and ends up with her throat cut?"

"Sounds more something for my old newspaper."

Flanner was not happy with him.

Bedford leaned near. "There are some aspects to this I haven't quite resolved. If I come upon anything involving France that might fit your needs, I'll let you know. I promise. But I'd appreciate it if you wait until then. Miss Smith was a close friend of Polly's and this is upsetting her."

He just then noticed a short black man loitering just inside the Dome's main entrance.

"Excuse me," he said.

◆

THE Negro man, who Bedford recognized from their wild auto ride with Man Ray through the streets of Paris, followed him into the men's room, which was otherwise unoccupied.

"Mr. Bullard found out what he could," he said.

"And what is that?"

"You are being followed by the flics."

"They must be good, because I haven't noticed."

"We noticed. We know some of them."

"Am I still a murder suspect?"

"No. Mister Bullard asked in the right places. He was told by a detective here that you and your lady friend are in the clear. That inspector in Toulon, Roche—he thinks someone else did both jobs. But he thinks that someone wants to rub you out, too. He's waiting for them to try."

"That's why he won't let us leave the country?"

"Guess that's so."

"We may anyway."

"You'll have trouble getting back in if you do."

"I'll call Inspector Roche. Maybe I can be more persuasive this time." Bedford washed his hands. "Did you find out anything about that motor accident outside of Nice?"

The man shrugged. "It was a motor accident."

"The police aren't saying anything about bullet holes?"

"Nothing about bullets."

Bedford took up a towel. "What have they done with the driver's body?"

"Don't know. Still on ice, I guess."

Bedford thought a moment, washing his hands.

"I need another favor from Mr. Bullard," he said, straightening his tie. "If you could wait in the café a moment, I'd appreciate it."

"Mr. Bullard says to do whatever you say."

Returning to the outside tables, Bedford noted with relief that Flanner had moved to the other side of the group. He sat down next to Sloane, who seemed almost in a trance.

"Are you all right?"

"I'll get by. We're leaving soon."

"I need to borrow two hundred dollars. I'd use my own money, but I need that for passage."

"Two hundred dollars for what?"

"I want to have Mr. Oritzky's remains shipped back to New York. His family probably can't afford it."

"I think they're very poor."

"It's the least we can do."

"Are you feeling guilty now, Bedford?"

"No. Just trying to show good form."

"All right." She reached for her handbag.

"You carry too much money."

"Sometimes it comes in handy. Like now."

Bedford slipped the bills into the side pocket of his coat, then put his hand to Sloane's shoulder.

"Are you calm?" he asked.

"Yes. Why do you ask that?"

"Say the word, 'calm.'"

"Calm."

"Again, please."

"Calm." Her voice was more forceful.

"Thank you."

BEDFORD reached Roche that night. The next morning, they went to the Gare St. Lazare for the boat train to Le Havre, escorted by the Hemingways.

"We'll see you in New York," Hemingway said. "I owe you a drink."

He shook Bedford's hand, then gave him a hug with several back slaps. Sloane received a much different kind of hug. Bedford felt a little embarrassed for Hadley.

As they started down the platform, Bedford halted at the sound of a woman calling his name.

It was Zelda. She turned up late, and without her husband, and now was hurrying after them with a package in her hands.

"Good bye, Beddie," she said, grinning, and placed the parcel gently in his hands. "It's a bon voyage present. Something I think you wanted."

Oblivious to the others standing behind her, she gave him a warm kiss, then stepped back, gave the Hemingways a smile and a wave, and ran off again.

After the train had left the station and they were well on the way to Rouen, Bedford opened the package. It was quite elaborate, but contained only a book and a large manilla envelope. Inside was a bound sheaf of papers covered with writing in Fitzgerald's neat, well-bred hand.

The book was Fitzgerald's new novel, *The Great Gatsby*. He opened it, read a few lines, and then kept on reading.

"Any good?" asked Sloane, after a few minutes. She was seated across from him in the compartment.

"He writes very beautifully."

"What's it about?"

"Folly. Desperate lives. And the north shore of Long Island."

"Oh dear."

"I suppose there are worse places."

He'd read a third of the book by the time they reached Le Havre. The rest he finished that night on the ship.

It was Bedford's custom to carry around old business and personal letters that were important to him in the left breast pocket of his coats, moving them from garment to garment as he changed clothes so he'd never mislay them. That was why he still carried Polly's postal card, and—as he recalled over a brandy in the Second Class lounge late that night— why he still had Nicholas Pease's letter to her, sadly undelivered.

He took it out and set it before him, studying the envelope's face, which bore only the word, "Polly."

Had he gotten it to her and she had opened and read it and it had turned up posthumously among her possessions, Bedford would have felt no compunction about reading it. But the supposed "gentleman's creed" that his father and grandfather had pounded into him now stayed his hand.

"A gentleman does not read another gentleman's mail," his grandfather would have said.

He could imagine the offense young Pease would take upon learning that Bedford had invaded and violated such intimate correspondence when its intended recipient had died horribly and been burned to ash before the words could reach her eyes.

The young man had already shown his small esteem for Bedford's sense of honor by offering him money to play the part of courier.

But there was someone who counted more than Nicholas Pease or any of his family in this. Bedford's obligation was to the young woman he had failed to save.

He tore open the envelope.

❖❖

I N the morning, he found Sloane out on the aft deck, leaning on the rail and staring after a headland that marked the Irish coast.

"I finished Fitzgerald's book," he said.

"Is it any good?"

"Yes. I also read the notes for it that Zelda gave me."

She was keeping her eyes from him.

"Why didn't you tell me?" he asked.

"I made a promise, Bedford."

"She's dead. That doesn't matter."

"Yes it does."

❖❖

A T the pier in New York, Sloane declined his offer to share a taxicab. She and her porter disappeared into the dockside crowd.

CHAPTER 22

JOEV D. was waiting for him outside the funeral home, wearing another of his purple suits with a blue and black striped tie and yellow shirt. It was raining, lightly, and he wore his gray fedora pulled low. In all, he looked more a character from Broadway than a New York police detective. That was doubtless how he thought of himself.

"Morning," he said, amiably. "Did you know you're a wanted man?"

"Good morning to you, sir," Bedford said. "'Wanted' for what? And by who?"

"French cops cabled us asking if we knew your whereabouts. Seems you left their country without permission."

"Must have misunderstood them. My French is poor."

"I'm sure they'll buy that line next time you pay la belle France a visit." He flicked his cigarette into the gutter, then stuck his hands into the side pockets of his suit coat. "Anyway, if you're not going to worry about that for a while, I won't either."

They were on Second Avenue, which had a steady stream of trucks and cars rumbling along it, adding their noise to that of the Third Avenue elevated a block to the west. Despite all the traffic, there was only one automobile parked at the curb.

"That's theirs?" Bedford asked, nodding to the small car.

Joey D. nodded. "Shouldn't be too long. They just went in."

"Both parents?"

"The mother and an uncle. The father's sick or something. Or maybe not interested."

"And the body?"

"It arrived nicely embalmed and in pretty good shape for a crash victim. I guess he's recognizable. I understand you paid for it all—embalming, shipping the corpse back here, all that stuff. I thought you were tap city?"

"Borrowed the money from Sloane."

"How is she?"

"Don't know. Haven't seen her for days."

They were interrupted by a piercing wail coming from the funeral parlor's open doors. D'Alessandro, who'd heard every manner of human anguish, was startled by it. Bedford was not.

Not long after, a short, round woman with gray streaks in her dark hair, wearing a voluminous black dress and head scarf, emerged from the doors, sobbing uncontrollably. She was supported by a thin, grim-faced man some years older.

Bedford and Detective D'Alessandro watched the two drive off, then turned as another plainclothes cop came outside, shaking his head.

"Not the guy," he said to Joey D. "The mother swears it."

"She seemed very upset," Bedford said.

"Yeah," said the other detective. "Whoever that stiff is, he ain't Norman Oritzky."

"So what now?" Joey D. asked, looking to Bedford.

"I think you should keep the gentleman on ice for a while. He's had a long journey and should rest awhile. But you might want to take his picture."

"Mug shot? He's dead."

"Say 'calm,'" Bedford said.

"What?"

"Say the word 'calm.'"

Dubious, the detective sighed, then said, "Calm. I'm calm. You're calm. That guy we thought was Norman Oritzky, he's real calm."

"Thank you," said Bedford. "When you say it, you pronounce the 'L.' Sloane, who's from Chicago, drops the 'L.' Most Midwesterners do. You pronounce the 'L' because you're from the East."

"East Twenty-Eighth Street."

"Norman Oritzky grew up in Brooklyn."

"I don't think I'm gettin' all this, Bedford."

"As his mother just observed, the body isn't Norman Oritzky's. I guessed right."

"So if he isn't Oritzky, why do you want to keep him on ice?"

"I want to know who he is. I'd like you to take his picture and send copies to the police in Detroit, Chicago, Milwaukee—maybe St. Louis, too. But I think especially Detroit. See if he matches anyone in their mug shot files."

"Why do that? All the laws this guy may have broken were in France."

"On the contrary, Joseph. In the city of New York, homicide is still a crime. And I believe he committed that crime."

"You said the girl was killed in Toulon, France."

"Something else I'd suggest," Bedford said. "You recall that young man who broke into her flat and turned up dead with her money and letters in his pocket?"

"Sure. Henry Schultz. Some street punk."

"Where are his remains?"

"Potter's field—on Staten Island."

"Good. You can go to a New York judge."

"For what?"

"For an exhumation order. I think you'll find it worth your while to have Mrs. Oritzky take a look at that one, if she can be persuaded. I think she might not agree that he is Henry Schultz, street punk."

"You ask too much, Bedford."

"I'm asking nothing, Joseph. I'm simply offering you the opportunity to close a murder case. That's not something you do every day."

"But what homicide does it solve?"

Bedford tipped his hat, and started walking away. "The murder of Henry Schultz, street punk."

CLAIRE Pell, wearing a very smart suit and crisp straw hat that perfectly matched the color of her hair, halted at the threshold, unwilling to enter, though it was her own dressing room. She paused to think upon the situation, electing finally to proceed as though nothing were amiss. The perplexed look vanished from her face and she stepped inside, closing the door and moving smoothly to her makeup table.

"Good afternoon, Mr. Green," she said, coolly, as she removed her suit jacket. "I wasn't aware you'd returned to our city."

"Just got back," said Bedford, who had risen to his feet in greeting. "Uh, Monday."

"And so you thought you'd surprise me," she said. "Two days later."

She sat down. Bedford took a finely wrapped small package from his pocket and set it on the table beside her.

"A small souvenir."

"Small, indeed." She opened it, and then the elegant bottle it contained, sniffing. "Coco Chanel. How sweet. Thank you."

Her voice had warmed little.

"I'm sorry," he said. "I've been busy."

"You and Miss Smith? Busy with your *art*?" Claire leaned toward the mirror, and began to do something to her eyebrows with a small brush.

He shook his head. "Sloane's gone. I don't know where, or even if she's coming back. I've been with Joe D'Alessandro, among others of his professional calling. It's about this Polly Swanscott girl."

"Yeah. I read about it in the papers. Something about a boating accident."

"She was murdered."

Claire's small brush strokes ceased. "That's awful."

"Yes it is. Not a pretty end at all, for such a pretty girl."

"Why are you here, Bedford? I have the funny idea you want something from me."

"What I want from you is you. I stopped by to say hello."

"Hello."

"But, yes, I do need your help again."

"You didn't get it from me the first time. Why do you expect it now?"

There was a clatter of high heels in the hall outside, and giggles—the chorus heading onstage to rehearse.

"I think that you didn't help me the first time because you feared I might cause trouble for your family or friends in Little Italy—especially if I learned who might have been the party who broke into Polly Swanscott's apartment or murdered this guy the police identified as Henry Schultz. It's a reasonable supposition. The building Polly lived in is owned by the mother of the man who runs the Broome Street Social Club—abode of the Sicilian Brotherhood. They do not take such transgressions lightly."

"It should be obvious then why I don't want to get involved."

"I know that no one in Little Italy was responsible for the break-in," Bedford said. "I'm positive of that. What I need to know now—for certain—is that none of them had anything to do with the killing of this Henry Schultz. They had grounds, in their way of looking at things. If the Brotherhood had done it—and it was done as a lesson to others not to trespass—that sort of thing should have pretty wide currency in Little Italy, but I don't think it does."

"Why don't you go down there and ask around yourself?"

He smiled, politely. "Some might consider that ill-advised, for someone with my lack of acquaintances in that precinct."

She made no reply. He rose and stood behind her, moving to massage her shoulders, knowing her dancer's muscles welcomed that, whatever the circumstance.

"I need to know for sure that the Brotherhood wasn't involved. I need to eliminate that from the equation—unless it can't be eliminated," Bedford said.

"And you have to know that from me?"

"Then I would know for sure."

He could feel her relaxing under his kneading fingers. Her head came back slightly. He leaned forward and kissed the top of her brow.

"And then what?"

"With this behind me, I'll be free to resume my delightful social life—centering, as always, on delightful you."

She growled. "Bedford . . ."

He dropped his hands. "Claire, I've got to go to her mother and tell her everything. She paid me to find her daughter—to try to bring her back, if I could—and I failed, miserably. At the very least, I owe her a thorough explanation of what happened. I don't want to leave her with doubts."

She leaned closer to the mirror, studying the lovely image as might an artist. "I must get ready now, Mr. Green. Thanks so much for stopping by."

◆

BEDFORD made a lengthy digression to Fifth Avenue and Scribner's bookstore, where he made a purchase, then returned to Broadway, heading straight for Lindy's. He didn't expect to find Rothstein there—gamblers were peripatetic fellows and kept odd hours—but was sure word would quickly reach the man that Bedford had come into the place, debts and all.

Smiling to friends, he took a prominent table, ordered a dish of rice pudding and coffee, then sat back to wait. It didn't take long.

Rothstein, accompanied by two gentlemen not quite as well dressed as he, rapped his walking stick on the table top just as Bedford was finishing up the pudding.

"I left a good game at the Astor Hotel to come here and see for myself if it could be true that you'd just walk in here."

"True enough, Mr. Wolfsheim."

"What did you call me?"

"Wolfsheim. As in Meyer Wolfsheim." He slid the book

he'd purchased across the table. "Here, I bought you a present. You've been immortalized in a great work of literature."

Rothstein pulled out a chair and sat down, picking up the book. His two associates, sensing there was no immediate need for them, slipped away into the general mob of customers.

"*The Great Gatsby,*" said Rothstein, turning a page. "This is a novel. How am I in there?"

"You're not by name. But the character named Wolfsheim in there is an elegant, well-dressed gambler famous for fixing the 1919 World Series."

Rothstein began turning the pages furiously.

"Here," said Bedford, taking back the book. He found the proper page quickly, then returned it.

As the gambler read, a waiter, unasked, brought him a cup of coffee. The aroma bore the scent of good bourbon.

"The son of a bitch," Rothstein said. "Who is this guy Fitzgerald?"

"Very classy guy—just like that Jay Gatsby he writes about. Only, Gatsby's a fraud. His real name is Gatz, and he's not a North Shore aristocrat. He's bootlegger and stock swindler, who does business with all kinds of criminals. One of them is the man who fixed the 1919 World Series—Meyer Wolfsheim."

Rothstein closed the book, shoving it aside. "Where does he get this crap?"

"Oh, Fitzgerald's a terrific researcher. Practically everything he writes is drawn from reality. He's a regular vacuum cleaner, sucking up all kinds of details about real people and spitting them out in his novels."

The gambler's eyes narrowed, as though he were studying cards in a game of seven card stud.

"I never met anyone like this Gatsby," he said. "Not even Legs Diamond is like this guy."

"No," Bedford replied. "He's young and good-looking, has charm and a great deal of moxie. But he also has manners and taste enough to pass himself off as one of the upper crust. Rather like Fitzgerald. And he's from the Midwest, like

Fitzgerald. You don't do business with anyone like that, do you Mr. Rothstein?"

"Who I do business with is my business. Which reminds me that you and I have some unfinished business."

The gambler grinned his gambler grin. It had an unsettling effect.

"Actually," said Bedford. "I think you do have a business associate like that. Not young and charming, but a bootlegger and swindler from the Midwest who's achieved some social prominence here in the East, even though just under the surface he's little more than a gangster."

One of Rothstein's associates, as sensitive to his master's moods as a faithful spaniel, appeared from nowhere, hovering near.

"What are you getting at, Green?"

"You know very well what I'm getting at."

They stared at each other, two pokers players trying to figure the other's hand.

Rothstein decided to bluff. "Nothing to do with me."

Bedford decided to call.

"There's a writer for the *New Yorker* in Paris who knows about half of this story and wants to use it in a piece about the murder of Polly Swanscott. If I were to supply the other half—which I think now I can do—well, it would make for some highly interesting reading, don't you think?"

"Like I say, it's nothing to me."

"If it were nothing to you—or your business partner—you wouldn't still be sitting here listening to me."

"What do you want, Green? You want me to tear up your marker?"

"No, Mr. Rothstein. As my grandfather used to say, a gentleman always pays his debts—though I do wish you'd be nicer about it until I get my gallery on its feet."

Rothstein nodded, curtly, then pushed back his chair. "Anything else?"

"Tell me if I'm wrong."

The gambler stood up, took up the book again, then handed it to Bedford.

"You better keep this, Green. Maybe this guy Fitzgerald

can answer your question." He paused. "I'll give you a little longer on your marker—just so you're not forgettin' it."

"No, sir."

Rothstein halted again. "There is something I can tell you. Not sure if you want to hear it."

"And what would that be?"

"You've got a friend, nice-looking lady, real class. Claire Pell."

Bedford feared threat here. "She has nothing to do with this."

"Didn't say that. What I'm saying is that, while you've been gone, she may have found herself a new friend."

"Who is that?"

Rothstein turned his back to Bedford and started walking away.

"Someone who knows how to treat a lady."

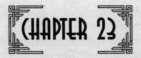

CHAPTER 23

BEDFORD went the next morning to his much-neglected gallery, finding it a sad and lonely place in Sloane's continuing and unexplained absence. If not solace, there was distraction in the undone work that awaited, and he threw himself into that, commencing with his unread mail and the task of arranging the bills in order of most urgent to pay.

It was a frustrating task, for they all seemed to be of compelling urgency.

To his amazement, he had two customers that morning, both sent his way by Stieglitz. One was a man looking for "something modern" for his fiancée. Bedford presumed that Stieglitz would not have made the recommendation if the fellow's notion of modern was indeed "modern." As a test, he offered up a nicely framed print of a tempestuous Art Deco nude by the Polish artist and voluptuary Tamara de Lempicka. The man's blush told all.

Bedford sold him instead a pretty watercolor with some Impressionist touches by a little-known artist from Mount Kisco who had studied under the great and utterly boring William Merritt Chase.

The other customer, an expensively dressed woman who

said she needed "something in blue" for her seaside cottage in Bridgehampton, bought all but one of a half dozen ships' paintings that had come his way from an estate sale in New London, Connecticut. At this rate, he might even be able to pay his rent.

He had thought seriously of abandoning the art business on the voyage home; now he was thinking again. Much depended on Sloane. His two sales seemed rather meaningless without her to share in them. She probably could have talked both customers into more major purchases.

On impulse, he went to Sloane's work table in the alcove and sat there a long while. There was a framed photograph of her with her parents on the near wall. She was barely smiling in it but looked very beautiful and very young. That the picture reminded him of the one Polly's parents kept in their Scarsdale house made him all the more melancholy.

The front door opened again but it was not another client.

"Mr. Green?"

"Yes?"

"It's Nicholas Pease."

Wearily, Bedford rose and went out front. The young man was standing in almost exactly the same spot he had chosen in his previous visit, as if he had no wish to proceed any further.

"I've been coming by every day, waiting for you to come back," he said. "Now here you are."

"I wish I'd brought back better news."

Neither said anything more for a long moment. Pease nervously began swinging his hat, then ran the back of his hand across his eyes.

"I can't believe it," he said.

"I'm sorry. There's no easy way to take a thing like this."

"It wasn't a boating accident, was it?"

Bedford shook his head, sadly. "She was murdered, Mr. Pease. The French police think it was either a sailor she'd taken up with or someone quite like him. But the sailor was also murdered—in very similar fashion."

"What *fashion*?"

"Never mind. It wasn't nice. Be glad you weren't there."

"I should have been."

"No, there was nothing to be done."

"What was she doing with someone like that?"

Bedford sighed, then went and sat behind his desk, wishing the younger man would seat himself as well. "You won't want to hear this, but she had a number of relationships with men in France, all brief and unhappy. Some of them were not at all nice."

"But why? She wasn't like that here. Certainly not at college."

"Some think she may have sought this end. That she was suicidal."

"That's nonsense. Over me?"

"No, over art. Perhaps."

Pease turned away, biting his lip a moment. He glanced up at a framed Gustave Klimt print Bedford had on the wall near the front window—a dark-haired, heavily rouged woman in Oriental dressing gown with a wicked, malicious, mocking, but very sensual smile and a bare breast exposed from a fold of silken cloth.

He looked back. "I haven't talked to Mrs. Swanscott. Is Polly . . . are there any services?"

"She was cremated. The Swanscotts haven't said what they plan to do."

"What do you think happened to Polly, Mr. Green?"

"I haven't made up my mind yet. There are still some things I don't know."

"What about Sloane?"

"She's gone away. All this upset her badly."

Pease began the swinging of the hat again. He was having trouble keeping a pleasant expression on his face.

"I want to help, Mr. Green. I want to do something. What can I do?"

Bedford got up and walked over to the Klimt print. He liked it, a lot, actually. He wondered what had possessed him to put it up for sale.

"You could tell me something," he said. "Truthfully."

The hat ceased its motion. "Sure."

"Your parents didn't approve of your marrying Polly."

"No. Truthfully, no, they didn't."

"Why?"

"They didn't think Polly would fit in."

"Did you?"

"Of course!" He was becoming indignant.

"How much did your parents know about her?"

"What you'd expect. That she'd gone to Smith. That her parents had a lot of money. That they were new here. That, that she had bohemian inclinations."

"What bothered them the most?"

"Mr. Green, what do my parents have to do with this?"

Bedford smiled, he hoped disarmingly. "Nothing, I'm sure. I'm thinking of Polly. I'm trying to understand what she went through before she left for France."

"It wasn't very nice, not here in New York." He paused. "Her neighborhood wasn't very nice." He looked out Bedford's window. "It was pretty awful. Her friends . . ."

"I have a neighbor down the street named Gertrude Vanderbilt Whitney," Bedford said. "She has bohemian inclinations, too."

"Mr. Green, I meant nothing by that."

"Do you suppose your mother approves of Mrs. Whitney?"

Pease drew himself up very straight. "I would appreciate it if you would not mention my parents in this context anymore."

"Just one other thing. To what lengths did they go to compel you to break off the engagement?"

"Mr. Green . . ."

"Did they threaten to disinherit you? Run you out of your father's firm?"

"They would never do that."

"Did they threaten her?"

"Mr. Green, this is intolerable." He went to the door.

"A moment, Mr. Pease." Bedford drew out the opened letter Pease had written to Polly and handed it to him. "I'm sorry for its condition. Polly's things did not fare well in this business."

"Did she read it?"

"I don't believe so," Bedford said.

"But you did?"

Bedford said nothing. Pease slammed the door behind him very hard.

J OEY D. called late in the afternoon.

"I don't know if we've solved any crimes here," he said, "but at least now we've got the right name on the victim."

"Mr. Schultz is Mr. Oritzky?"

"Yes he is. Or was. We had the uncle come out and view the exhumed remains. He didn't enjoy it much. I didn't think we needed to put the mother through that again."

"No. Too many weeping mothers."

"You're a clever guy to have figured out the Oritzky switch, Bedford. You oughta get in my line of work."

"No thanks. I don't like the hours. Anyway, I haven't accomplished very much, really. We still don't know who that fellow in France was who said that he was Mr. Oritzky."

"We sent copies of his picture out to the Midwest on the Twentieth Century Limited. They must have got there by now."

"But no word."

"Nope. So where does this leave us?"

Bedford sighed. "I really don't know."

"Something else funny about all this."

"And what would that be, Joseph?"

"There was another grave out there, dug about the same time as Oritzky's. Wanted to make sure we got the right guy, so we took a look at that stiff, too."

"But it wasn't Warren G. Harding."

"No. An ex-copper. Quit the force to become a private investigator. Specialized in divorces and domestic stuff like that. He was reported missing a couple of months ago."

"Murdered?"

"Yeah. Looks like it."

"Too many bodies."

"Yeah. Gotta go, Bedford."

◆◆

HE had a third sale that afternoon. The commission was enough for him to pay back the money he'd borrowed from Sloane in France and reduce some of the principal on the marker Rothstein held.

Closing up immediately afterward, Bedford went to Sloane's Grove Street flat for the fifth time since his return, hoping she'd at least be willing to join him in a celebration of the day's success.

But once again, she was not there.

Turning uptown, he went by Dayton Crosby's Gramercy Park townhouse, where he quickly found himself in a game of chess. He just as quickly lost. Crosby took him uptown to the Harvard Club for dinner by way of consolation. The subject turned to Sloane.

"What do you know of her family?" Bedford asked.

The older man's brow crinkled. "Isn't that a question I should ask you? After all the years she's been your friend and colleague?"

"She's never talked about her family much."

Crosby pursed his lips. "Father's a bond lawyer—respectable, but dull. Mother's the daughter of an equally dull architect, specializing in overlarge houses. Both are very keen on the tribal customs of their class—such as they have them in Chicago."

"They don't like what she's done with herself."

"What young woman's parents do these days?"

"They're very stern about it. A very strict sense of propriety."

"That's plain and simple pretentiousness, Bedford—based on very, very little. So many of them are like that. Gustavus Swift, the meat packing tycoon? Did you know he got his start selling raw meat out of a cart? Potter Palmer bought swamp land and sold it to immigrants. His partner Marshall Field started as a seller of dry goods. And the shoddies! So many of those 'finer families' founded their fortune selling shoddy goods to the Union Army in the War between the States. It's all a great joke, this strutting of theirs."

"Nothing like that here."

"On the contrary. New York society is even worse. The first Commodore Vanderbilt began his career skippering a Staten Island garbage scow. Astor was a musical instrument salesman. John D. Rockefeller's family were penniless Hugenots who came from some vermin-infested little village on the Rhine. Now, they are *grand*."

"And the Peases? The parents of Nicholas Pease?"

The great, bushy eyebrows shot up. "They're the exception to everything I've said. They've been in America for at least a million years—and they've been in the Social Register even longer."

He laughed. He was enjoying the evening.

"They never sold meat out of a cart?" Bedford asked.

"If they did, it must have been immediately after the invention of the cart, and it was only for the briefest of times. *Trade*, don't you know?"

"Would they be the sort of people to have their son's girl-friends investigated? By a private detective? If matters got too serious?"

"If they didn't know her family, certainly."

"Hmm."

They went into the gentleman's lounge for brandy.

"I don't think Sloane cares for *grand*," Bedford said.

"One of her many virtues."

"I think it's something she had very much in common with Polly Swanscott."

Crosby raised his glass. "To them both, then."

They clinked glasses. Bedford took a sip of his cognac, which was excellent. "I wish that was all they had in common."

"Don't fret, Bedford. Sloane's a sensible young woman. More sense than you, most of the time."

"Most of the time isn't now."

❖

LATER that night, after Crosby had taken a taxi home, Bed-ford drifted over to the theater district. He went by Claire's stage door, but it was too late for her to still be on the premises. Rothstein was not at Lindy's, or any of his other haunts. Bedford encountered a number of friends, but none of much help to him.

◆

T HE next day passed much the same as its predecessor, except for the lack of paying customers at the gallery. Late that night, in an unexpected place, Rothstein found him.

Bedford had stopped by the circular fountain in the square opposite the Plaza Hotel, looking up at the classical nude who stood in modest, romanticized fashion atop the pedestal in the center. She was one of his favorite sculptures in the city, and he liked to look upon her even now, with the hotel windows beyond all ablaze with light, rendering her more a silhouette than a figure in three dimensions.

"Nice-looking lady."

Startled, Bedford turned to see Rothstein standing behind him, elegant in a pale striped suit and spats.

"Yes she is," Bedford said. "It's a wonderful sculpture. I didn't figure you for an art fancier."

"I knew her," said the gambler. He was holding a cigar and paused to light it.

"Knew the statue?"

"Knew the model who posed for it. Her name's Vera. Actress sometimes; artist's model more nowadays. She's spooked by theaters. Her husband died in the Iroquois Theater fire. Heart of gold, that one. Heart of gold."

"Sounds like you knew her well."

Rothstein changed the subject.

"I've been looking for you, Green. All over town. I was just having dinner at the Plaza and was going to head down to your place in the Village again."

A chill crept over the skin of Bedford's back. Had he pushed the man too far? Rothstein had never gone to his flat or place of business. What did he intend?

"I've got some good news for you," Rothstein continued.

"You had enough down on American Flag to pay me what you owe."

Bedford had forgotten what day it was.

"American Flag won the Belmont?"

"Never any question."

"But you wouldn't let me bet on him. You wouldn't take any more markers. All I had on the horse was a fiver I placed with a bookie at my old paper."

"Yeah, maybe so. But I got a heart of gold, too. Green. I changed my mind at the last minute and put down a couple thousand for you."

Bedford decided not to ask what would have happened if the horse had lost.

"Well, thank you. Sir. You're a true gentleman."

"That's a nice compliment, coming from you. But let's just say I'm a smart businessman. Let's look upon this as an investment in the future. A future with nothing very interesting to read in the *New Yorker* magazine."

"But there's always something interesting to read in the *New Yorker* magazine."

Rothstein's eyes were not merry. "Don't crack wise, Green. Not about this."

"All right," Bedford added. "That's aces with me. But I have to keep on with this. I'm going to do right by that dead girl."

"You're a regular Sir Lancelot."

Rothstein put his arm around Bedford's shoulder, turning him and walking him toward Fifty-Ninth Street. The gambler liked to conduct business he didn't want anyone to know about on the move.

"With regard to the dead lady," Rothstein said, "I've got answers to a couple of your questions. One comes from our mutual friend Miss Pell. She says to tell you there was no involvement in the recent death of a burglar over north of Little Italy by anyone from the neighborhood. Friends and relatives out there have told her this. You're supposed to know what that means."

"I do. Why is she passing this on through you?"

"And here's this," Rothstein said, ignoring the question.

He stuck a folded piece of notepaper into the breast pocket of Bedford's blazer. "Now we're completely even. On the square. And I want to keep it that way."

"I'm in your debt, Mr. Rothstein—I mean, I'm obliged. Thank you very much."

"A pleasure, always a pleasure," Rothstein said, and ambled on toward the street.

Bedford quickly pulled out the slip of paper and unfolded it. There was on it only the name of a man and the name of a Midwestern city—not the one Bedford had expected.

He looked up to see Rothstein getting in the rear of a long blue limousine. There was a woman waiting for him in it.

She looked away.

❖

He finally came upon Sloane at last in the most predictable place—one he'd been avoiding because it reminded him so much of her sadness, and his own.

She was alone at a small table in Chumley's, her back to the front wall at the right of the stairs. Had he only glanced in the doorway, he would not have noticed her.

A glass of what looked to be Pernod was on the table before her, and she was gazing into it as though it held some deep secret she couldn't quite make out. Both Henri de Toulouse-Lautrec and Gustave Caillebotte had painted women in just such a barroom pose.

Bedford stood in front of her, waiting until she looked up.

"Have you come back?" he asked, softly, when she didn't.

It was a quiet night at Chumley's, with only a few customers in the room.

She took a deep breath, exhaled, then touched the chair beside her.

"Join me, Bedford," she said.

"Where were you?"

"With friends in Bridgehampton—until I could bear it no longer."

He pictured her with other young women in white summer dresses, sipping cocktails on the lawn of a large, white house with young men in blazers, talking idly about nothing at all.

"It's no place to go when you're feeling miserable," she said. "I tried spending time on the beach by myself but some smiling idiot would always hunt me down like a stray sheep and haul me back to the frolic." She drank some of the liqueur, making a face. "The ocean made it worse, actually. Reminded me of the South of France and what happened there."

Bedford waved to the bartender, raised two fingers, and pointed to Sloane's glass. Then he leaned closer to her.

"I've become much better informed on that unpleasant subject," he said.

"How so?"

He explained, leaving out nothing. She wiped the corner of one eye, then gulped down what remained of her drink. Staring at the table top, she ignored the second Pernod Bedford had ordered for her when it came. She was a statue.

"What would you like me to do, Sloane?"

"What do you mean?"

"I want to finish this—in hopes that you can get it behind you and come back to your old life here; your present life. With the gallery. And me."

She continued to avert her eyes.

"I want you to do whatever is just. Sometimes you're a fool, Bedford. Sometimes you're stuffy and sometimes a snob, but you are always just, and I love you for it."

"I will need that choker. The blue ribbon with the gold arts medal on it."

"That's all I have left of her. What do you want with it?"

"To be just."

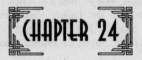

CHAPTER 24

THERE was a light rain falling, glistening the road. With the top and side curtains of her yellow Packard up, Tatty's view of the traffic around them was perilously obscured, but she drove as fast as ever.

"Why are you sitting like that?" she said. "You look like a propped-up board."

"Perhaps it's because I'm afraid of becoming one after we make an intimate acquaintance with a tree."

"Bosh and piffle, Bedford Green. My driving is improving all the time. At all events, I'm exceedingly cross with you. You kept me waiting twenty-two minutes at the curb, as though I was a taxicab or something."

"Sorry. I had no choice. I placed a call to Toledo and it had just come through."

"Toledo." She pronounced the name as though it were a place near Kazakhstan.

"This won't take long."

"I'll bet it does," she said. "And even if it doesn't, it will seem like it does. Tell me again why my presence is so obligatory?"

"I want to be well received, for as long as I can. You have

such wonderful cachet with them. Among your many attractions, you belong to the Woods Golf and Tennis Club."

"What has that to do with anything?"

"They've applied for membership."

"Oh dear." She actually slowed the car a moment. "Will they both be there?"

"Yes."

"You're going to go through this entire dreadful, ghoulish business in front of the mother? The poor woman must be in a terrible state. Her only daughter. Good heavens, her only child. Why not simply deal with the father?"

"It's to her I have to make my report. She paid me money."

They skidded out of a curve. Tatty shifted down, then accelerated as the road straightened and they crossed the Saw Mill River over a rickety wood and metal bridge.

"Bedford, I do wish you were rich. Then you wouldn't have to go through this kind of bother to make ends meet."

"Some of this bother is interesting."

They were nearing Scarsdale.

"Actually, Bedford, I'm a little scared," she said. "I've never had dealings with gangsters before."

"You probably have, but didn't know it. Theatrical producers don't get all their investment money from kindly little old ladies with a bent for culture."

"Are you carrying a gun?"

That was unexpected. "Why do you ask?"

"I'm not sure. It just occurred to me."

"As a matter of fact, I am. The one I keep in the gallery."

"Are we going to shoot our way out of Scarsdale, like Butch Cassidy and the Sundance Kid?"

"I hope not."

"Now I am scared," she said.

She passed a chuffing Model T truck in a wide swerve.

"I only mean it as a conversation enhancement."

"Enhancement?"

"I'll feel more comfortable."

She fell silent. Her speed fell off—an involuntary manifestation of reluctance.

"Would you rather go back?" he said. "I can do this my-self. I'll get a taxi and . . ."

"No, Mr. Green. Game girl that I am, we'll play the entire set. I just don't think your having me along is going to ac-complish very much."

$\int$ HE managed to miss the Swanscotts' flower beds and shrubbery this time, but pulled into the driveway too fast, throwing up a swash of muddy water and gravel. The car's engine shuddered as she turned off the ignition, as though from relief.

"I guess we've announced ourselves," he said.

Tatty took his arm as they mounted the front steps. He used his other hand to ring the bell.

A maid answered the door and quickly admitted them, leading them down the hall and into the sitting room they'd been in before. Everything was precisely as Bedford remem-bered, except the framed picture of Polly in vacation clothes had been moved to a prominent place at the center of the mantel.

Several minutes passed, then Mr. Swanscott entered, mo-tioning them to chairs. He was dressed in golfing clothes, which ill fit him. Bedford feared Tatty might giggle.

Swanscott settled into a big chair by the fireplace. He sat leaning forward, his elbows on his knees, his legs slightly splayed.

"Talk," he said.

Bedford and Tatty had settled side by side on a small divan opposite.

"I want you to know how terribly sorry I am about the way things turned out," Bedford said. The words sounded id-iotic as he listened to himself speak them.

"Yeah. Thanks. Does a lot of good to hear that."

The man spoke in such a growl that his sarcasm was a bit hard to detect.

"Where is Mrs. Swanscott?" Bedford asked.

"She's upstairs. She doesn't much feel like hearing whatever it is you have to say and she doesn't like coming into this room anymore." He paused. "It was Polly's favorite. She used to sit in the corner over there by the window. She liked days like today—when it rained. She'd sit there and watch it rain."

Bedford glanced in that direction, then looked to the hall, seeing only a maid with a feather duster tidying up the room beyond.

"Mrs. Swanscott engaged me to locate your daughter," he said.

"Yeah, I know. Five thousand bucks. And then you locate her dead."

"Five thousand dollars?"

"My wife told me everything, Green. Including what a lousy detective you are."

At that moment Bedord had to agree. But now, at least, he understood everything.

He hesitated, then proceeded, cautiously. "As she did engage me, I feel obligated to tell her what I've learned. I won't consider my duty done until I do."

"We'll feel real bad around here if you don't get to consider your duty done."

"There's something I need to ask her about the club," said Tatty.

"What club?"

"The Woods Golf and Tennis Club. I believe you applied for membership there? I'm on the women's committee. And the admissions committee."

Swanscott sat without speaking, drumming on the chair arms with his stubby fingers. He had a large ring on the little finger of his right hand, which caught what light there was in the room.

"All right. I'll get her. Then you can say what you have to say to both of us."

MRS. Swanscott entered the room dabbing at her eyes with a handkerchief. She put it aside to briefly shake Bedford's hand, and Tatty's, both in limp, unfriendly fashion. Then she seated herself in an oversized chintz-covered armchair on the other end of the chamber, near a large window that looked out onto the misty garden. The handkerchief returned to her face.

"What can you tell us, Mr. Green?" she said, in a voice leaden with melancholy.

"Are you acquainted with F. Scott Fitzgerald, the writer?"

Her handkerchief came away from her face. She blinked. "Is he mixed up in the death of my daughter?"

"Not at all," Bedford said.

"Yes, I know who he is. They came to one of our parties, once. I think they were living in Connecticut. Mrs. Fitzgerald was very . . ."

"Uninhibited," Bedford interjected, politely. "Have you read Mr. Fitzgerald's new book, *The Great Gatsby*?"

"I don't believe I've read any of his books, Mr. Green."

"This one's quite good," Bedford said. "It's about a man named Gatz, who changes his name to Gatsby and moves to the North Shore of Long Island."

"Just what the hell does this have to do with my daughter?" Mr. Swanscott asked.

"I ran into the Fitzgeralds in France," Bedford continued. "They were very helpful to me. Put me in touch with some useful people."

"Get to the point, Green. What happened to Polly?"

Swanscott reached into a drawer of the table beside him, taking out a long letter opener that resembled a ceremonial dagger. He began striking his palm with the flat blade.

At least it wasn't a gun.

"I'm not sure you want to know everything," said Bedford, with a quick look to Mrs. Swanscott.

She met his eyes unwaveringly.

"I'll tell you what I learned so far," he said. "Your daughter was murdered, as of course you know. Her body was found in the waterfront district of the French port of Toulon. She had gone there by boat with a sailor she had met in Napoule, a village on the sea where she rented a little house.

A shed, really. Two rooms, which did for living quarters and artist's studio."

"How was she murdered?" said Swanscott.

His wife had not moved a fraction of an inch.

"Her throat was cut," Bedford said, "I'm sure she died very quickly. I don't think she suffered much."

"And the sonofabitch who killed her?"

"A sailor was found dead not many blocks away. He also was cut up, but probably with a knife. The French police have assumed he was her killer because several of her possessions were found on him."

"And was he? If it hasn't occurred to you, that's what we'd really like to know."

Bedford looked down at the rug, which was Persian and extremely expensive, but its weave was turned the wrong way for the light.

"There was a gang of waterfront thugs," he said. "We were set upon by them not far from where the sailor's body was found. One of them tried to stick me with a knife, but happily did a rum job of it. My party included a man who's a good boxer. I don't think our assailants counted on that. At all events, they ran off. The police never caught up with them."

"So this sailor bastard killed my daughter, and then got rubbed out by some waterfront punks, and they tried to rub you out. And they got away clean. That's all you've found out? For five thousand dollars?"

"That's what the official Toulon police report says. That's what we're supposed to believe. But I suspect there is more to this than that."

Tatty was getting fidgety. Mrs. Swanscott sat as still as a stone.

"Go on," Swanscott said.

"There's another theory. As the postal card picture I showed you earlier indicated, I don't think Polly was a very happy young woman. She despaired of ever being taken seriously as an artist—even by you, her own parents. Moving to Europe didn't change matters. In frustration, she became increasingly self-destructive. Drank a lot. Took up with some pretty rough men. You could almost say that what happened to her was inevitable, given the course she embarked upon. You might even call it suicidal."

Swanscott stopped slapping his palm with the blade of the letter opener. Now he simply held the weapon, blade high.

"All right. My daughter was unhappy," he said. "But she wouldn't do anything like that. Anybody who knew her would tell you that."

The slapping of the letter opener resumed.

"I think you're probably right. There was a Dutch artist who also went to the South of France, and killed himself there—Vincent Van Gogh. Polly was like him in many ways, but she hadn't reached that point. That's clear in her art. She was looking for something—desperately—but it wasn't death. Someone else brought that to her, uninvited."

"Like you said, the sailor."

"No. Someone else."

Bedford felt nailed to his place by both parents' unmoving eyes. He wished he had taken a seat closer to the hall.

"I was once a police reporter, Mr. Swanscott, and I was in the war. For the wounds that were inflicted, there was comparatively little blood found around either body."

"Bedford, do you have to talk about these things?" Tatty said. She had moved close to him. Her arm muscles were very tense.

"Go on," said Swanscott.

"I think they were killed somewhere else and then brought to where they were found. I don't believe that gang of thugs had anything to do with either death. I think they were hired—to go after me. One of the many curiosities in this is that one of them put a knife in my pocket, apparently the one used on the sailor. It suggests a compelling fiction: I was hired by you to find your daughter. When she was murdered, I killed the man who did it—on your behalf. I would have gotten away with it, had I not been fallen upon by ruffians."

"What do the French cops think?" Swanscott asked.

"I doubt that they found the compelling fiction very convincing, for they let us go—after keeping us in jail for a night. They would have preferred that I stayed in France until this was settled, but they haven't raised too much of a hue and cry. Whatever they may say, I think they're keeping the case open."

"But no suspects?" Swanscott was sounding very impatient.

"Actually, I have one; more than a suspect," Bedford said. "After Toulon, Polly's friend Sloane Smith and I . . ."

He was interrupted by a sharp intake of breath from Mrs. Swanscott. "Sloane was with you? You took that lovely young woman to France, into those places? You didn't tell me you would do that."

"Mrs. Swanscott, it would be more accurate to say she took me. At all events, after we left Toulon, we returned to Polly's place at Napoule to collect her paintings and personal things to bring back to you. There was a man there. He said he was Norman Oritzky."

"I knew it!" the mother said, her face coloring. "I knew that no good bum would be trouble. I warned her. Time after time. She wouldn't listen. She just ignored me."

She began sobbing, behind her handkerchief.

"Later, this man tried to run Sloane and me off the road—over a cliff and into the sea—while we were driving up the coast to Nice. As it turned out, he met that fate himself. I'm told the local police found a gun on him. And a substantial amount of U.S. currency. But they've not connected him to anything, and don't seem to know that Sloane and I were there."

"He must have robbed her," Mrs. Swanscott said. "Taken Polly's money. That was what he was doing in her house . . ."

"I understand you were not fond of him, Mrs. Swanscott," Bedford said. "But please hear me out. Norman Oritzky committed no crime. He was the victim of one."

"How's that?" asked the husband. "You just said . . ."

"The man who went over that cliff identified himself to us as Mr. Oritzky. He even had Oritzky's New York State motor vehicle operator's license on him when he was found. But he wasn't Oritzky."

"How on earth could you know that?"

"The police put his death down as an accident and

informed the American authorities. I paid to have the body shipped home to his family here in New York."

"And?"

"They viewed the body and said it wasn't Oritzky. They were demonstrably positive on that point. The police dug up another body in Staten Island, originally identified as a Henry Schultz. The family identified that corpse as Norman Oritzky."

Mrs. Swanscott was speechless. "Staten Island?" said her husband. "Schultz?"

"Your daughter's apartment in Greenwich Village was broken into and vandalized shortly before she went to Europe," Bedford said. "I was curious about that because the building is owned by one of the Sicilian crime families down there and they have low tolerance for that sort of thing on their property. When this 'Schultz' was found, it was assumed he was the burglar and that he'd paid a price for his indiscretion. But that man wasn't 'Schultz.' He was Norman Oritzky, your daughter's boyfriend—and the Sicilian crime family had absolutely nothing to do with it."

Letter opener still in hand, Swanscott rose and went to the fireplace, standing near the framed photograph of Polly. "You ex-police reporters know all about the Little Italy crime families, do you?"

"Let's just say I have acquaintances who do. People whose word I trust."

"So where does that leave us?"

"I am convinced—and my friend Detective D'Alessandro is convinced—that young Oritzky was killed by the same man who followed Polly to France and murdered her and the sailor. The same man Sloane and I found at Polly's place who claimed to be Norman Oritzky. The same man who broke into Polly's apartment in the Village."

Swanscott was standing less than six feet from Bedford. The doorway to the hall was four times that distance.

"Why would he do that?" Swanscott said. "Bust into her apartment. Go all the way to France and hunt her down? What did she ever do to anyone?"

"Perhaps it wasn't what she did so much as what she might have done."

"What the hell do you mean?"

"Perhaps she knew something, something she threatened to reveal."

Swanscott took a step closer. "Polly? All she wanted to do was paint pictures. She wouldn't threaten anybody."

To his dismay, Bedford felt the first tinges of physical fear begin to creep over him, something he hadn't really experienced since the war. He stood up, hoping to feel less apprehensive, but the gathering rage apparent in the man's face was too intimidating.

"The body I had shipped back," Bedford said, taking a step away from Swanscott, "the man who posed as Mr. Oritzky—we know now who he is."

He waited. No one spoke or moved.

"His name is Richard Scarzetti," Bedford said. "He was a professional criminal. His arrest record included burglary and assault with a deadly weapon, including an attack with a razor. He was from Toledo, Ohio."

The look on Swanscott's face now became quite murderous. At that moment, Bedford would gladly have been in Tatty's car, thundering along the highway at a hundred miles an hour. But he pressed on.

"Your wife hired me. Did you by any chance hire a New York private investigator, too?"

"I hate those guys," said Swanscott. "I wouldn't hire them to clean a toilet."

"Do you suppose one might have been investigating you?"

"What the hell for?"

"I'm not sure we'll ever know. The one I'm talking about turned up dead in the same pauper's graveyard as Mr. Oritzky."

Swanscott turned away from him, toward the mantel. He stared fixedly at the picture of Polly, then down at the hearth, both hands gripping the edge of the mantelpiece.

"I think I'd like you to go now, Mr. Green," he said, his voice now strangely subdued.

"I'm not quite finished, Mr. Swanscott. There's the matter of Polly's paintings. I brought them back with me. They're down at my gallery. Six of them. All self-portraits."

"Are they like the postal card picture you showed us?" Mrs. Swanscott said.

"Variations on that theme."

"You keep them. I don't care what you do with them. I don't want them in this house."

"There was another painting. A Picasso. A gift to her from the artist. Under the circumstances, I thought I should give it back."

"I told you to go, Mr. Green." Swanscott still wouldn't face him.

"Just one more thing," said Bedford.

He reached into his pocket and gently took out the silk ribbon with the gold arts medal on it that Polly had worn around her neck as a choker. Slowly, as he might bear some precious jewel to a monarch, he brought it to Mrs. Swanscott, happy to note Tatty rising from the divan behind him and moving to the center of the room.

"I'm sure she valued this more than anything she had," he said. "We thought you should have it."

The mother's eyes widened, filling with a mix of horror, fascination, and grief.

"I'm sorry," Bedford said, handing the medal to the woman gingerly. "The ribbon's still stained with her blood. There was no way to remove it."

The woman gulped, then turned toward the window, pushing Bedford's hand away.

"Give it to me," Swanscott said.

Bedford approached the man warily, handing him the morbid object at arm's length. Swanscott accepted it reverentially, holding it with both hands.

"You're right," he said, his voice cracking. "She was so goddamn proud of this thing. It meant more to her than anything we ever gave her."

He brought it to his lips as he might a holy relic, then carefully folded the ribbon and set the medal on the mantel next to the photograph. He remained there, a hand over his eyes.

"We'll leave you now," Bedford said. "Again, I am so sorry about your daughter."

He took Tatty by the elbow and started for the doorway.

"Wait," said Mrs. Swanscott. "There was something about the Woods Club."

Tatty and Bedford kept moving until they reached the hall.

"Oh yes," Tatty said, from the doorway. "I'm afraid your application for membership has been declined."

"What do you mean?" Mrs. Swanscott's words came out as sharply as gunshots.

"There was a discrepancy. You put down your name as Swanscott. It's really Schwamm. I'm sorry, but putting false information on an application is automatic grounds for rejection."

Mrs. Swanscott began to wail, the sound rising like a siren, and struck at the chair arm with her fist.

"I think we'd better go," said Bedford to Tatty quickly. "Step lively."

THEY hurried down the front steps. Bedford for once forewent his practice of holding Tatty's door for her, snapping open his own on the passenger side instead. She was in the driver's seat by the time he shut his door. The engine started easily, as it did not always do, but Tatty just sat there.

"Let's go," he said.

"I can't, Bedford. They've closed the gates."

SWANSCOTT came down the steps slowly, but moving with great deliberation, and looking a hungry bear. A large young man who was either servant or business associate followed behind.

Bedford quickly considered his alternatives, and found none. He opened the side curtain. Swanscott leaned in. Bedford was surprised to see tears running down his cheeks.

"What do you want, Mr. Swanscott?" he said.

"You haven't told me all you know."

"I didn't wish to be impolite."

"Be impolite. Now."

"Very well, sir. I know that you're an immigrant who came here with his family from Germany. And that you ran with a street gang on the North Side of Chicago before going to night school and learning bookkeeping. When Prohibition came in, you worked with Bugs Moran and other bootleggers, and then opened your own operation in Michigan using a chain of drugstores as a front. You subsequently came East and got into the stock market. You style yourself an investor and many people think you respectable, though I've heard you may be involved in some kind of stock swindle."

Bedford paused. "And I know that Polly knew all this."

Swanscott gripped the top of the door with both hands. If he had a weapon, he didn't seem ready to use it. Bedford's small pistol was in his jacket pocket, not easily reached.

"And something else," Bedford said. "I did not receive five thousand dollars from your wife. My compensation was six hundred dollars. Plus some extra expenses. That was the figure she stipulated in the beginning. The remainder of that money went elsewhere."

Swanscott lifted his eyes to Bedford's. "I understand." He leaned in closer, scaring Tatty all the more. The young man behind Swanscott was watching her intently, in a chillingly businesslike way.

"You said you know Detective D'Alessandro—the one who calls himself Joey D.?" Swanscott asked.

"I do. I also know a certain Mr. Rothstein, who I believe is a business associate of yours."

"Will they vouch for your word?"

Bedford thought upon the woman in the back of Rothstein's limousine.

"Yes," he said.

"Then I want your word that you won't ever talk about this to anyone. For Polly's sake, for my sake, and for your sake. Yours and that young woman who went to school with Polly. And this woman here. All right?"

"Yes."

"Your word?"

"My word."

Swanscott nodded to the young associate, who went to the driveway gate.

"Okay, Green. Good-bye. Don't come around here again."

As soon as the gates began to open, Tatty shifted into low and moved the long car forward.

<hr />

I DON'T understand," Tatty said, once they were back on the highway.

"Mr. Swanscott's wife is from Toledo."

"And so?"

"And so that explains everything. I shouldn't be surprised if Mr. Richard Scarzetti turned up in her high school yearbook."

"Good God," said Tatty, with a shudder.

She slowed, and then stopped for a traffic signal. The electric wiper on the windshield was performing badly, leaving a smear of rainwater. There were no cars coming in either direction on the intersecting street. Tatty ground the Packard into gear and roared on through the stop signal, hell-bent for any place but Scarsdale.

"Are you going to leave matters at that?" she asked, shifting into high.

"No, I'm certainly not." He looked into the side mirror, to see if they were being followed—relieved to see they were not. "You might say I'm leaving matters to the workings of the criminal justice system."

CHAPTER 25

SLOANE did return to the gallery, as Bedford never gave up hope she would. But it was for a grimmer purpose than re-assuming her old duties.

A short while after opening time a few mornings later, she appeared in the doorway, then marched up to his desk and laid before him a copy of the morning newspaper, folded open to an inside page.

She thrust her index finger at an article, in as forbidding a manner as the beckoning hand of the Ghost of Christmas Yet to Come in Dickens' *A Christmas Carol.*

"I haven't looked at the papers yet," Bedford said.

"You should." The finger jabbed again. "Read this."

He bent forward, the headline sending a small *frisson* over his flesh.

"SOCIALITE FOUND DROWNED IN LONG ISLAND SOUND."

Bedford looked up. Sloane's face was a cold, beautiful mask.

"Read it."

He did, slowly, careful of each word.

RYE—Mrs. Murial Swanscott of Scarsdale, wife of financier Haskell P. Swanscott, was found in the waters of Long Island Sound early today, an apparent drowning victim.

Police said she was wearing evening clothes. Her body was discovered by two fishermen, floating in open water off Milton Point.

According to her husband, Mrs. Swanscott had been feeling despondent over the death of their only child, Polly Ann Swanscott, in a boating accident in France last month.

Mrs. Swanscott was active with the Westchester County Horticulture Society. Services will be private.

Sloane's eyes were still hard upon him when he looked up.

"What does this mean?" she said. She trembled a little as she stood there.

Bedford gently pushed the newspaper aside and got to his feet, taking her by the arm.

"Let's go for a walk, Sloane. Just to the square."

◆◆◆

H E found a bench with no one near it a short way in from MacDougal Street. It was beneath a high elm that dappled the walk with its shadows. There were mothers pushing babies in prams and barking dogs in the park. The water from the high fountain in the center glittered in the morning sunlight. But the happy setting was lost entirely on Sloane. The anger had gone from her but Bedford almost wished it back, so deathlike was her face.

"Mrs. Swanscott would have been pleased by the newspaper article," he said. "It portrayed her as everything she always wished to be. Not a word about her past as a hootchy kootchy dancer in a Maumee, Ohio, roadhouse."

Sloane made no response, though he saw a faint blush of color in her cheek. He wanted very much to touch that flesh, to gently brush away a curl of hair that had fallen over her eye.

"As obituaries go, it was one almost worth dying for," he said.

"I said you should be 'just,' Bedford," she said. "I didn't mean for you to be cruel."

"All I did was tell them the truth. That's what Mrs. Swanscott paid me for."

"And then she went and drowned herself."

Moving away from him, she put her face into her hands, shutting out the beautiful day.

"I don't feel sorry for her," Sloane said. "She was a horrible woman. Do you know she drew up a list of rich boys she wanted Polly to sleep with? She made a place for these seductions in their little summerhouse. She didn't want her using the back of a car."

"How genteel."

"God. I can't bear to think of any of this."

"Mrs. Swanscott didn't drown herself," Bedford said.

Birds were singing sweetly in the elm tree. One of them flitted down to the sidewalk, and hopped about, pausing to study them quizzically with its head to one side. Then it flew off, toward the fountain. An organ grinder was playing in the distance.

Bedford put his arm around the woman who was his dearest friend, pulling her nearer.

"I know your secret, Sloane," he said, quietly.

"What do you mean?"

"What you wouldn't tell me about you and Polly."

"How can you possibly know what I haven't told you?" Her voice quavered.

"It was mostly a guess at first," he said, "but now I'm certain."

Her muscles stiffened, but she showed no sign of moving away from him.

"You told Polly to do what you had done with your own parents," Bedford said. "You told her that, if her parents wouldn't let her lead the life she wished, she could gain her freedom by threatening to reveal their secrets. Given the criminal nature of their secrets, it was a formidable weapon."

"She was so desperately unhappy, Bedford. She was so envious of the life I led . . ."

Her words subsided as she took a deep breath, but it failed to help her keep control. The anguish and guilt and despair that had inundated her spirit ever since the morning she came upon the "weeping woman" postal card now came forth in a great flood. She turned toward him, as might a terrified child, having no other place to go. He held her with both arms, very close, very tight, until the sobs at last began to subside.

"God damn me," she said. "Damn me to hell. I shouldn't have said a word to her. I knew her father was a gangster—that gangsters kill people."

He stroked her hair. Her cheek was moist against his. A nursemaid holding two small children by the hand came by, pretending not to notice them, hurrying her charges along.

When they had passed, Bedford straightened, lifting Sloane's face so that he could look upon it.

"You did nothing wrong," he said. "Nothing at all. No one in her life tried to help Polly as much as you did. You could not possibly have known that that ridiculous mother of hers would turn out to be a creature who ate her young."

Sloane pulled back. "Her mother? It was her father who sent that terrible man after her. A gangster—just like him."

"It was Mrs. Swanscott who hired that man. He was someone she knew from Toledo."

"But why?"

"Polly threatened to tell things—if only to the parents of Nicholas Pease. Polly had nothing to fear from her father. He loved her. He's made that very obvious."

"Then why didn't he help her? Why didn't he do something about her wretched, social-climbing mother?"

"Ultimately—as we see—he did."

Sloane stretched out her legs and tilted her head back until she was looking directly at the sky.

"I thought I was helping her."

"You have nothing to feel guilty about," he said.

"Yes I do," she said. "And so do you. We were wrong to dismiss her art."

"Yes we were," Bedford said. "But I wouldn't now."

"Too late."

"Not quite."

"What do you mean?"

He stood, extending his hand to her. After a doubtful moment, she took it, rising.

"Let's walk a little longer," he said.

"All right. It doesn't help much. I've been doing it for days."

With his arm around her shoulders, he steered her toward the arch and Fifth Avenue.

"I didn't know what to do with her portraits," he said. "Her parents wouldn't take them—especially not her mother, who needed no such reminders of what she had done. So I showed them to our neighbor, Mrs. Whitney."

"Gertrude Vanderbilt Whitney? She wouldn't want Polly's paintings."

"On the contrary. She's quite taken with them. Immensely so with one of them. She dropped by last night and I showed them all to her. She asked for the one."

"But what will she do with it?"

"She says she'll exhibit it in her Studio Club. She says she plans to open a museum some day, and will add it to the collection. Think of that."

Sloane's eyes were on the hazy city skyline to the north.

"What I think of," she said, "is decades from now, people looking at poor Polly's face in that picture, wondering why."

"No," said Bedford. "She was really a very gifted artist. They'll know why."

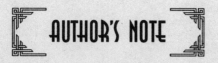

AUTHOR'S NOTE

THIS is a work of fiction. The principal characters in this murder mystery—Bedford Green, Sloane Smith, Tatty Chase, Claire Pell, Dayton Crosby, Joey D'Alessandro—are purely fictional. But it is intended also as a literary conveyance that might transport the reader back to one of the most enthralling and exciting periods of the modern era. To enhance that effort, I have included a large number of actual people from the period—people a man possessed of as many parts as Bedford Green would quite likely encounter in his several walks of life. I have drawn them as closely to real life as research enables me, and put them where they actually were at the time, doing what they did. Ernest Hemingway strangled pigeons to feed his family, yet vacationed with Gerald and Sara Murphy in the South of France. Zelda Fitzgerald actually did have an affair with Edouard Jozan, and did throw herself off a terrace balcony. Her husband Scott did base a character on Arnold Rothstein. Lindy's, Harry's Bar, La Coupole, and Villa America certainly were no strangers to this kind of drama.

ACKNOWLEDGMENTS

I AM indebted to a number of quite wonderful people without whom I should know very little about the many different but overlapping worlds my detective Bedford inhabits: the late Cleveland Amory, Marian Probst, Lisa Anderson, Tammy Grimes, Paige Price, Betsy von Furstenberg, Christiana Besch, Elizabeth Wilson, Marie-Gabrielle Schecher, Randy Jurgensen, Connie Fletcher, Nancy Jennings, Frank Bowling, Dianne deWitt, and Margaret Schwarzer, in great particular.

I am beholden to Gail Fortune and Dominick Abel for their peerless performances in their respective callings. I am grateful to Steve Shlopak for keeping Chumley's so splendidly alive for future generations.

I am grateful to my wife, Pamela, and sons Eric and Colin as only they can know.